The Horse In The Mirror

Lisa Maxwell

Other Books by Lisa Maxwell

The Horse Who Walked Through Time

The Horse In The Mirror

Lisa Maxwell

Published by:
Lisa Maxwell
2017

First Printing: 2017

ISBN 978-0-9987421-0-6

Sugar Creek Publications
www.frenchclassicaldressageforall.com

For my sister Jane, my heroine.

I would like to express my heartfelt thanks to my editor, Julie Abbott, and to my tech support guru, Daniel Palmer.
Thanks also to Kelly Takacs and Dirty Hooves Photography for the cover art.

Chapter 1

Yesterday Is had been able to handle the stallion with just a rope attached to the ring of his halter. Today she would need to use a chain wrapped around his sensitive nose in such a way that it would cause some discomfort if the horse pulled against her. By tomorrow pain would not subdue the horse. It would enrage him.

Is watched the horse circle his stall impatiently as she prepared his feed. Suddenly he snaked his neck out, raking the wall with his teeth for no apparent reason. A grim little smile stretched Is's lips. Today she would pour the feed through the slot. Yesterday she had walked into his stall carrying the feed and the horse had nuzzled her while she scratched his neck. But no more. From here on her life depended on how well she read the horse. He could kill her if she made a mistake.

While Is poured the grain the stallion attacked. Charging across the stall, he hit the iron bars in front of her face with enough force to rattle them. Is jerked back. Those teeth would not rip like canines; they would bruise and crush. The horse was not really biting; he was punching, and a punch like he'd delivered to the bars would knock her to the ground where his hooves could kill her.

Unable to reach her, the stallion attacked his grain. His hooves hit the wall as he lashed out savagely with both hind legs. Is had seen the work other war horses' hooves had done to those specially reinforced walls. She would probably have to replace the inside boards after this horse left too.

Sadness threatened to overwhelm her. She had trained this horse since he was two years old, forming a deep bond with him. She had always known this day would come, but her heart had never believed it. She had loved him. But she must not give in to sadness now. Impatiently she pushed a strand of her shoulder length dark brown hair behind her ear. She was slight-built and wiry, her motions efficient and smooth. Her work with the horses left not an ounce of fat on her. Living alone as she did she was negligent of how she looked, wearing heavy-duty jeans that were none too clean and a faded blue jacket that had seen better days. In spite of that she was pretty, with brown eyes that were ever-so-slightly slanted and clear skin that was always tanned.

She would have three days, at most, she decided, watching the horse. Then the berserker would arrive. She had trained the horse to be a weapon, while others had trained a man. When horse and man met, it would be as though she no longer existed. Even now the bond Is had with the stallion was weakening. By tomorrow he would be a weapon without a master. The next day he would meet the man who was genetically engineered to be his master. They would have a bond, instantly, that would overshadow the one Is had worked to develop since the horse had been a gangly-legged colt. The tie between horse and berserker was designed into their genes. Is had forged hers with hard work, patience and talent. It had served its purpose and now it was time to let go she told herself sternly.

She felt the sadness that always wanted to overwhelm her when one of her horses was taken, but she put it away harshly. From here on there would be no time for emotion. Her life would be on the line every moment she was with this stallion. The day the berserker arrived to claim the horse would be the worst. Considerable tact was required to get a man, who was nearly as dangerous to her as the horse would have become by then, mounted on that horse and on their way.

Still Is lingered, watched the stallion eating. His neck arched as he bit into the grain as though it were an enemy. His blood-bay coat, that she had spent so many hours grooming, rippled over well-developed muscles. His eye, which had looked so intelligent and kind yesterday, was hard and cold today. He struck the bars again. Wet grain splattered from his mouth unheeded.

Is turned away. She had the rest of the horses to feed. Along with the bay stallion, she was training three younger horses. As each one matured, a berserker would come to take it. Is was not allowed to name any of the horses; she was supposed to remember they were not hers to keep. Yet the only time she remembered that was when a berserker was coming. So today while she fed "her" horses she felt the loss of all of them although only the blood-bay was leaving.

She took time over her own breakfast. Sitting on the porch of her small house she could overlook the paddocks where the three younger horses grazed. Behind them the mountains rose in a jagged wall, green and gold and brown. She loved living here, with just her horses for company, at this final outpost before the range of mountains they called the Boundary.

When Is returned to the barn the bay was more subdued. He came over to see her, ears pricked and eyes interested. She felt the old bond that united them. This morning would be the last time, but she shoved that thought aside. It would only lead to sadness and inattention that could get her killed.

She was careful, reaching between the bars and snapping the lead to the horse's halter before she rolled the door open. His ears flicked back at the sound and his eyes turned hard. Quickly Is gave the lead a jerk. "Stand."

As he stood, ears in neutral, eyes on her, Is breathed a sigh of relief. His training was still good this morning. No, she corrected herself. His training was still good for that moment. It could change anytime, or from moment to moment. Anything could set him off. She had not lived this long by being sloppy, but she had not stayed in this line of work by being overcautious either.

She kept well to the side as the stallion came through the door, never presenting herself as a target. His massive shoulders towered over her as she walked beside him.

In the aisle Is cross-tied him with a rope snapped to either side of his halter so he could not turn his head far enough to bite her. He would not allow her to groom him, twitching his skin, pinning his ears back, and stamping his hooves. He was a good seventeen hands tall, with legs like pillars and hooves the size of dinner plates. Is put the brushes away and brought out the saddle. The stallion stood like a rock while she tightened the girth. He put his head down, yawning his mouth wide to accept the bit like some kid's pony, but his head alone was as big as her torso.Before leading him from the barn, Is snapped a long canvas line to his bridle. She would exercise him around her in a circle on the lunge line before mounting. This would let him warm up his muscles and get rid of some of his freshness. She had another reason too. She wanted to see him one last time proud and athletic at the very peak of his power. By tomorrow it would no longer be safe to work him this way. He would attack her if he saw her on the ground. No voice commands or show of force would stop him.

He moved off on a circle around her, trotting with his wonderful swinging gait. His dark red-bay coat gleamed over fluidly moving muscles. He tossed his head now and then with good spirits. Despite his size, he seemed to float over the ground. His black mane lifting from his neck caught the breeze with each stride. His black tail arched from his beautifully muscled rump like a proud flag, the end of it swaying softly in the tempo of his trot. Behind him the autumn-colored ridges and the more distant snowcapped giants of the Boundary formed a backdrop of breathtaking beauty. Is absorbed the beauty, letting it soak into her very pores. She felt her connection to this horse, this moment, this place.

She made an almost imperceptible motion and the stallion bounded into the canter. Now he snorted rhythmically in time with his strides. The soft wuffling of his nostrils, the soft landing of his hooves was like music completing the moment.

Is would never tire of watching and he seemed to delight in his own movement. Sadness threatened her again but she drove it away. She would not lose these precious moments to outside thoughts.

She called him down to a halt. One moment he was bounding, the next he was standing as still as though he had been there all day.

He allowed her to approach and remove the lunge line, but he showed an edge of impatience and Is knew better than to take too long or try to fraternize with him. Today he was the king, allowing her to mount because it

9

suited his purposes. This day she would not delude herself into believing otherwise.

He moved off before she signaled him but she did not dare stop him. His neck reached before her and his body was a coiled spring under her. Her heart surged with a sudden wild joy at the feel of his incredible power beneath her and she was aware that she controlled that power only because he allowed it. If she came against his will too much she would find out just how puny her human strength was against his. He could bolt and she would never be able to stop him. He could easily throw her from his back. All the years of training she had put into him were nothing to him today. He allowed her presence because it made him happy to do so.

She had barely to think she would like to canter and he was off, bounding high and light into a slow gallop. Is's heart soared with his strides. She merely had to think what she wanted and he did it as though she was the mind and he the body. They went through all the preparatory exercises as if playing - trotting in place, turns on one spot at the canter, flying changes of lead. But this was a horse of war and these were only the preliminary exercises Is had taught him to get him ready for his real training. Now she asked him for those movements, the movements of war - rearing, leaping forward, leaping into the air, and lashing out with his hind hooves - movements of death.

For the first time the stallion's whole heart was in these exercises. Before, he had done them out of obedience to her. Today he seemed to understand them. Today he leapt higher, kicked harder.

Sadness struck Is like one of the horse's hooves. He was what he had been bred to be, and what she had trained him to be. He was ready. She had done her job well, but deep in her heart she knew it was wrong.

Horses were not meant for war. Even these magnificently bred stallions would only fight because of the link they had with their berserkers. Oh, two stallions might fight, but rarely to the death and not with this kind of preparation and premeditation.

Is quieted the stallion to a walk and when he saw they were done for the day, he relaxed, stretching his neck and striding forward. He could have been a lady's hack for all his seeming gentleness now but Is knew what lay just beneath the surface. She reminded herself of the necessity of training her stallions to this peak. Without the berserkers to drive them back, the Blueskins would come out of the Boundary and attack the farmers. Blueskins had killed her parents.

After their deaths Is had wished that the Alliance could send a bunch of berserkers to kill all the Blueskins. But without the Blueskins to keep them in check other terrible "things" would come out of the Boundary, killing the farmers, destroying the land, and disrupting the whole chain that allowed all the people in all the cities to exist. And so an uneasy truce had been reached. The berserkers went into the Boundary singly and engaged the Blueskins' best warriors in battle and if the berserkers exhibited enough of the qualities that the Blueskins prized, including showing no fear of death, then the Blueskins honored the truce another season.

When the horse was cool Is groomed him and he leaned into her currying, enjoying the massage. She spent extra time stroking his glistening coat with soft brushes and soft cloths. She could see the reflection of her own colors, her hair as dark as a shadow hidden in the rich red/brown of his coat, the oval shape of her face erased by each brush stroke and returned again as the brush passed. She could have groomed him forever, holding both of them thoughtless in the euphoria of their ride. But she had to return him to his stall before his mood changed.

She spent the rest of the day grooming the other horses; she had no heart for working them today. The two-year-old colt was frisky and pushy in the cool autumn weather, his honey-colored coat flashing in the sun. He tossed his neck while she curried him, grabbing at anything that came near his mouth. Today it was beyond her to chastise him.

The four-year-old was more disciplined and easier to groom. Even though Is had always given him as much love and attention as the others, he seemed to have little use for her, remaining aloof and disdainful of her ministrations. She ran her fingers through his chestnut mane losing her hand in his thick red hair, losing her thoughts in the mindless stroking of her fingers through his mane.

She left the six-year-old for last. Whenever she glanced at him in his paddock, he was watching her with dark intelligent eyes. When the bay stallion was gone, Is would concentrate her training on him.

His liver chestnut coat was the color of rich soil and it shone with the warm sheen of polished leather. For a while Is lost herself in grooming him. He was the most docile stallion she had ever handled and she had trouble imagining him as a fully trained war horse viciously attacking anything that came near him. But he would. It was programmed into his brain, to be triggered when he was fully mature and his berserker came. *You have no choice,* she told him silently. *Just like me.*

She didn't dare give in to the sadness she felt. The questions she had begun to ask were more insistent now, demanding she look at them. But she could not. Not now. The next two days she had to survive.

She heard the bay kicking during the night and incorporated the sounds into her dreams where horse after horse left her care to be killed. Some were galloped to death by their berserkers. Some were slain by weapons their

---

hooves and teeth could not match. Some were betrayed by their riders. All were betrayed by her.

She awoke before dawn feeling as though she had received the kicking of the horse's hooves. She lay until light came, listening to the horse attacking his stall.

He charged the bars when she came to feed him and she did not stay to assess his temper but went back to her house and ate her own breakfast slowly, keeping her thoughts on how to exercise the horse. At this point she was always tempted to leave them in their stalls. But she couldn't. The way the stallion was acting he would damage himself in there. She could not explain to a berserker that there was no horse to carry him. The horse had to be ready.

He tried to take her arm off when she reached between the bars to snap a lead on his halter. She snubbed him to the bars with one lead and got another one on the other side of his halter, effectively cross-tying him in the stall.

When she rolled the door back he reared and struck out with his deadly iron-shod hooves. Is didn't even try to groom him. She held the saddle out before her so he could see that it was the one she used for galloping him. He tossed his head, ears still pinned against his neck, but he did not rear again. She moved into his stall, slowly, but not too slowly. If he sensed fear, he would attack her. She had to keep her mind on the immediate moment, every movement.

He allowed her to swing the saddle onto his back. The girth fell twisted and she had to reach farther under his belly than she liked to straighten it, but he stood. Today she put the bridle on over his halter so she didn't have to untie him until she had the bit in his mouth.

The moment of truth came when she unsnapped him. She undid the far side quietly with no fuss so he wouldn't take notice. Then she slid outside the stall, around the corner of the door, before unsnapping the near side. He came forward immediately. If she had been in front of him he might have attacked. She let his head and neck pass her as he came through the door. Walking at his shoulder she reached up and took the reins and some mane in her left hand, and as they approached the end of the aisle she grabbed the saddle with her right hand and jumped up. He was too tall for her to vault cleanly onto his back. She had to settle for jumping high enough to put her left foot in the stirrup and then swing over. He accepted this because they had practiced this routine in preparation for today. She never allowed herself to miss that jump.

He broke into a trot as soon as they were through the door and Is didn't try to restrain him. If he had been on the edge of unmanageable yesterday, today he was well past any point at which she could control him. In a moment he was off in the canter and in a few strides he had extended into a gallop. Is gave him the signal to slow, which he ignored, so she crouched over his neck like a jockey and let him run. He allowed her to suggest the direction and she steered him into flat bottomland along the river. She had galloped him here frequently to condition him but this was different. Today Is had no power over him. He ran as she had never allowed him to run before. In spite of all her years of galloping horses her heart surged with adrenaline. She had no command of his speed; his strength was unbelievable. Then suddenly she broke through her fear, enjoying herself with a fierce kind of joy that erased everything else.

She had to let him run enough so he would be ready to let her stop him, but not so much that he would exhaust his best energy for tomorrow. She wanted to slow him to a walk long enough to arrive at the barn cooled out, but not walk so long that he might become uncontrollable again.

Is rode him right into the barn before slipping from his back. He was relaxed and happy after the gallop, giving her a few minutes to untack him. But there was no grooming today. He had to be back in his stall before his mood swung.

Today she did not even want to handle the other horses. Grief about losing her bay horse and fear about the berserker's arrival warred within her. It took all her control to keep from giving in to either. Today she would do all the chores she had saved – repairing paddock fencing, digging out the runoff ditch, patching her roof. Tasks that she usually hated and would put off in favor of playing with her horses were what she needed to get through this day.

When she let the other horses out into their paddocks, the two younger horses immediately moved off to graze. The liver-chestnut stayed, watching her expectantly with his wide-set expressive eyes until she went to stroke him. She leaned against him and without warning began to cry. She had never done that before, never, and it felt awful but she could not stop. She had no choice but to hang onto his neck while she shivered and sobbed.

Afterward she was mad at herself. She understood the necessity for berserkers as well as anyone. Without them, innocent people would die the way her mother and father had died. It was better to sacrifice a few specially trained men and a few horses than to allow the slaughter of innocent people.

From time to time, as she went through the mending and repairing that she'd saved for this day, she heard the bay kick. Already he was no longer her beloved companion. He wanted only to fight and he would get that wish. There was no point in mourning him. She told herself that repeatedly.

That night she slept lightly, waking each time the stallion's hooves hit the walls. She could almost track the berserker's progress by the restlessness of the stallion.

By three a.m. she was too nervous to stay in bed any more. She got up and began to disguise herself for the berserker. A tight undershirt effectively bound her breasts. The heavy work shirt that went on over that was baggy and sexless and hid how slight her frame was. She twisted her dark hair into a knot on top of her head and pulled a floppy-brimmed hat low over her eyes. Heavyweight jeans, lace-up men's boots and a man's thick leather jacket finished the disguise. She looked as much like a man, or at least a boy, as it was possible to make her slender body look. There was no way to make the delicate features of her face appear masculine. There was no help for her voice either. She would simply not speak. Her best hope was to get the berserker off the horse he would be riding and onto the stallion and away as quickly as possible. Usually that was exactly what the berserkers wanted too. Her mind was filled with images of other berserkers she had handled and all the things that could go wrong.

He came just after dawn. Is was alerted by the bay's whinny and went out to watch the man approach. The horse he rode came forward at a shambling trot, his once proud head low to the ground, his toes dragging lines of dust up from the unpaved road. He was too spent even to answer the bay's challenge, trumpeted repeatedly and interspersed with the crashes of his hooves hitting the walls.

Is ignored the bay and watched the berserker. He spotted her standing on the porch of her house and kicked his horse toward her.

The poor beast picked up his head and broke into a canter, unable to disregard a command from his rider. He stumbled to an exhausted halt in front of her house. Is clamped harsh control on her feelings and looked directly into the rider's face. His eyes were glazed over and unreadable in some way that made her shudder inside. He was further gone into his trance than most who arrived here.

He stepped down from the saddle and stood staring at her. He was at least seven feet tall, with width to match his height. The tight-fitting riding breeches he wore revealed his powerful thighs. A light mail vest exposed his bare arms bulging with well-developed muscles. His face would have been handsome except for those eyes. They stared fixedly at something Is couldn't see.

Had he been any other person she might have assumed he was in a state of exhaustion. With a berserker it was never safe to assume anything. The blood that coursed through his veins was highly augmented with hormones to forestall fatigue, pain, and fear, and strongly laced with chemicals that could be instantly tripped into rage or lust.

He looked even bigger as Is came down off the porch. He was standing on his horse's left, so Is went to the animal's right side, took the reins and started for the barn. Usually this worked.

Sometimes the horses refused to follow her. Even as close to death as this one appeared, if his rider got mad, the horse might well attack her. Although he was a galloping horse, not a war horse, he was linked to the berserker's brain in the same way and easily had the strength and size to knock her to the ground and trample her.

But this horse followed quietly as she led him toward a stall at the far end of the barn away from the bay's. The bay stopped his challenging when he could see the other horse. He pressed his nostrils against the bars, sniffing deeply, bowing his neck and making a rumbling sound in his throat. The horse Is was leading didn't respond. The berserker did.

He went past her, slamming her against his old horse. The horse staggered, went to his knees, and stayed there swaying as though trying to decide whether to get up or just go ahead and fall down.

Is overrode her feelings for the horse. If he went down, she might not be able to get the berserker's saddle off him. Quickly, while the horse was still on his knees, she undid the girth and pulled the saddle from his back. As though that gave him more will he tried to rise, but faltered, careened against the wall, scrambled a few more steps on his knees, and then somehow found his footing and stood, legs wide, head low, nostrils flared, and sides heaving.

The berserker paid him no attention. He stopped in front of the bay's stall. The stallion had quieted and was standing with ears pricked looking at the man. If only the berserker wouldn't open the door, or do something else stupid, Is might have a minute to deal with this poor horse.

The horse's head hung at her knees, his eyes sunken with dehydration. His coat had been soaked with sweat and had dried into a crusty mat. He was beginning to wobble on his widely placed legs. Not wanting him to go down in the aisle, Is gave the reins a tug. She was afraid to speak a word of command to the horse because the berserker would hear and know she was a woman.

The poor horse lifted its tired head and staggered after her into the stall she had prepared for him. The clean straw rustled loudly as the horse dropped to his knees. Quickly Is slipped his bridle from his head. She always tried to do this before they went down. It was her way of telling the horse he had accomplished his mission, and it was the final praise this horse would get. His hind legs buckled and he fell heavily on his side.

Is had to step over his legs to get to the door. She was careful. Sometimes the horses went into convulsions.

At the door she looked back. The horse looked so huge lying flat out, like an already bloated corpse. His flanks heaved with the effort of breathing. Mud was caked on his legs and under his belly. A thick layer of white chalky sweat had dried between his hind legs.

He was finer of bone than her bay, more of a galloper, while the bay with his heavier legs and bigger hooves was designed for the rigors of rearing and kicking. Is could imagine the horse that was lying before her standing, sleek and full of himself, his chestnut coat gleaming the way the trainer must have kept it before the berserker came. She could almost see him raise his head, his eyes intelligent and trusting instead of the way they were now, half-open and staring. She turned away before the questions could come, but her body shook with suppressed rage.

The berserker's back was to her. His hands gripped the bars of the bay's stall as though he would rip them out. Muscles stood out on his shoulders, biceps, and forearms. For a moment she was too mad to be afraid of him. A rational part of her mind knew she was in deep trouble. The augmented senses of the berserker would pick up her pheromones of anger.

The berserker spun so quickly Is had no time to move, not that it would have done her any good. His huge hand closed on the front of her coat and he pulled her toward him. His eyes were focused now. He laughed, revealing large flat teeth that reminded her of the stallion's. His grip constricted the coat around her torso, and she was thankful for its thick leather. It kept him from feeling the way his hand was twisting her breast. She wanted to cry out with pain but she fought to stay silent. If he didn't realize she was a woman he might kill her, but he wouldn't rape her. She tried to keep this coat heavily saturated with a man's scent by making Brandy wear it every time he visited. Now she prayed the berserker wouldn't smell her woman's fear.

Behind him, the bay whinnied, rearing up and striking the bars with his hooves. Distracted, the berserker shoved Is away. Her feet flew off the ground as if she weighed nothing. Her back slammed against the wall across the aisle from the stallion's stall. Her head snapped back against the bars and she crumpled to the ground.

. . . Nothing hurt. Not really, though it seemed as if something should. There was a loud ringing in her head. If it would just stop, she could find out about the rest of her body. There were other sounds too. Crashing, and the ripping of wood, like a horse kicking down a stall. But her eyes could only see black. She should move anyway. Maybe back into the dying horse's stall. Standing up seemed out of the question. *Crawl.* Her body had lost the technique of it. Fear hit her with a rush of adrenaline that took her over the edge of dizziness into unconsciousness.

Chapter 2

Brandy found Is two days later curled up to the horse's stiff corpse.

Brandy was the cleanup rider who came after the berserkers. He was supposed to be a doctor among other things, but the only medicine he seemed to know how to administer was brandy. Thus the name.

Most of the time it didn't matter if he wasn't a real doctor. Trainers who made a mistake with the stallion or the berserker usually died. Brandy would drink with the ones who had survived. He buried the others. He buried dead horses, repaired barns, brought new stock, and he brought news. For most of the Border Station trainers he was their only contact with the rest of the world.

By the time Brandy found her, Is had a fever as well as a concussion. When he managed to rouse her she was not particularly rational. The dying horse had kept her warm for a while, but now it was cold and stiff. Is had been unable to get up and tend the other horses and that was all that was on her mind. Brandy had to see to them before Is would stop fighting him and let him put her to bed.

Brandy used his horse to pull the dead horse out of the barn. His horse was accustomed to such work. The weather had been cold and the carcass was holding together well, so Brandy just kept dragging it all day. When it got dark he unhooked the corpse, retrieved his rope and headed back, relying on his horse to take him back as surely as a compass to the other horses and the feed waiting at the barn.

Usually Brandy buried the horses. It wasn't good to have predators around a barn area, especially this close to the Boundary. But there was too much work to do this time.   The barn was a wreck. The one super-reinforced stall was almost immune to both horse and computer-augmented human berserker, but the rest of the barn was of ordinary construction. Sturdy enough for other horses, it had been like kindling to the enraged berserker. Is had been lucky that he had taken it out on the barn and not her.

It took eight days to repair the damage. The first two days Is was too weak to get out of bed. Brandy had to help her to the bathroom and she hated him for it. She was furious at being ill, furious at the berserker and, Brandy suspected, furious at the system.

Whenever Brandy went out he saw carrion birds circling where the dead horse lay. This close to the Boundary there might be other "things" feeding on the horse too. It hadn't been very smart to leave it above ground but it was done now.

By the third day Is was out of bed and insisting on helping him. They used up the stockpiled lumber repairing the barn. Brandy would have to send in a wagon crew to cut more and Is wouldn't like that. She was one of the most solitary trainers he dealt with.

Trainers were an odd lot anyway, living alone most of their lives, suspicious of people and devoted to their horses, but Brandy got on with them mostly. For some of the women his occasional visits were their only sexual contact. But not Is. Her family had been killed by marauding Blueskins when she was little and Brandy could guess how that had been. Blueskins didn't usually harm children, but they had raped her mother. Is would have seen the whole thing.

He felt bad for Is. The Alliance could have fixed her. He knew enough about medicine to know that, but the Alliance needed her the way she was. The trainer's life required a certain kind of toughness. They had to stay alone in these outposts facing the difficult and sometimes dangerous task of training the war horses, and then they had to face the berserkers' visits. But hardest of all they had to send the horses they loved to their deaths. They must believe those deaths were necessary.

There wasn't any way to lie to these Border Station trainers. They saw how the berserkers treated their line horses. Farther from the Boundary it wasn't so bad. The implants hadn't caused the berserkers' brains to release their chemicals yet. But the closer they got to the Boundary, the harder they pushed their horses and by the time they were within three days' ride of the Border Stations their computer-augmented minds were picking up the magno-electric output of the stallions' specially equipped brains. From then on, rider and horse fed on each other's emotions. By the time the berserker arrived at the last stations neither rider nor horse was entirely sane.

The rider was damn near as dangerous as the horse at that point. Brandy didn't envy the Border Station trainers their jobs. But it was too bad about Is. She would be beautiful if she'd take a care about it. When she was with her horses she radiated such vitality and caring . . . that shouldn't be wasted on horses. Brandy sometimes fantasized about her turning that look on him. But it would never be.

As long as he stayed in his role, Is was willing to accept him. She'd talk about her horses and show him their progress, all animated and beautiful, and he'd want her so badly. But if he ever made any move, offered any hint that he'd like to change things, she'd retreat with a coldness he knew hid fear. While he played in his mind with how it would be to break through that fear and seduce her, he knew he would never try. She was one of the Alliance's best Border Station trainers and his job was to keep her that way.

Chapter 3

Brandy watched Is working the liver chestnut stallion. He was a beautiful animal with sloping shoulders, great muscular hindquarters and a lovely arched neck. Except that his head was a little large and a little Roman-nosed, his conformation was nearly perfect, showing the best mix of the bulk of the draft horse and the refinement and speed of the native breed. Brandy could see the horse's training had come a long way since his last visit. There was a special communion between Is and this horse. That wasn't good. Brandy knew the danger signs.

You could lose a good trainer a lot of ways. Sometimes they got hurt one time too many by the horses and lost their nerve. Sometimes they got too scared of the berserkers' visits. Sometimes they became too attached to a horse. And worst of all, sometimes they started questioning the system.

Is had at least two of the danger signs. She was too attached to this horse. And, Brandy suspected that a lot of the anger she had held against the marauders who killed her parents had swung around to be focused against the system that took her horses from her and made her vulnerable to the berserkers.

Sometimes it helped to remind the trainers how important they were to the success of the entire Alliance. To the rest of the population the trainers were heroes. Not only could they handle the much-feared war horses, but also they were the only thing standing between the people and the marauders who would destroy the farms on which everyone depended for food.

The horse trainers were usually picked from the children of the upper classes. It was easy for Brandy to appeal to the patriotism that was so inculcated into them. But Is was an anomaly in the system. As the orphaned daughter of farm parents she had not been of a high enough station to receive the benefits of the culture she now worked to protect.

Brandy knew it was time to bring Is in. He also knew that short of drugging and tying her he'd never make it. Once Is saw the way of things, she'd go rogue and it would be ten days to a place where Brandy could count on getting help with her. He couldn't handle her alone for that long.

He thought about knocking her out and taking the horses. She'd be on foot then and she'd either stay here and the Alliance would pick her up for reconditioning, or she'd trek off and hide and probably perish. The important thing was that Brandy mustn't let her take the horses and run.

In the end Brandy decided on the course he usually took, the course of least resistance. He got Is to drink with him.

She usually wouldn't drink more than a few sips, but Brandy was quite skillful. He pretended to be getting drunk and started telling Is the kind of stories she'd want to hear, rumors about how the whole berserker system might be shutting down. He wasn't supposed to tell her this, oh no. But who could she tell? And with drunken sincerity he made her swear to secrecy anyway. Then he told her how the Alliance had found a better way to control the Blueskins.

As with the berserker system it would avoid an all-out war that would decimate the Blueskins, for the Blueskins did serve a purpose. Their savagery kept all the other things that lived behind the Boundary in check.

The new method would appeal to the Blueskins' primitive awe of a superior warrior just as the berserkers did. But unlike the berserkers, the new plan would not risk the lives of horses.

Brandy could not tell Is more about it. He wasn't even supposed to tell this much and he changed the subject to how war horses were going to be kept in state. They had been such an important part of the Alliance for so long they would still be bred and trained, but for show and display only. They'd be honored for all time for the role they had played in making the Alliance a safe place to live. Of course the trainers would go with their horses. Who else could show them? Surely not the berserkers. There'd be no more berserkers made. The trainers would be glorified for the part they'd played in defending the Alliance. Brandy knew that didn't matter to Is. What mattered to her was that she'd be allowed to stay with her stallions.

He managed to get two drinks into her that night. With her armor somewhat relaxed, Brandy set the hypnotic induction field and Is went under easily enough. It was a different Brandy who spoke to her then. His voice was cultured. His cadence was exactly fitted to the field for maximum strength. Even so he didn't try to do too much He just told her to stay here, better days were coming soon, and he reminded her of the dangers that lurked in the Boundary, elaborating on the childhood horror stories all children were told.

The next day, when Brandy was leaving, Is asked him how long it would be before he sent the lumber crew to repair the barn. That was the only clue she gave him.

He paused to think about his answer, then told her he had to visit the station to the east of hers before he headed back to the Alliance. It would probably be two weeks before he got to where he could *fast* the order, then maybe another two or three weeks before the wagon arrived at her place.

He headed out in the proper direction, put two ridges between them and turned abruptly south toward the Alliance.

Is waited until the next day, then she took the liver chestnut for a ride and found where Brandy's tracks turned south. She rode home slowly. In her heart she had known Brandy was lying to her. Things were not going to change, not soon. Brandy was heading back to where he could *fast* his order immediately. He had deliberately built more time into his plan to mislead her. It would not be a lumber wagon that came and it would not take the four plus weeks Brandy wanted her to believe. Is didn't know exactly what was happening. She only knew she had lost her last horse to a berserker.

With that decision came a sudden upwelling of her spirit. Delighted by the unexpected feeling of freedom, Is put the stallion into a gallop. He went effortlessly, his long strides springing them over the rough ground as if it were cushioned meadowland. For a time Is let the stallion's rhythm carry her, her body working in unison with his. She loved the power and speed that were suddenly hers, the horse's body an extension of her own. She thought nothing and immersed herself in the pure animal pleasure of galloping.

By the time she had walked the stallion cool her mind was working again, frantically.   It was one thing to decide to steal a war horse and run; it was another to do it. For one thing, Is was terrified. The only direction open to her was into the Boundary. There was no doubt in her mind that the Alliance would hunt her down and punish or kill her if she stayed in their territory. Stealing a war horse would be considered an act of treason. Her only hope of escaping the Alliance lay in going into the Boundary.

She didn't know if the Alliance would send troopers, or maybe even a berserker after her. But it was the other things that lived in the Boundary she found herself fearing most.

The Blueskins were first on her mind. She knew what they did to women and she feared them deeply. But at least they were human Except for the bluish cast to their skin they looked like other men, just larger and stronger than most But the other things that were said to live in the Boundary ... Is had no idea how she could face them.

The great lizards could run down a horse over a short distance. She knew of their voracious appetites. Then there was something that stood on its back legs like a man, with long hooked claws on its hands and the strength of a berserker. Even more frightening than that, there were forces that could manifest as winds, or rock slides, voices where there shouldn't be voices, fogs that could drive you off your route and drive you crazy, rivers that were poison, eagles large enough to consider her prey, and other things, more evil and less understandable. She found her mind full of them.

She tried to tell herself that death at their hands wasn't any worse than awaiting her fate with the Alliance. She believed herself. That didn't make her any less fearful.

She thought about how it would be if she got the stallion killed and that almost stopped her, but his fate with the Alliance would be no better.

Horses didn't want to be weapons. Left on their own horses ran away from danger.   Running away would be her strategy too. This stallion wasn't as heavily built as some of the war horses she'd trained and he was faster than most. She'd do everything she could to protect him. Surely that was better than letting him be ridden into attack by a man who cared about nothing but attack.

Somewhere along the line Is found that she had decided not to take the other two horses. The liver chestnut was "hers" in some way the other two weren't, so it wasn't so much like stealing.

She waited six more days before leaving, needing a head start on whatever troopers Brandy had sent for her, but not wanting the other horses left alone too long. They would be safe in their paddocks for the two or three days the troopers should be behind her, she reasoned. She'd leave them more than enough hay for a week, in case she'd miscalculated. They would soil and waste a lot of it, their pens would be a mess and they would be high-spirited, but the troopers could handle them. If she were wrong about the troopers coming, the horses would starve to death. But her guts told her she was not wrong.

She spent the intervening days getting ready. She sewed her quilts together to make a sleeping bag. She fashioned a tent and tarp from the waterproof grain sacks.

She packed rice, beans and flour but she knew she would have to learn to live off the land even more than she did now. She took her hunting knives, skinning knives, rope for snares and other purposes, and extra leather for repairing tack.

The things that would be most irreplaceable were metal: a bucket, the knives, a rasp for the horse's hooves, a hammer, a bowl, spoon and cup, the axe. It helped that she had already lived a simple existence close to the land all these years.

When she finally turned the stallion's head north he looked more like a pack animal than a proud war horse. The two younger stallions were in the paddock where she often left them when she rode the liver chestnut. When they crested the first ridge she stopped and looked back. For some reason both the young stallions raised their heads and whinnied. There was no way they could know she was not coming back. It was just coincidence she told herself.

She was sadder to leave them behind than she had thought she would be. She took one last look at the valley where she had lived. The grass was still showing green in irregular splotches, but the bushes and trees were mostly leafless. Their bare branches had a reddish cast. A few bright yellow leaves still clung here and there in clumps, adding dashes of color. The taller grasses where the horses hadn't eaten were shades of bay and chestnut. It was not a good time of year to be setting out across mountains.

The house, barn and paddocks nestled in the middle of the valley, a little village unto themselves. Is had stood down there and looked up at this ridge how many times? She had watched these mountains in all their moods, survived their winters, celebrated the springs, cursed the mud, hated the ice as she'd broken it from the water buckets in the stalls, and basked in the heat of late summer afternoons with her horses grazing all around her. Over the years she'd watched colts grow and change from gangly, uncoordinated yearlings to beautiful, intelligent beings as she sculpted their bodies and brought out their capacity to learn with her training. That was her life.

It called her now to return. But she knew it was already changed. Troopers were riding toward her as she should be riding away from them.

Is turned the stallion down the back side of the ridge. They kept to a northerly direction, letting the lay of the mountains determine their course. She had never gone more than half a day's ride in this direction and was soon in new territory. But she knew the berserkers always went this way so there must be a pass through which they could ride a horse. Her plan was to get through that pass as quickly as she could, then bear east or west and try to find a sheltered place to spend the winter. Maybe if she didn't go too deep into the Boundary nothing would bother her.

From the top of the next ridge she studied the land ahead. The mountains rose like a barrier, sheer and uninviting. There was only one notch in their formidable facade. It had to be the pass.

That evening they camped near a little creek and Is let the horse loose to graze. She thought they were too far from home for him to head back there so he would probably stay with her for companionship. If he wouldn't, it was as well to find out now.

Is ate a cold dinner. She would have no cook fires until she was sure there was no pursuit. She did not know when that would be.

In spite of being tired she was lonely and nervous. She could not bring herself to go inside a tent where she could be trapped. She pitched only the fly, unrolled her sleeping bag and lay awake a long time imagining all the things, natural and supernatural, that could kill a horse. He was truly her only friend now.

Horses had been her only friends for a long time. When she finally slept, her dreams were full of horrors from a time before that was true.

. . . Her father had taken an axe when he went out to meet the Blueskins. He hadn't limped. It was the only time Is had not seen him limp on his gimped-up leg. When the Blueskins saw that he would fight they dismounted. They towered over her father. Their bare chests painted in slashes of blood red and rock-sickle orange made their skin look even bluer.

Her father's axe glinted in the morning sun, raised above his shoulder. Is saw it begin its forward, downward stroke . . .

The scream ripped across her dream. Her mother's scream. The harsh grunts of the men ... the blood across her mother's bare thigh . . .

Absolute stillness.

. . . The sun not moving in the sky. The heat pressing her to the ground. The weight of the shovel in her hands. The over-loud scrape of its bite into the gravelly soil. An eternity passing, one shovel full after the next, after the next.

. . . The grave grew until it was deeper than Is was tall. A moon lit the sky above her but in the grave it was dark and very still. She slept there when her body stopped moving. The earth was cold. She should be cold. She felt nothing.

. . . Morning was almost as dark as the night had been. Fog seeped over the edge of the grave and flowed down into the hole with her. It looked like a waterfall frozen in slow motion. When she threw a shovel full of dirt out it fell back in. She had to climb out to move the dirt away from the edge so it wouldn't keep falling in. A sound drew her attention. A horse came trotting out of the mist. It was gray like the mist, with a black leather harness and blinkers on its bridle, pulling a flatbed wagon. Another horse, dark as a shadow, and its rider followed behind.

When she saw the two men she felt relief. It didn't occur to her that they would take her away. She didn't realize she couldn't stay at her home anymore because she was only twelve years old and they couldn't leave her there alone. She was just relieved they had come because they would know how to get her mother into the grave. She had been dreading that. The thought of having to touch her mother's stiff and violated body was terrible enough. But the thought of having to drag her across the ground, which was the only way Is could move her, and then watch her fall into the hole, made Is feel panicky.

And then there was her father. The Blueskins had cut his head off with his own axe and Is was afraid to pick it up with her hands. She was afraid of it, afraid of him . . . but these men wouldn't be afraid to pick up a man's head and put it in a grave.

She was relieved when they told her to get into the wagon. She thought they would finish burying her parents and she wouldn't have to watch their bodies falling into the hole or the dirt being thrown in on top of them. Instead, the wagon started to move away. That wasn't right. The man driving told her to stay right where she was. She did not want to disobey him but then she looked back and saw the smoke. They had not buried her parents. They had burned them and the house and everything.

. . . She heard the man running behind her and ran as hard as she could but he grabbed her. She fought as her mother had fought, but he was too strong. He carried her back to the wagon and tied her in it.

The other man was angry when he caught up to them riding his horse. The two men argued. The second man asked her to promise not to run away again so he could untie her.   She wouldn't promise anything to a man who'd burned her home.

Is stirred, crossing from dream into wakefulness without leaving the dream behind. It had happened half her lifetime ago, but the dreams kept it as clear as yesterday.

She shifted her position, trying to shift her thoughts, and another memory took her into sleep.

. . . The man's footsteps echoed in the stone hallway as he walked in front of her. She had to hurry to keep up with him in this strange cold place.

He stopped at one in the endless row of doors they had passed. "Go in." These were the first words he had spoken to her except "Follow me."

There were probably ten kids in the room. They were sitting on a bench, and they all stared at Is as she walked in.

The door closed behind her and she stood, uncertain what to do.

Finally one of the boys got up and sauntered over to her. He was a lot taller than she.   He had a haughty belligerent air about him as he walked around her. Suddenly he reached out and jerked her shirt, ripping it.

"What kind of clothing is that?" he asked scornfully.

"It's rags," a girl answered. She unfolded gracefully from the bench. She was tall and beautiful and at least three or four years older than Is. But her tone and posture were insulting.

"It's what peasants wear. Ain't you never seen a peasant?" she said to the boy.

It was a shirt Is's mother had made for her. It was the same woven fiber that everyone wore where Is came from. But these kids were dressed in some materials Is had never seen before. They were neat and clean and their hair was done in fancy ways, not the braids Is wore. She knew she didn't belong here and she wanted to leave as much as the other children seemed to want her to leave, but the man had said, "Your parents are dead, do you understand that? They are dead. Gone. Your home is gone."

They had been in a room with a high ceiling and wood panels covering the perfectly good stone walls, because they were so rich here they could have both.

"You have nowhere to go except where we tell you to go. You don't own anything.   You don't have any rights. You're a ward of the Alliance. That means we're going to feed and house you and you're going to learn to do something useful to earn your keep. You understand that? Earn your keep?"

He was a very stern man with down turned lines at the corners of his mouth. He seemed to be angry at her for being there although Is didn't want to be there any more than he wanted her there.

"You can make this easy on yourself, or hard," he said. "Your folks would have wanted you to do what you're told, learn to earn your keep."

On her family's farm everyone had earned their keep. But on the farm there had been love and happiness and sharing. Is could already see that it wasn't going to be like that in the government school.

She woke to what she thought was the absolute dark of the windowless dorm room where she had lived those first years in the Alliance. Then she smelled the trees sleeping all around her and felt the cold damp air. She was free of the awful school, free of the Alliance. A strange, defiant joy filled her. This might not last long, it might not end well, but for the moment she was free!

She had spent six horrible months in that school before she had been picked to go to the equestrian academy. The contact with the horses had come as a great relief. Although her poor farm parents had not been allowed to own a horse, Is had been around plenty of other animals. She knew their basic natures and she knew they would always be true to those natures. If you understood that, an animal would never betray you. It couldn't betray its nature.

To Is, horses were the most beautiful of all animals. The way the government restricted their use and breeding made them even more thrilling because they were unobtainable. On horseback, one would be taller, faster, more beautiful, and surely smarter, more pure, and more courageous than ordinary mortals. But beneath all the romanticism in her heart Is knew horses were animals. So she had applied herself to learning their true natures while she worked at cleaning their stalls, grooming them, feeding them, and learning to care for their medical problems. But through it all she had never missed a chance to watch the riders being trained.

Lowly apprentices, like Is, had to work for years before they were allowed to train as riders. She slid back into an uneasy sleep, her mind reliving the horrors of those years when her only relief had been the quiet moments spent grooming the horses.

Is broke out of her memories to the song of a bird, a meadowlark. It was morning although still very early. A mist had formed a few feet above the ground, like a blanket.   But when she stood up, her head rose above the fog. The morning was outrageously beautiful. The sky was deep blue, not a cloud anywhere. The peaks rose all around, snowcapped against the sky. A creek gurgled, unseen, As Is walked, the mist swirled about her legs. Then she saw the stallion and her heart leapt. He had stayed with her. Is had not allowed herself to realize how important that was to her. Suddenly the whole thing seemed possible. They might get somewhere and find a place to live, and it wouldn't be much different from life at the station except the horse would never be taken from her. She could be happy.

She waded through the mist to the horse. He was resting one hind leg, sleeping in the way horses do, aware of her approach but not truly awake. She spoke to him and touched his neck. His hair felt damp and she could see how moisture had collected in little beads on the tips of the long hair he was growing for winter. When she stroked it, her hand left a wet swath. He turned his face to her. His eyes were so kind and trusting that Is was suddenly overcome with the feeling that she had done the right thing. He towered over her but he was all gentleness. She stroked his ears the way he liked and let herself feel her love for him. The meadowlark called again, clear and achingly beautiful. The stallion turned his head, ears pointed to listen.

"Lark" she said softly, explaining to him that it was just a bird, nothing to fear. Then a funny feeling passed through her. "Lark," she said again and it was his name. She had never named a horse before. It was against the law. But now the law had no hold over her.

With the name she confirmed herself. Outlaw. It was as simple as that.

Chapter 4

The trail into the pass was beginning to seem like a highway. Is had to rethink her strategy. Not only would the troopers know this route but anyone coming out of the Boundary would probably take this path too. The thought of meeting a party of Blueskins affirmed her decision to turn aside.

The only other place that looked slightly passable was a high saddle between two snow-covered peaks, so she set a new course of landmarks to steer her in that direction.

Halfway through the morning it began to rain, just a drizzle, but the mist that came with it obscured the surrounding mountains. In time, plodding through the gray, featureless landscape had a stupefying effect on Is. Huddled into herself she may have missed some warning signs. The first she knew of trouble was when Lark's head came up and he stopped in his tracks. From his body posture Is guessed he was hearing other horses. Any moment he would whinny and give them away. Abruptly she turned him back the way they had come and set off in a trot.

That might have worked ... if the other horse hadn't whinnied first. Is heard the high tones, distant and questioning, dampened by the fog. Before she could do anything, Lark's neigh rang out, impossibly loud in the hushed damp land. For long seconds it rolled away into the distance like thunder reverberating off the hillsides.

Is kicked Lark into a gallop. If he was running maybe he wouldn't whinny. Maybe the echoes would confuse pursuit. Things were moving too fast for any real planning but she knew they would have to get off the ridge they were on and down into the forest to hide. Before she could act, riders burst from the trees below and slightly ahead on the left. They were traveling at a quick trot in the same general direction Is was galloping. In an instant she would catch up to them. She pulled Lark back and tried to turn him before it registered that the riders hadn't seen her.

There were five of them, not government men. She clearly saw the telltale bluish cast of their skin.

Lark's hooves clattered on the rocky ground as he tried to obey Is's command to check his speed and turn. If even one of the Blueskins looked up, they'd be on her in heartbeats. In the interminable seconds it took Lark to sit back on his hindquarters and turn, none of them looked up. They were all staring straight ahead and trotting as though they had somewhere to go. As Is sent Lark plunging down the other side of the ridge, her last impression was of the blue-skinned riders, bare from their waists up, on weedy thin horses hardly bigger than ponies. But those small scrappy horses would be quicker and more maneuverable than her massive war horse on this steep rocky terrain.

Her mind registered all that in a flash while her body dealt with trying to slow Lark before they plunged into the trees, but he could not obey her. He was skidding hock-deep in a landslide of mud, rocks, and loose debris. The rocks hit the trees first. One airborne fist-sized stone bit a chunk out of a pine with a sound like a dull explosion. Then more rocks and mud arrived, rattling the trees like a hurricane and making a noise Is couldn't have screamed over. The Blueskins on the other side of the ridge would surely hear that. But she had more immediate problems. If they hit a tree at the speed they were going, Lark could break his neck. There was no time for further imagination. The first branch hit her - just a little offhand slap across the ribs - that nearly knocked her off Lark, a reminder that she could get hurt too.

She felt something snag Lark's hind leg just long enough to reorient him sideways on the slide. If he lost his footing now he'd roll. Instinctively, Is dropped off his uphill side and landed on her feet but only for an instant. The mud was cold and wet and full of hard rocks, moving very fast. For a little piece of eternity she had enough of her own problems not to worry about Lark. Then her hands caught hold of a root and she anchored herself against the worst of the slide in time to see Lark lose his footing and roll. For an awful moment his legs thrashed wildly in the air before he flipped all the way over. He got his feet under him just in time to broadside a tree. He hung there a moment, two legs on either side of the trunk, while the worst of the slide went by. Then the tree began to bend, slowly, until it stopped at about forty-five degrees.

Is slid-skittered down to him, starting a little spill of her own. The slope was wiped bare of anything large and loose, so she was mostly skiing on raw clay. Lark heaved himself upright and stepped free of the tree. Is had time to note that he seemed steady on all his legs before she was consumed with stopping herself from sliding under him.

Most horses would have been spooked out of their wits. He greeted her like a long-lost friend, snuffling her all over as though reassuring himself of something. His pupils were big and Is could see the muscle in his left hind leg trembling. She put her arms around his neck, suddenly shaking so badly she couldn't stand without his support. She clung there a moment trying to get control of herself. This was no time to go to pieces with Blueskins behind them, and more must be ahead. The horse that whinnied had been ahead of them. And Lark might be hurt. That thought galvanized her into action.

She went over Lark with her hands. He was covered with red clay and she couldn't see anything. If he was scraped or cut, at least it wasn't bad enough to bleed through the coating of mud. If nothing else he was bound to have some pretty sore muscles.

Her own hands were scraped raw and would be sore too once the adrenaline settled out of her system.

Lark's saddle was probably all scraped up under the mud that covered it, but she'd have to find out about that later. The packs that held her gear seemed intact. The reins had broken and the headstall had been pulled off one ear. Is righted that and led Lark by the piece of rein still dangling from one side of the bit. He seemed willing enough to move. She'd have to get him on level ground to be sure he was really okay ... get him to a stream . . . wash him down . . . check out the tack.

The thought she'd been avoiding finally surfaced. Why hadn't the Blueskins come? They had to have heard all that noise. Had they thought it was a landslide and not wanted to be anywhere near it? Had they not heard it? Mountains could play tricks with sound. Suddenly Is had to stop. Her legs just wouldn't go any farther. Everything could have been over as quick as that! Lark could have been terribly hurt and she'd have no way to help him. Was it really worth the risk of breaking his neck to try to save him from the Alliance?

What if the Blueskins caught her? They'd rape her and beat her and stab her like her mother. She could see the blood. She would never forget the smell of it, or her mother's cries and the harsh grunts of the men. Never! Any sort of death was preferable to that.

She could go back and turn herself in. She didn't know what the Alliance would do. Punish her? Retrain her? The horror of the years in the government schools filled her and she knew she could never go back to that. Death was better.

She had not really understood what it would be like to be pursued. Somewhere deep inside she had believed that since she was saving Lark's life she would be lucky. Everything would work out because she was doing the right thing for the horse.

She leaned against Lark's neck and considered what would happen if the government caught them. They would take good care of Lark, until they sent him out to die.

If the Blueskins caught them, they might try to take good care of Lark, but he would not do well on the harsh, sparse diets that barely sustained their small mountain ponies. Is had no idea how the Blueskins felt about their animals. Were they just creatures of utility to be abandoned when they were sick or hurt? She had no guarantee they wouldn't kill Lark and eat him.

She started to walk again. The Blueskins must be well gone by now. But the initial whinny had come from the other direction. It couldn't have been one of the ponies in the band she had seen. There must be more Blueskins up there. She turned downhill.

There might be a stream at the bottom to wash Lark and she needed to repair the bridle. Is had reached her decision. She would not be captured even at the risk of both of their lives.

A cold rain began to fall. The mud sloughed off her and Lark and ran down their legs in brown rivulets. As much as Is feared stopping, moving on was impossible. It was getting dark. The ground was slippery and the exposed rocks were beginning to ice so when she stepped on one she slid and nearly fell. She found a spot that seemed protected by big trees and pitched her tarp.

Soon she discovered that sitting around in the miserable damp was worse than walking, soaked through, had been. The cold made Is hungry, and once she had mended the reins, she had little to think about but her hunger and how hopeless her situation really was. She ate sparingly from dry rations, longing for hot food and a warm, dry place to be. The night was long and miserable. Her mind drifted back to the first days in the government school.

. . . She was following the boy with red hair. She had never seen hair that color. His skin was mottled with red spots too, like a hound her father had kept. She had tried not to stare when he'd been introduced to her. Jacob was his name. Even his eyelashes were red.

He was fifteen and he was in charge of her. Someone had to be in charge of her. She had no idea how to get around in the world in which she found herself. She was used to a rough cabin that offered peace and quiet, where meals were cooked in a stove heated by burning wood.The cafeteria was bigger than the inside of their house and barn put together. And the noise! So many people making so much noise just to eat! She followed the boy inside. People stared at her and stopped talking.

The food tasted bad, soft and overcooked. The noise and hostility and strangeness kept Is from being able to eat anyway. Where she came from you didn't take what you couldn't finish. But some angry-looking women shoveled the food onto her plate – plop, plop – and Is had been afraid to protest.

After Jacob saw she wasn't going to eat it, he reached over and switched his empty plate for hers and ate her food too. She'd thought he was doing her a favor. Later she learned he was breaking the rules by having two lunches. But that day she'd been too naive to know she could have sold it to him in return for protection, information, or something else of value. Instead, she'd just let him take it and people had seen and thought she was stupid.

Jacob was supposed to show her around so she'd know where the rooms were when someone told her to go to one of them. Is followed him and tried to remember, but mostly she was lost. The buildings were so big and most of the rooms didn't have windows. There was no way to find her direction from the sun and the plants and the wind. She felt intimidated, but the atmosphere was so hostile she could not allow herself to show it.

One of the rooms Jacob showed her was a library. Stepping through the door, Is was suddenly surrounded by books from wall to wall. Books from floor to ceiling. Books so high up there were ladders and walkways to reach them. Books like the ones her parents had told her about, but that she had never gotten to see. Books that a farmer would never get to read because farmers couldn't read. Farmers weren't allowed to learn to read.

Is's parents had wished that she could have a better station in life than theirs. Is hadn't cared. She'd been completely content. Yet she had understood how much her parents revered books and education. Now it seemed their dreams for her were possible. She might learn to read.

A whole world opened up before her. She walked slowly into the room, not even aware of having done so, drawn by something too strong to name. Seeing the books meant more to her than anything she could remember since the death of her parents.

"Isadora! Isadora, pssst." She didn't hear Jacob's urgent whisper before the two men who sat reading raised their heads and stared at her. She would never forget the look of cold contempt in their eyes. Even in the cafeteria the hostility had been minor compared to this. She froze.

"What dare you in here, student?" It wasn't a question. It was a denouncement.

Is could not answer. What had drawn her into the library was opposite to what she faced now. She could not explain the fascination she had felt. She had wanted to know how it felt to look inside a book and learn something just by seeing. How would it feel not to have to put your hands into it, or lift with your back, or get covered in its smell, or feel it through your whole body. How did it feel to learn just through your eyes? Just sitting still?

After long seconds the man turned his angry gaze on Jacob who had stayed at the door behind her. "Explain."

No one had ever used that tone of voice with Is before. Her father at his angriest, at some thoughtless or harmful mistake, might have demanded an explanation from her. But he would listen to it. She knew these men would not. They were not simply asking why she had come into a room she had not known she should not have entered. Instead, they seemed intent upon showing her how stupid and ugly and worthless she was. Evidently Jacob understood this too because he did not respond.

"Your name, student."

"Jacob Onry, sir."

Is heard the fear in Jacob's voice. But there was something else there too. Something conniving, dishonest, and just plain wrong. The man fixed his eyes on her.

"Your name, student."

Is understood with all her heart the injustice of what this man was trying to do to her. She understood how reprehensible it was of Jacob to allow this man to do that to him. For one blinding instant she understood the wickedness of the whole place.

"Isadora Drey," she answered, and it came out like a challenge. *I am my parents' child. They were better people than you, and I am better than you.* But that small act of defiance was before, before they'd had her long enough.

She rubbed her face as though she could scrub away the memory. Why should she think about that now? She had never been able to reconcile her inner knowing – something she seemed to have learned from her parents – with what was expected of her at the school.

She had sensed something terribly wrong. But her child's sense of correctness had been pitted against all the people at the school. All the adults Is should have trusted and honored, and all the older, wiser students couldn't all be wrong. So Is had come to doubt herself. She had tried to do what she thought her parents would want her to do, to behave by the rules of her new home. When that had proven impossible, she had learned to do what was necessary to survive.

Eventually, despite the cold and wet she dozed. But her sleep was filled with strange dreams, inspired by the ceaseless wind and her old confusion was with her more relentlessly than it had been in years.

By morning the rain had stopped. The sky had been washed to the palest of blues as though color had bled from it with the rain. Everything had a washed-clean feeling to it. Lark's coat was soft as a newborn foal's after its rain bath, soft as Is's own hair. She was glad to see that he moved freely, without favoring any leg. In spite of their situation her spirits rose.

She draped yesterday's wet clothes over Lark's rump and shoulders, tucking the ends under the saddle so they wouldn't blow off as they walked. It was the only way the clothes were ever going to get dry. He looked like a peasant's clothesline, her proud war horse, but there wasn't anyone to see him. She hoped.

The wind continued all morning. Wispy clouds scudded overhead and by afternoon the mountaintops were shrouded again.

So far they had seen nothing unnatural and not even any of the larger natural predators had appeared. Is hoped it would stay that way. Whenever she heard a meadowlark call she thought it was good luck.

It was hard to guess how much land they covered. The saddle, which had seemed to be only over the next ridge, now seemed farther away as a stretch of open land came into view.

They kept going and days began to blend into each other. As they gained altitude there was very little grazing and Lark was noticeably losing weight. Is promised him a rest in the first good pastureland they came to once they'd crossed the saddle.

The day they finally crested the ridge was hot and sunny. The sky, bleached almost to white, offered no shielding from the sun. There was a silence and stillness to the air as though it was too tired from the heat and altitude to carry any sound. Even Lark's hooves on the rocky ground and the saddle leather's soft squeaking seemed distant.

Is found herself staring into space, thinking nothing, immersed in each plodding step of the toiling horse. They were almost in the midst of the riders before Is saw them.

Blueskins. A dozen of them with their backs to her in a rough half circle. And facing them, four government riders, their sleek proud animals dominating the Blueskins' scruffy ponies.

Is should have already whirled Lark around and galloped away as fast as she could, but her mind was taking in all sorts of conflicting observations. All she managed was to jerk Lark to a halt. And even that was odd. He ought to have seen the horses first. His head should have come up. He should have whinnied.

They were close enough that one of the other horses must see him. No doubt they would at any moment. *I should be galloping away,* Is thought. *Why are Alliance troopers talking to Blueskins? I should be galloping away.* The riders were so much at ease that even their horses were dozing. Several of the Blueskins' ponies had their hind legs cocked, resting. Their tails swished leisurely. The government horses were every bit as relaxed. One rider had swung a leg over the front of his saddle and was leaning his elbow on his knee. He must have felt very much at ease with these Blueskin "enemies" to sit that way.

All of this information went into Is's mind in an instant. What she did next made no more sense to her wildly yammering nerves, which were screaming at her to turn and run, than the scene in front of her did. She turned Lark right and walked him forward. Her course would take her in a big circle around the riders, but she would be out in the open all the time. There was no cover.

Lark went without the slightest hesitation. He didn't even try to turn his head to look at the other horses. Is didn't look at the riders again either, pretending that if she didn't see them they couldn't see her. It was a child's game, totally irrational, and likely to get her killed. She was so tense with listening for the first shout of discovery her head ached. When she finally did look back she had gone farther than she'd realized. There were no riders in sight.

For a moment Is was relieved. Then she began to question if she had really seen them. The whole thing seemed so impossible. But each horse and each rider was etched in her mind's eye. Details she had not been conscious of seeing came back to her – the long, cruel-looking shanks on the Blueskins' bits, their animal-skin saddle pads, the paint pony with the scraggly tail. Then the visions of her mother came, as real and detailed as the riders with their blue-tinted skin and long, braided hair. Is was suddenly in no mood to question anything. She sent Lark into a trot, the fastest pace she dared on the steep shaley slope.

When darkness came Is could not bring herself to stop. It was not just the riders behind her that kept her going. She could not face being still with herself, trapped in a tent, cut off from her horse and from movement. The questions she was trying desperately not to ask herself would overcome her. They'd ask themselves if her mind was not busy with riding.

The horse could see well enough in the dark and there was no grazing, or water here to rest him anyway. It would be better to get down to cover before daylight, she rationalized. She let Lark pick the way. As long as they kept going downhill they couldn't go too wrong.

Eventually he brought them to a little stream. Is took his bridle off, lay flat out on the ground and fell asleep while he grazed. When she woke, Lark was standing nearby with his head hanging above her. Smiling, she turned over and slept some more.

Later the birds woke her. Lark had moved away to graze. Is could hear the rhythmic tearing of grass, the occasional swish of his tail or stomp of his foot as the insects found him. She could have stayed there, in that dream place with only the horse she loved, the land, and no great need to do anything. But there were also Blueskins, government troopers, and winter coming. She stretched and picked up Lark's bridle.

Chapter 5

Is called the valley Safehome, hoping it was going to be both of those things. As she rode down into it old-growth forest had given way to immature trees - branches low to the ground and boles close together - possibly because those acres had burned.

It was exactly the kind of place not to ride a horse, but Is had gone down into it anyway, coaxing Lark to squeeze between trees and duck under branches where no horsemen would go, not government troopers and not even the Blueskins on their smaller horses. And she had been rewarded beyond her greatest hope as the nearly impenetrable trees had opened into a meadow that the forest hadn't reclaimed yet.

The meadow was an elongated egg-shaped bowl, surrounded on three sides by steep land and miles of the sort of trees that would turn horsemen away. On the fourth side the bowl was shallow, but opened to a forbidding snow-covered range that was too steep for horses.

With the days getting shorter and colder Is hurried to build a shed for her and Lark, cutting trees with the axe she had brought and having Lark drag them like a common plow horse. She had not really kept track of the days, but the moon had been waxing when she left her home, and it had been full and waxing again before they found the valley.

It was full again before Is finished the shed. Above Lark's stall she had built a half loft for herself. She and Lark would be protected from the worst of the wind and snow, and Lark would generate enough heat to keep them both from freezing.

The peaks around them had already assumed their winter mantle of snow. The wind was often strong in the surrounding trees, sounding like a rushing river, or fiercely driven rain, but the valley seemed to be protected from the worst of it.

The day the first snow fell in the valley Is took time off from her winter preparations. She had started the tradition of celebrating the first snowfall of each winter when she had lived at the border station.

Keeping the usual holidays made no sense. Either she felt sad remembering good times with her parents, or sad remembering the horrible times at the school where holidays had become just one more chance to be humiliated and embarrassed.

So Is had invented her own special occasions. First Snow was one of her favorites. She could entertain herself for weeks looking forward to it and trying to guess what day it would come. It certainly kept her from dreading it, which she might otherwise have done.

She'd had different ways of celebrating, but they always included a ride, just to enjoy the changed landscape, and usually she would dive into her stores of winter food and find something special to eat.

This year she had no stash of powdered chocolate or carefully rationed sugar to make herself a holiday treat but she didn't let that bother her. She saddled Lark and set off for the far end of the valley. Large powdery flakes settled on Lark's mane like jewels. It was cold enough that they didn't melt but formed a white crest which he occasionally sent flying with a shake of his head.

Winter turned out to be a delight. On the coldest or stormiest days they stayed indoors. Is listened to Lark chewing the dried grass she doled out to him while she repaired leaks in the roof or worked the hides of the small animals she'd killed. Sometimes, when the snow was too deep for Lark, Is would leave him in the stall and go hunting on snowshoes she'd made herself. She hunted rabbits mostly, as they were numerous and she identified with the other small predators that hunted them.

So the winter passed and spring came. They celebrated the thawing of the ground with progressively harder workouts. Although they were alone, Is decided not to give up Lark's training because it was so much fun to work with him. Besides, Is needed the riding to keep her spirits high.

She discovered a wide place in the stream that ran near their shed and took her first bath of the year. It was very cold, and invigorated from it she took Lark for a long gallop.

So spring passed. Summer took hold of the land and everything slowed. The land dreamed its summer dream, and Is dreamed with it, living one day at a time, moment by moment, slowly, in pace with the land.

Chapter 6

In mid-summer they were hacking lazily back from a ride that had taken them out of the shallow end of the valley, when they came upon the mare so suddenly neither of them had any warning. As they crested a rise, Lark's head snapped up and he stopped abruptly, jarring Is from her day dream.

Not twenty yards away the mare's head jerked up in response. Both animals stood frozen at the unexpected sight of each other while Is sat equally immobilized. In an instant she took in the mare's refined head, her expressive eyes and fine bones. She was a dark bay, with black mane and tail – much too fine to be the horse of a Blueskin or a berserker. This mare did not belong here in a way that sent Is's heart racing.

She wore no bridle, and though she wore a saddle it had slipped off to her left side as if she had thrown her rider and run loose.

Lark lowered and raised his head several times, trying to focus the mare better. It was odd, the way she seemed unwilling or unable to move as though her leg, or the dangling stirrup, was caught in the scrub juniper that blocked Is's view.

The mare broke the deadlock by nickering. To Is it sounded like a plea for help. Lark lowered his head and Is felt him relax. He made a soft wuffling sound of reassurance as he walked forward.

Lark was reaching out his neck to sniff noses with the mare when Is saw the man. She wanted to jerk the stallion's head away, and flee, but it was too late. The man would have already seen them. In the next instant Is realized he was not lying in ambush. He looked dead. He lay sprawled on his face, one arm thrown out and the other under him. His body was turned at the hips and his foot twisted in the stirrup. He must have resisted falling, clutching the saddle so hard he nearly dragged it off with him. Whoever had trained the mare had obviously instilled in her a trust so deep that all she could do with this terrifying situation was wait for help. Is's heart went out to her. She was gallant, and beautiful, and in trouble.

Is had to step over the man to position herself where she would have enough leverage to get the girth undone. The mare stood like a statue while Is struggled with it. But the moment the saddle was off she stepped carefully away from the man and began to graze. By then Is had taken in enough clues to realize the horse had stood like that for hours, maybe a day or more. Everything she could reach without dragging the man had been eaten. She was starving to avoid stepping on him.

It took an incredibly talented trainer, and a special horse, to achieve that kind of trust. The man who was lying at her feet could be that trainer, but such a horseman wasn't likely to have a fall like this. More likely this man had stolen the mare from some very expensive stud. She was certainly a quality animal.

On the other hand, the mare was wearing no bridle and there were no broken pieces lying around. The inescapable conclusion was the man had been riding without one. That was no rookie horsemanship.

Is had been so caught up in the mare's plight, she had ignored the man. If he was not already dead, he was probably so badly hurt she couldn't help him anyway. She didn't really have any intention of trying. Whoever he was, he was dangerous to her. But the thought that he might be the horseman who had trained this incredible mare made her hesitate.

She knelt by him and gingerly touched his check. It was warm. She jerked her hand away, heart racing. She knew she should try to help him, that was the right thing to do, but she was terrified.

She stood, marshalling her courage. The two horses were grazing together like old friends, the mare tearing frantically at the grass and Lark grazing sedately beside her. The scene helped to calm Is. Someone had trained the mare to go without need of a bridle even in the rough terrain of the Boundary. If it was this man he must have a kind nature for no one could train a horse to that degree by using forceful or cruel methods.

Is freed the man's foot from the stirrup and rolled him over. If his back was broken, he would die anyway. She wasn't concerned about doing further harm. It might be best if he did die. Kind or not, he was going to be trouble for her. He was either an outlaw who had stolen the mare, or he was someone high ranking in the Alliance, for only they could ride horses.

One side of his face was caked with dried blood and mud. His skin was pulled tight from dehydration making his face look like a skull. His hair was blond almost to the point of being colorless. Behind their closed lids his eyes looked sunken, like the eyes of a dehydrated horse. The skin around them was dark, almost bluish, and bruised-looking.

Is watched his chest rise and fall. His breathing was shallow compared to hers, but regular. She started to feel for broken ribs and then stopped. She had to decide whether to try to help him, or not. She could just ride away.

If he hadn't stolen the mare, he had to be some sort of government official because no one else could have such a quality animal. He wasn't wearing a Trooper's uniform, and Is had never heard of a bridle-less school within the government, but that didn't mean there wasn't one. If he had found her, she should be getting away before others followed him. Is glanced around nervously, and her eyes came to rest on the mare. If she tried to leave, the mare would probably follow. But if this was the horseman who had trained the mare, she belonged to him in a way that made taking her seem like stealing in a way that taking Lark had not. *If* this was the man who had trained her.

What if he was a thief who had stolen the horse? Maybe he had murdered the mare's rightful owner.

But he had been riding without a bridle. That was not something a horse would do for just anyone. The mare must know this man well and trust him.

If he recovered he'd be trouble for her. He'd try to take her in, or report her at the very least. Or if he was a criminal he might try to steal Lark. Enslave her. Nothing good could possibly come of helping him.

While her mind ran through all that, and her body begged her to run, Is watched the horses and knew she could not take the mare and leave the man to die.

She rigged up a travois, using pieces of her tack, pieces of the man's tack, and two small trees. The mare quietly accepted the harness and the strange contraption of poles with a rope hammock tied between them. Although the man wasn't very tall, it was hard to move his dead weight. Is gave up on trying to be gentle and dragged and wrestled him onto the travois any way she could. Maybe the man would have the good grace to just go ahead and die. Or, maybe the mare would take off galloping and kick the whole thing to splinters, the man included. Is didn't have any idea how to control her without a bridle except to lead Lark and expect her to follow. That arrangement seemed fine to the mare. She followed along, nibbling a few bites of grass here and there.

The man didn't die on the trip. So Is dragged him to the back of the stall. She couldn't have gotten him up into the loft if she'd wanted to. She felt funny going through his stuff, so as soon as she found his sleeping bag, she stopped. It was a marvelous bag, thicker and warmer than her makeshift one, but not a third the weight. Only a very important man, high in the government, would have something like that. Is berated herself for bringing him here and trying to help him. But here he was, and he would die of dehydrated if nothing else, so she rigged up a stomach tube to get water into him. He choked and gagged as she forced the tube down his throat but he didn't vomit. When she blew into the tube, he didn't cough, so she guessed it had reached his stomach, not his lungs. She dribbled a little water down it and that didn't kill him either.

That wasn't the worst of it. The worst came a day later when his bladder started working again. Is gave up on modesty and wrestled all his clothes off, then rigged up a tube to that end of him too. Getting the tube on, and getting it to stay on, were no easy tasks. She was thoroughly disgusted with the whole thing until the next time his bladder let go and it ran down the tube and out of the stall, and she didn't have to clean it up. Then she was sort of proud of herself.

Other than the fluid, and a general cleanup of the man's cuts - none of which seemed serious - Is didn't know what to do for him. She wasn't going to try to feed him. If he was that far gone, let him die. She'd done her part.

The mare settled happily in with the stallion. Over the next few days, Is spent a lot of time watching them. She imagined the colt they would produce, and thought about where the mare had come from, and about where to bury the man, who didn't appear to be getting better. But she didn't let herself think about what she'd do if he lived, took the mare and left.

On the fourth day the man started having convulsions. They terrified Is and she was sorry she'd ever gotten involved. She hadn't done him any favor. He would have died of exposure by now if she'd left him. That night she had nightmares about him suddenly rising up out of the bed and attacking her, or the horses. She planned ways to defend herself, while she knew it was all quite illogical.

The next morning she decided to go through the man's saddlebags. The clothes she found were high quality Alliance material. She recognized packets of dehydrated food. And then she found the tools. She couldn't even guess their uses. Common people had axes, shovels, picks, things like that. His tools were sophisticated, smooth things with no apparent purposes. If he had stolen them as well as the horse he must certainly be a wanted criminal.

The convulsions lasted, on and off, for two days. Then the man seemed to sleep differently, unlike the stillness of a comatose state except it went on and on. Three days later he woke up.

Is had come into the stall to get Lark's bridle. Halfway across the room, she felt the man's eyes on her and froze, afraid to meet those eyes. Every berserker she'd ever dealt with flashed before her vision – their cold, deadly, unreachable eyes. She knew this man wasn't a berserker. He wasn't built like one. But it didn't matter. She was afraid his eyes would be like that. She had to force herself to turn and face him.

He wasn't what she expected at all. His face looked much kinder with his eyes open. His expression was soft. "Beatific" was the word Is thought. He looked as if he'd opened his eyes on heaven. She couldn't quite look away. If dying was like this, she'd never fear it again.

His eyes closed and the breath went out of him like a sigh. Is stood frozen, watching for the sleeping bag to move to tell her he was still breathing. She was hoping very hard, but wasn't sure what she was hoping for, that he would breathe again or that he wouldn't. After a moment the man's chest began to rise and fall again, and Is breathed too. Her legs felt rubbery as she walked the rest of the way across the stall. Her hand shook as she reached for Lark's bridle.

Whether the man was an Alliance official or a criminal, if he lived, she would have to leave her safe little valley. She was mad at herself for having helped him, mad at him, mad at fate. She hadn't been doing anyone any harm. True, she'd stolen Lark, but damn it, she'd saved his life. The Alliance had lots of other horses. She'd been happy enough living with just Lark. Maybe that couldn't have lasted. Maybe because she'd known that one way or another it couldn't go on forever, she'd cherished every moment carefully. But there was nothing else for her.

The man woke again in the night. Is heard him trying to get up. She listened, holding her breath, almost holding her heart still. He didn't make it far. She heard him fall, then silence. She knew she should go down and see if he was all right, but she couldn't. For once fear won over discipline. She wasn't going down until it was light. She knew he couldn't make it up the ladder, and yet she couldn't sleep, fearing him and being angry at herself in turn.

In the morning Is saw that he had made it to the middle of the stall. He looked like a little boy curled up on the floor. His skin was even whiter than she remembered and his face was innocent in sleep, gentle enough to be the man who had trained the mare. He'd gotten the tubes off, and she wasn't about to put them on again. He looked cold, nude, curled up with goose bumps on his skin. She got his sleeping bag from the corner, threw it over him and went out to the horses.

The horses were not far away. Is touched Lark's neck in greeting. His shoulder towered over her. The mare raised her head from grazing and came over for some attention too. Is had come to love this mare for her loyalty and manners that were as delicate as her conformation. Is tried to imagine how leaving her behind would feel. But she couldn't go just yet. The man might still die, and Is was pretty sure she'd have to lock the mare in the stall to keep her from following Lark. She'd starve if the man wasn't able to take care of her. Is put her head against the mare's withers and began to shake. By staying, she was giving up her own best chance to survive.

When she went back to the stall, the man was gone.

Adrenaline flooded Is while she fought for rational control. He was only a very sick, very weak man. He couldn't do anything. But she was out the door to check on the horses before she could convince herself. They were grazing as placidly as they had been when she left them.

She saw the man's footprints in the wet grass. He had gone around the side of the shed. Is took several deep breaths before she could put on her best sauntering, confidence-exuding walk and go after him.

The man was sitting with his back against the shed, legs sprawled in front of him, eyes closed. The morning sun on his face, lit his blond hair to white. Dark circles showed like bruises under his eyes. His cheeks were sunken and his ribs stood out. He looked frail and very much in need of her help. It had been so much foolishness to be afraid of him.

He heard her and opened his eyes. They were gray, like the mist on the mountains. Soft. He tried to smile, expressing his gratitude and apologizing for his continued need more perfectly than any words could. He reached his arm out toward her, asking for help to rise. Is knelt, put his arm around her shoulder and helped him up, surprised at how natural and easy it was to touch him like this. They began to walk back around the shed. He was as thin as a skeleton, and as light. He had to stop every few steps to rest, but he seemed completely unashamed of his nakedness, and so Is ignored it too. When they got inside, he collapsed into his sleeping bag and fell asleep instantly.

Is heard him get up again in the night and listened to his slow, staggery steps as he chuffed through the dried grass with which she bedded the stall. His steps stopped near the door, and after a while she heard him making water. Then he had to rest awhile before he could make it back to bed.

In the morning, Is took the forked stick she used for cleaning up after the horses and pitched out the straw he'd soiled. He watched her from his bed and smiled with a little embarrassed, apologetic grin when she looked at him.

"Don't worry about it," she said. These were the first words she had spoken out loud in a very long time. She realized that the man had not spoken to her at all and she wondered if he couldn't speak.

Over the next several days Is fed him broth and then the gruel she made for herself   from the cereal heads of various grasses. By the third day he was strong enough to sit up at her fire outside. He never spoke to her and so she didn't speak to him. She was used to silent communication with the horses and felt comfortable communicating the same way with the man.

Is remembered the food concentrates in the man's pack and thought they might help him gain strength. Again, she felt strange going into his things, so she brought the whole pack out to him. But he had leaned back against a rock and seemed to be dozing, so she decided to go ahead and have the food ready for him when he woke.

She had the water hot and was about to pour a packet of mix into it when she heard something behind her. She turned just as the man lunged for her. There was no time to get away. She struck him flat-handed against the chest in a reflexive action that all her years of handling the rude young stallions had honed, before she realized that he wasn't going for her, but for his pack.

Her strike knocked him back. He crouched on the ground, gripping the pack he had snatched from her, and started to say something. But the sound that came out of his throat was like the cry of a hunting hawk. Startling enough from a bird, it was disturbingly inappropriate from the man.

He turned away with a harsh movement, and his fist slammed into the pack with a sound like a fist hitting flesh.

Is jerked in reaction to his sudden violence. She moved away from him, closing her hand over a rock. She had left her knife by the fire and was afraid to try for it now.

The man upended the pack and shook everything out. Then he scrabbled through his belongings and flung the food packets into the fire. The flames sputtered under the onslaught and turned green. A foul smell reached Is. Poison? Had he been poisoned? Was that why he'd had the fall? Why he'd been sick? Is wanted to ask, but she was too afraid of him now.

Even sick and weak he might be stronger than she was. And now he didn't look rational. His hands shook and his eyes were wild. He started to restuff his pack, but his movements were jerky and uncoordinated. He seemed to be losing control of his body. After a moment he gave up and sank back on his heels gripping his head with clawlike hands as if he were in terrible pain. Torn between fear and pity, Is had to break the tension.

"It was poisoned, wasn't it?"

He spun on his knees to look at her, frightening her with the crazy wild mix of emotions she saw in his eyes.

Maybe the people from whom he had stolen the mare or the tools had hit him over the head. Or maybe they had tried to kill him with the poison. She couldn't imagine anyone trying to murder a high government official, so he had to be a thief.

He must have realized how frightening he appeared for he tried to give her a reassuring smile, but it was so filled with conflicting emotion it failed to calm her, apologize, or explain anything. He reached toward her with a conciliatory motion.

Is couldn't help herself; she drew back. The man attempted to speak. His mouth opened and his throat worked but this time instead of the hawk scream he began to laugh, a high-pitched, hysterical giggle. He twisted around so his back was to her but he couldn't stop the sound. It built higher and more frenzied, while he beat on the ground with his fists and kept laughing.

The noise jerked Is's nerves tight. She couldn't stand it. She got up and moved away from the fire, but it was too dark to go far and she could still hear his horrible laughter. When it finally died down, she couldn't go back to the fire.

She watched him all night, from a distance, unable to sleep. He eventually curled up by the coals and when Is was sure he was asleep she slipped in and retrieved her knife.

In the predawn light she walked by the stream and tried to think what to do. The man was crazy. If his moods could swing like she'd seen, and he could so totally lose control, she couldn't trust him. She had to get away from him, but how? Would he try to follow? And once she left this protected valley there might be Alliance troopers and Blueskins, and other horrors. She was sorry to the depths of her soul that she had saved his life.

She wandered farther than she had intended, thinking deeply. When she finally turned her steps for home, she had decided to take Lark and slip away that night. If the mare followed her that might be best, it would leave the man on foot.

She was only halfway home when she heard Lark's frantic whinny. She left the stream bed and cut across the open field sprinting at top speed. As she topped the rise she could see that the shed door was closed. She heard the thud of Lark's heels hitting the wood. Memories of war horses gone berserk raced through her mind, adding speed to her legs. But Lark was not a trained war horse feeling his berserker approach. The only explanation was that the man had taken the mare and left Lark behind.

Is flew down the hill to the shed, pounding over the uneven ground and leaping the small bushes. The man could have taken Lark too! She'd been such an idiot to leave Lark like that. She skidded on the gravelly ground in front of the stall, crashing into the door. With her hand on the latch, she took a deep breath.

"Lark. Stand." She put as much command and calmness into her voice as she could, out of breath as she was. Then she rolled the door open only enough to admit her, not enough to let the horse out. In his excited state he would go after the mare with no thought of Is. It was dark, even in daylight, in the shed with the door closed. Is found Lark's bridle by memory. He quieted while she tacked him. Then she ran upstairs and threw a pack together. She didn't know how much head start the man had. Whether she found him or not, she better not come back here. If he couldn't talk, he could still lead the authorities back to her. Even if he was some sort of criminal himself, he might do that if there was a reward on her. She couldn't risk it.

She heard Lark pawing as she assembled her pack. It was easier than it had been last time. She just took everything she had.

She let Lark pick the way, moving off at a fast trot and then opening into a gallop. She didn't try to control him until they had crossed the valley and gotten onto rocky footing. The man had gone out the shallow end of the bowl toward the mountains. Lark seemed sure of where he was going, and Is occasionally saw hoof prints to confirm his conviction.

It might be just as well if they didn't catch up to the man, but Is wanted to know which way he'd gone. She expected him to turn back toward the Alliance lands but he kept going straight into the mountains instead. There was no way he was going to cross those jagged, snow-covered peaks on a horse. Was he just crazy, or did he know a way through?

Is would have been content to follow at a distance but Lark was desperate to catch up to the mare. It was the nature of horses to want company. It was their need for companionship, and their ability to live within a herd hierarchy that made them trainable. Is's company had supplanted that of other horses, and Lark was happy with that until it was tested against the real thing. Once Lark became convinced that the mare was gone, he would be happy with human companionship again. But for now Is needed to find out what the man was up to.

They climbed the first ridge and turned north, deeper into the Boundary. That was the wrong direction for the man to be going if he was planning to report her.

Lark was moving steadily now, not panicked, but determined. From the top of the next ridge she saw the man. He and the mare were halfway down the other side, moving at a steady walk. Lark called. Is wondered if the man would try to outrun them. Instead he turned the mare around and waited for them to pick their way down to him.

Is wasn't sure what to say or do. She let Lark touch noses with the mare. Both horses made small throaty sounds of greeting. The man sat like a sack of potatoes, not a horseman of the caliber of the one who must have trained the mare. And yet the mare wore no bridle, and he had gotten her to leave the other horse behind. Is was even more confused about him. He sat regarding her with those soft gray eyes in a face that was still hollow and sunken, and somehow too hard to contain those gentle eyes.

"Where are you going?" she asked.

He turned and looked north, and then back at her.

"Why north?"

He grinned suddenly, a harsh baring of his teeth that was not a smile at all. He made some small movement with his body and the mare turned and began to walk. Is let Lark pace them.

"Are you going to turn me in?" If he couldn't answer the broader question, perhaps he would answer less general ones, but he didn't look at her.

She didn't know why she asked. If he did answer, she couldn't let herself believe him. The mare came to an abrupt stop. The man twisted around in his saddle, reached into his saddlebag, and came up with one of the shiny, metal "tools" Is had wondered about. He twisted the end of it, pointed it at a piece of deadwood lying several meters away, and the wood burst into flame.

Is stared at it. She had heard of wonderful tools like that. She had seen the cutters the lumbermen used to fell and split trees to make lumber for her barn. This was something like that.

Suddenly the man turned and pointed the tool directly at her chest. For a moment Is was too shocked to believe the threat, but one look at the man's eyes convinced her. They were wild. His lips were parted in a tight grimace. His hand shook with emotion, but it didn't shake enough to make Is think he would miss. If he meant to kill her, he could.

Instead, he turned the tool away from her, gave it a twist to disarm it, and put it back in his pack. Is sat, stunned, while the mare started to walk again. When Lark began to follow, Is let him. Her mind reeled about like a drunk. The man could have killed her. But then he'd put the tool away. Was he trying to say he meant her no harm? Was he trying to tell her not to follow him? But he had done nothing when Lark started following again. Maybe he was just crazy. Is had never seen eyes like his, tortured and frightened and angry all at once. They couldn't be the eyes of the same man who had smiled his appreciation for her help, or an apology for his needs. They did not look like the eyes of the man who had sat stroking his mare's ears, even though the effort of lifting his hand that high had made his whole arm shake. Is had to know what she was dealing with.

She gave Lark a short pressure with her legs that sent him in front of the mare, and wheeled him about to block the man's path. The mare halted patiently. Is had the man's attention. His eyes questioned her, sane and rational, nothing like the man who had held the weapon.

"Look, I don't know who you are. I don't know where you're going. But if you take this mare into those mountains, there won't be enough grass, it'll be too cold, and she'll die this winter."

He took in her outburst without expression and just sat until Is felt foolish, then he gently steered the mare around her.

"There won't be enough grass," Is called after him. "She'll starve."

He kept riding.

"There will be too much snow. She won't grow enough coat. She'll freeze."

But he kept going.

"Damn you! She's too nice a mare. Don't do that to her." Is sent Lark in front of the mare again and blocked her. The man met her eyes. He tried to turn the mare aside, but Is made Lark block him again. The man's mouth worked as though he were trying to speak. The crazy look was coming into his eyes again. Is remembered his weapon. But he didn't reach for it.

His voice was high and strained. "Dread, thread, tread," he said, fighting for each word and surprised at them as though he meant to say something else entirely. Then his voice broke into a high, hysterical giggle. His face worked as he struggled to say something. He seemed almost to conquer himself. His eyes were desperate with some emotion Is couldn't understand.

He threw his head back and shrieked laughter to the sky. Lark pinned his ears back and fidgeted nervously. Even the mare reacted, tossing her head in an uncharacteristic way. Lark's prancing moved him out of the way, and the mare began to walk again. Is let them go. The man was insane and dangerous in some way she could not comprehend. Lark pulled at the reins to follow but Is held him back. He fretted and whinnied as they watched the mare move out of sight.

Chapter 7

At first Is was only going to follow the man for a couple of days. Then she would turn aside and find another place to live. It was late summer, and there would still be time to get ready for winter. There had to be.

But Lark wasn't happy with following. He pulled, impatient to catch up to the mare, and that evening Is had to tie him for the first time.

Partly to calm herself, and partly because she needed the food, she took her knife and went hunting. Hunting had become a ritual for her. Learning to take the lives of small animals had not been easy, but that first winter she had become desperate. Initially she had tried snares. But the animals were trapped, not killed, and suffered horribly until she came. So she had taught herself to kill with the small slim knife she had brought with her.

The knife was a clean death, very quick. The most wary, intelligent animals probably escaped. She liked to believe that.

She had learned a lot about the rabbits she hunted and had come to love their quick frightened temperaments. They could detect a predator with senses Is wished she had. The best way to hunt them was to wait, in a sort of non-waiting mode, for them to come to her. It was like a meditation. She had to keep her mind still, not wanting, expecting, or hoping. The animal would come, or not.

Is found a little trail and settled herself comfortably, dismissing all thoughts and worries. Lying in the grass, waiting in her special way, she found the peace the land always brought her. The problems the man had introduced into her life receded. Enveloped by the smells of the ground and the grass, she heard the birds begin their evening songs, the rustling of insects, and finally the movement of a small animal. The rabbit came grazing his way along the trail. A few steps, a hop, raise his ears a moment, nibble a few mouthfuls, step, hop. His nose twitched constantly as he watched for foxes, weasels, or owls – not expecting a being he had probably never seen before. Besides, Is wore clothes patched with rabbit skins and saturated with the smells of the ground.

Is always felt kinship with these small hunted animals. But that kinship contained the knowledge of their role as prey animals, just as she was prey to larger animals, and her own kind. The killing was not just for food, it connected her into the chain and that made her own death more acceptable somehow.

She carried the small warm corpse back to where Lark was tied. He had pawed a deep hole in a thwarted attempt to go to the mare. His neck and chest were wet with sweat. Is felt sorry for him. She didn't mean to upset him, but he couldn't understand. She stroked his ears, trying to comfort him, but he had little attention to spare for her.

She began to question herself. Maybe she should go with the man and take her chances. At least he was not going back to the Alliance. But he was crazy and probably an outlaw. Still, he hadn't stolen Lark when he could have and he hadn't hurt her, only frightened her with his odd behavior. Lark finally decided the matter for her by letting out a ringing neigh that reverberated off the mountains. He neighed again and again, echo overlying echo. Is couldn't have that. The noise would draw someone, Blueskins or Troopers.

It was almost dark by the time she caught up to the man. He had pitched his tent and was standing by it, alerted to her approach by the mare even though Lark had stopped calling. He did nothing to invite her to stay or to suggest he wanted her to leave. She was on her own with this decision. She dismounted and untacked Lark, who went immediately to graze with the mare.

The man had chosen his campsite well. There was water nearby and grazing for the horses. His tent was pitched on high ground, but sheltered from any unexpected storm by the lay of the land. He was apparently sane enough to use good camping skills.

He had a small fire going, and some water warming in a pot. Is took the rabbit to the fire and began to skin it. The man sat down near her and watched. Is ignored him. She was in her own world again. As she prepared the rabbit she gave thanks to the animal for dying for her. In that mood of thankfulness her awareness expanded until she felt communion with her own life, and her own death. She was part of the chain.

But the man intruded into her moment. He took the guts Is had set aside and slit them open and began sorting through the grasses and leaves the rabbit had eaten but not yet digested. He meticulously attempted to unfold and piece together each leaf and blade.

Is could no longer ignore him. His behavior frightened her all over again. When he began to eat the contents of the rabbit's stomach, it was too much for her.

The ritual had been ruined. More than ever, she regretted saving his life. Now she didn't know what to do about him. She spitted the rabbit and sat in gloomy silence while it cooked. When it was done she offered the man half but he waved it away.

Is pitched her fly and spent a restless, wary night wondering what the man might do next. It was a relief to get moving in the morning.

The man's camp breaking was efficient and thorough. He took considerable care with dismantling the fire, soaking the coals and scattering them so they couldn't start a fire and would sink quickly into the ground, replenishing it. Also there would be no trace of their camp. Is wasn't sure which consideration motivated him.

She watched him ride, trying to figure out if he could be the horseman who had trained his mare. She could not decide. He slouched in the saddle in a way good horsemen did not. But he might still be too weak to sit up, or he could be in some kind of pain.

They were wending their way through a canyon when suddenly the man slipped from the mare's back and scrambled up the rocks. Fearing ambush, Is twisted around in her saddle but saw nothing. Meanwhile, the man crouched like some wild animal, scraping frantically at the rocks with his knife. When he lifted the knife it was covered with bright yellow-green fungus. The man ran a finger along the side of the blade and slid all of the poisonous-looking glob into his mouth.

He started to scrape again but in a moment he dropped the knife. It clattered down the rocks as he pitched forward onto his hands and knees and vomited like a dog. Is sat on Lark and watched dispassionately. Perhaps he had poisoned himself and would die.

He didn't die. When he'd finished being sick, he slid down the rock, re-trieved his knife and remounted the mare. He gave Is a wan little smile and started the mare walking. Is let Lark follow. She could not make sense of the man. He would not eat good meat. He ate the partially digested con-tents of the rabbit's stomach and now this.

The ground became increasingly steep and rocky as they continued throughout the clear, calm day. The trees had shrunk down to miniature forms the height of Lark's belly. Their gnarled roots and twisted trunks told a story of great wind and hardship.

As they continued to climb they left the last of the little trees behind. Now the soil was a thin coating of pebbly stone over heartrock, the only vegetation a mossy sponge-like mat. When Is looked up she could see a saddle between the peaks that lay ahead outlined against a sky that was so deep blue it was nearly purple.

The summit looked close enough to touch but never seemed to get any closer as they kept plodding steadily uphill. Eventually they stopped to rest, dismounting and loosening the girths to let the horses relax.

Is stretched out on the ground under the cloudless sky. The sun bore down, pinning her to the earth. There was a silence here that was unusual in nature. Even the wind that usually haunted these high places was still. The rocky ground was warm against her back and the incline just right to let her overlook the stupendous view without having to lift her head. Ridge after ridge of tree-covered mountains faded away into the distance.

The exhausting effects of the altitude made Is lethargic. Below her an eagle circled lazily. She could see the sun glinting off the top of its wings. Such an unusual perspective on one of the great mountain birds gave her a sensation of flying. She could feel the slow wheeling around of the world under her. Dizziness seized her. She pulled her attention away from the bird and concentrated on feeling the solid rock under her back. She slipped into a dream so smoothly she didn't even realize she had fallen asleep.

She was surrounded by horses as refined and delicate as the man's mare. She caught her breath at their beauty, and something else . . . less easy to name, a sort of royalty. Their presence was an honor they bestowed upon her, letting her see them, ghost silent, dream real. It was as though they wanted her to know something.

The scrunch of Lark's hooves on the gravel woke her. She sat up too fast, startled from the dream. The landscape spun and stilled, empty of a herd of horses.

The man was lying not far from her, asleep. With his features relaxed, he looked so kind and gentle. Is wished she didn't know another side of him.

Lark and the mare were standing head-to-tail, each resting a hind leg, sleeping. Their heads hung low. Their tails swished gently from time to time, swiping the flies from each other's faces. Is hated to disturb such contentment, but they needed to crest the ridge and get down to the tree line on the other side to find water and grass for the horses.

Is deliberately scuffed the gravel. The man's eyes came open. He sat up and looked around, taking in the view. For a moment Is thought he was looking for her ghost herd of horses. But of course he would not have had the same dream. As his eyes met hers, he smiled that gentle, beautiful smile Is needed so much to see. He seemed to share her feelings – relaxed, at peace and euphoric on the top of the world.

But, Is reminded herself, he wasn't a trusted companion and they weren't on a pleasure ride. She stood up and went to Lark. She checked his hooves for rocks and the man began going over the mare as well. When he mounted they started up the incline again.

At the top of the saddle the wind hit them. It was surprisingly cold and in minutes they both had to don their coats. Now they really were on top of the world. Behind them there were only lower ridges. Ahead were taller mountains but their summits were eclipsed by clouds. It would be snowing on those peaks.

Behind them was a beautiful, hot day. Ahead of them was winter.

As they started down the backside of the saddle the clouds began to move toward them. Soon they were riding in a cold mist. The temperature dropped and kept dropping. Snow came whirling out of nowhere, stinging against their faces, driven on the wind like hail, and even Lark faltered.

The wind grew stronger and the snow continued to come, obscuring everything. This was no little snow shower; this was a serious winter storm. The horses slipped and slid on the partially frozen ground and rocks that were quickly being covered with ice. Is could see nothing but the dark shape of the mare in front of her. The mare slipped badly and nearly sat on her haunches sliding down a rock face that had been invisible in the snow and gathering gloom. Is heard her frightened snort and then a grunt of effort as she lunged back up on the trail. Is tried to guide Lark around the rock but he wallowed suddenly in some sort of hole Is couldn't see, dropping out from under her with a gut wrenching sensation. For an instant she didn't know if they were falling off the mountain or just slipping a short distance. Then he lunged up, clawing his way up a bank Is couldn't see. It was all she could do to stay centered in the saddle not knowing which way he would go next, but she had to trust his superior night vision and let him find his own footing.

Though it was crazy to keep going, they couldn't stop on such a steep incline in the open wind. At times the descent was so steep Lark's hindquarters were above his shoulders and Is had to lean back to keep from falling on his neck. He kept his hind legs tucked under him and his front feet stretched out ahead. In that posture he took small steps punctuated with stretches of sliding. It would have been a scary descent in good weather. In this blizzard all Is could do was trust Lark completely.

Suddenly Lark leveled out. The wind checked and the snow swirled instead of driving blindly. They had reached a pocket of almost level land, a little protected from the wind although it roared above them, sounding like some monstrous force bearing down on them but never quite arriving.

The snow was deeper here. Even if ice lay underneath, it was too deeply buried to bother the horses. They immediately formed up side by side, rumps to the wind and heads hanging low, too tired to go on.

The man dismounted and started unpacking his tent. Is knew her makeshift tent was no match for this kind of wind and snow. She didn't even bother to get it out of her pack. Instead she helped the man with his. He had a handy tool that forced the stakes right through ice and rock.

They crawled into the tent bringing snow in with them as there was no way to keep it out. Closing the tent flap against the wind was a struggle, and once it was closed, they were engulfed by darkness. The tent shook and shuddered with each new blast of wind. The small bent poles that held it up bent more and snapped back into place with ominous creaking and popping sounds. But the strange too-thin fabric didn't tear.

Is couldn't see the man and couldn't hear what he was doing. But she couldn't squat there all night, dripping snow and getting colder by the second. She needed to get out of her wet clothes and into her sleeping bag.

The man bumped into her as she was struggling out of her jeans. He caught hold of her and she froze. Still unable to see him, she didn't know if he was on the verge of one of his crazy attacks or not. She was trapped in a tent, half-undressed, half-freezing . . . and then he let go of her.

Hands shaking, she rummaged in her pack and found the small knife and set it where she could reach it. By the time she had gotten into a dry shirt and long johns and crawled into her bag she was freezing. Her hands were so numb she could barely feel the knife as she checked to make sure it was still within reach. She could cut herself and not even feel it, so she placed the knife just outside the bag where she hoped to be able to find it quickly. Her legs hurt with cold. Her feet were frozen lumps. Her hands were so cold that when she tried to use them to rub warmth into her feet she couldn't feel her hands or feet. She put her hands under her armpits to warm them, which made her colder than ever. She began to shiver and couldn't stop. Her little homemade bag wasn't meant for this kind of weather.

She lay there feeling miserable and worrying about the horses. Lark was tough-skinned and hardy. If the cold didn't last too long he would survive. But the mare had a fine coat. They had both been sweating with the work of getting down the slope. Now they would be shivering. They had had no food since mid-morning, which made a big difference in how much cold they could withstand. Being grazers, they were designed to have food passing through their systems all the time. They had not eaten well even the day before. Between the cold and the lack of roughage they could colic and that could be life-threatening.

There was nothing Is could do. She huddled in her sleeping bag in her own misery and worried. She was far too cold to sleep. Shivering swept through her body in waves. Instead of getting warmer she seemed to be getting colder.

She suffered for what seemed the entire night, until finally she couldn't take any more. She crawled out of the bag and felt her way over to her clothes. They were stiff with frozen snow. Her pants cracked as she got into them. At least they were too frozen to be wet. She finished struggling into her clothes as quickly as she could. The cold made her have a desperate need to urinate.

She got the tent flap open more by luck than anything else. Outside it was still snowing, not quite as windy, but bone-chilling cold. The bright snow made it possible to see a little although it was very dark. Is moved cautiously. She was afraid of falling into a drift, or losing her way, so she didn't go very far. She fumbled with her pants with fingers that were stiff and unfeeling. Once she had them down it was too cold to let go. She had to stay that way quite a while before her body became convinced.

She could make out the shape of the horses. Lark seemed to be resting quietly but the mare was hunched and shivering. When Is laid her hands on the mare she could feel the muscles of her shoulders and hindquarters quaking but there was nothing she could do for her. She attempted to put her hands into her pockets and got a shock. She felt nothing, no sensation whatsoever. She tried to do the motion by memory. Her arms moved vaguely, as though they were asleep. Her heart raced with uncontrolled fear. She'd been cold many times before, taking care of horses in winter, her hands aching, red and swollen but she'd never lost control of them like this.

She made her way back to the tent. In the dark and with no sense of feeling in her hands it was hard to get the flap open. She was beginning to realize that her life depended on doing it. A strange stubbornness came over her. She forced her hands to work in the way she remembered they needed to work, and somehow she got the door open.

She thought she heard the man move in his sleeping bag.

"It's me," she said. Her frozen face and lips didn't work right. Even if he couldn't make out the words, he would recognize her voice. She had her back to him, concentrating on getting the flap sealed, when there was a sudden flicker of greenish light. She spun around, her mind full of the horrors she'd heard about this land, lost her balance, and fell ungracefully on her side. The man sat up in his sleeping bag holding a small tube in his hand. It cast a weak greenish glow that made his skin and hair look green and turned his eyes into strange dark shadows. Is fought down her fear, the light was just Alliance technology and the man was trying to help her, but she had to get out of her jeans again and she wished he'd turn it off.

Is did the only thing she could do, privacy wise. She didn't look at him. Getting her jacket off took total concentration. The buttons on her pants nearly defeated her. By the time she had gotten down to her underwear she was quaking all over and her sleeping bag wasn't going to be any help.

The sound of the seals being released on the man's bag startled her. When she looked at him he was lying back holding the bag open to her, inviting her in.

Her body cried out for relief from the cold, but her mind screamed its fear. She couldn't move. A very long time seemed to go by. He didn't move either. He must have be getting cold, his arm getting tired, holding the bag open to her but he didn't change position. Is got up the courage to look into his eyes. They were soft, concerned, waiting. Her body was screaming to take the offered warmth. Her mind was losing.

She moved before she was aware of having made any decision and slid into the bag with the man. His body was like a furnace at her back. She must feel like ice to him. She tried to keep from touching him, but the bag was not meant for two people. There was no way to avoid lying against him. Though she tried to keep her feet away from him, he deliberately brought his body into contact with hers along its whole length and touched his feet to hers.

His arm lay across her waist holding the bag shut. It would not seal with both of them in it.

Is lay rigid, feeling scared, guilty and more scared. She thought how terrible it must be for him to curl up to someone as cold as she was. He'd expect something in return. Surely there was a price on this. He was still weak. Maybe she could fight him off. Did she have any right to take this warmth then? She lay in turmoil. He lay still.

Eventually the warmth seeped into her body and the tension began to fade but her mind was not ready to relax. Her thoughts took her back to the government school and inevitably to Riding Master Masley.

It had come as a relief when she had been sent to the Equestrian School to be trained. She had loved the horses immediately. Of course there were still other kids, and they were all above her and delighted in tormenting her. Yet somehow it wasn't so bad because of the horses.

Until Riding Master Masley.

. . . She heard his footsteps coming up behind her and quickly tried to think if she was doing anything wrong, or could be doing something better. She was carrying a saddle and bridle to the tack room to clean them after the morning workout. She was carrying them properly, moving quickly enough. She could think of no way she could be doing this better.

She turned into the tack room and breathed a little sigh of relief. The Riding Master would go on by. Instead he came in too.

Is busied herself setting the tack up for cleaning, pretending she did not know he was in the room with her. That lasted only a moment.

"Junior Apprentice Drey," he said.

"Yes, Riding Master." He would probably send her on an errand. Instead he came

over and perched one buttock on the edge of the table where she had laid out the saddle soap, sponge, and polishing cloth. She stopped disassembling the bridle. It would be rude to continue now that he had spoken to her.

He didn't say anything else for a moment, just rested there with one buttock on the table. He was wearing the black riding boots that came below his knees, and the tight-fitting stretch pants of his profession. He had just come from riding one of the horses. One of his hands rested on the table, one on his thigh.

"I have been noticing you," he said.

Her heart sank. It was never good to come to anyone's attention, even if it wasn't for something bad. Anyway, a Riding Master would hardly be the one to reprove her for some sloppiness in cleaning tack or mucking a stall. There were senior apprentices for that, and above them junior riders and then senior riders. The Riding Master oversaw the senior riders and trained horses. It would be years before he should take any interest in Is.

"You are eager to begin learning to ride?" he asked.

Her eyes leapt to his before she could control herself. Yes. But so was everyone. Why single her out? Maybe he'd seen her watching the riders. Maybe, somehow, he knew she'd have more talent than the others. Maybe there was something about the way she handled the horses when she led them to the arena for the riders? Her heart was full of impossible hope, and her mind quick to find ways to believe.

He began to smile. He reached out and settled his hand over hers.

"Sometimes there are ways a student might pass to the riding phase without waiting four years."

His hand felt very hot on hers. She wanted to pull away, but didn't dare. She couldn't think of anything to say. She couldn't look at him.

"Do you understand me?" he asked.

She didn't answer. She wanted to ride, but she couldn't do what he was asking. She couldn't. Although she knew many kids did it, she could not. She didn't know what was wrong with her.

He swung his bent leg forward and wrapped the toe of his boot around the back of her thigh, hooking her with it so she couldn't move away. His other hand came up and his fingertips touched the side of her face and ran down her neck. For a moment his hand cupped her breast, squeezing it, not hard but as though measuring the size of it, deciding if it was interesting enough to him, as he might size up a horse's potential. His hand felt unpleasantly hot. The lines his fingers drew down her body burned into her flesh. She hated him, and desperately wanted to move away from his touch, but she didn't dare.

"Come to my office after lunch," he said. Then he released her and walked away.

She couldn't do anything for a moment. She was terrified and furious. Then

she heard a small sound and looked around, frightened that someone had seen what had happened.

Suzanne was standing behind the saddle racks. She had seen the whole thing. As a senior apprentice, she should have been next to move up to rider. Her face red with hatred, she walked toward Is as if she might strike her. Instead, she brushed by and spat on Is's chest.

Is wanted to scream after her. "I don't want him! You can have him! I hate him!" But she didn't. It would not matter. Suzanne would hate her anyway, maybe even more because the Riding Master was chasing her when she wasn't trying to attract him. No matter what Is did, the other kids would hate her.

Is did not go to the Riding Master after lunch. She wondered how much trouble she was getting herself into, but she didn't go.

The next day she was standing at the sink in the tack room washing a bit when the Riding Master came in. He walked right up to her. Pretending to reach around her for the towel, he leaned his whole body against her, pushing his hips against her backside and pinning her to the sink. She couldn't get away from him.

"Today," he whispered, his lips practically touching her ear. His breath blew her hair, and she felt the heat of the air he expelled against her check. Then he walked away.

Is stayed at the sink, head down, pretending to wash the bit. There were at least three other apprentices in the room. When she couldn't stay at the sink any longer, she moved to the table and began reassembling the bridle. She kept her eyes down.

This time it was Elsa, Suzanne's friend. She swaggered past Is's workstation and knocked a can of leather conditioner over, spilling it on the tack Is had just cleaned.

"Oops," she said.

Is was too slow to stop the catastrophe. She would have to clean up the mess and reclean the bridle. She would probably be in trouble for wasting the oil. She didn't care. Maybe it would take all of her lunch break to get the bridle back to perfect condition.

The next day was the worst because it was the most public. Is led one of the horses to the ring for his rider and as she turned to leave, the Riding Master came by on a horse he was training. Just as she was certain the horse was going to pass without stopping, the Riding Master vaulted from its back, landing right beside her. His whip came down with a whack on the rail in front of her, and his body blocked her on the other side. She was trapped.

"Why didn't you come to my office?" he boomed.

There was no escape.

"Why?"

"I had extra cleaning. I didn't get done," Is mumbled quickly. All the riders were looking. Even the apprentices back in the stalls would hear his voice.

He took his time, considering her reply, while the tension built unbearably for Is. Everyone was looking at them. The Riding Master had absolute authority in the manege, but Is had hoped that some fear of higher authority in the system would help keep him in check. Although some instructors were known for advancing students through sexual favors, it was not supposed to be done. But if he dared to humiliate her this openly, Is saw no chance of appealing to higher authority.

"Are you slow?" he asked.

Is didn't know how to respond. He tapped the whip, bringing it down with solid whacks on the railing, waiting with exaggerated impatience for her answer.

"Well?" he demanded in his Riding Master's voice, which could be heard throughout the arena and the entire stable area.

"Do you think you can ignore what I tell you to do?"

"No, sir," Is whispered. "I hadn't finished my work. I couldn't...."

"You are slow," he bellowed. "Don't you realize you must be very quick to be a good rider?"

"Yes, sir." Her voice was tiny in his presence. At least he was making the situation seem like an infraction of the rules rather than what it had been – a refusal of his sexual advances.

"If you do not like it here," he said, changing tack abruptly, "I do not think you belong here."

Is's heart nearly stopped. No! He could not throw her out of the Equestrian. She could not survive without her horses. She had no other friends, no other reason for living. Her eyes leapt to his, pleading. She must stay with the horses. She saw a cruel grin lift his upper lip and knew it was too late.

"We have no use for you here." He waited long enough to see what she would do. Plead for another chance, cry, promise to do anything he wanted, but she was too stunned to make any of those "proper" responses. He turned away and remounted his horse. He would ride away and her life would be over. She was furious that one man could hold such power over her. It didn't enter her mind that she could change what was about to happen. "Pack," he said over his shoulder. "You will go to the Berserker's Barn."

Under any other circumstances, Is would have been terrified by his decision. But at that moment it was a reprieve. She didn't care about the rumors. People got killed at the Berserker's Barn. The stallions were impossible to handle. The berserkers, who were being trained to ride there, were dangerous beyond description. She didn't care. She would get to stay with horses.

. . . Escaping from her memories, Is discovered that she had warmed up enough to stop shivering, but she could not relax. The man's body was solid against her back. Any moment he might make a move and Is didn't know what she would do. Even in his weak condition he was stronger than she, and she had seen him when he was not in control of himself. He had not harmed her, but she knew he could. It would probably be best not to fight him. If he was a thief, he was a very good one to have gotten away with such a fine horse and equipment. If she pleased him, he might be willing to help her hide. Or, maybe if he was a high government official he could break rules for her if she got in his favor. Maybe she could even return to the Alliance and not be in trouble at all.

But to her heart, none of that mattered. Whatever she might think she should do to improve her position, there was only one decision her body would accept. She thought carefully about where she had left her knife and how quickly she could reach it.

But the man didn't move, and finally the warmth did its work and Is relaxed too.

She woke to a feeling of peace like none she had known since she was a little girl. She had turned in her sleep and was curled into the man's chest, and both his arms were wrapped around her. She lifted her head to find him looking at her. His eyes held a peace so deep . . . it could not be rational.

Suddenly Is wanted to cry. He was some sort of crazy person. The peace and security she felt sleeping in his arms were as false as the security her mommy and daddy had offered. Worse. They had at least been stable, rational people trying to give her love and a home. It was not their fault the events of the world were too big for them to protect her against. It was not their fault they had been killed. But it had taught Is the truth of the world. No one could protect you.

She sat up quickly, before her thoughts could carry her into old grief. The man didn't make any move to restrain her as she got out of his bag and struggled into her crusty clothes. When she looked back at him, there were tears on his face. Silently, and unexpectedly, he was crying.

Is could not bear to look at him. Whatever pain he was feeling, she would never understand it, as he would never understand her pain. She jerked her gaze away and went out before he could start doing something crazy again.

The wind had stopped. The crystalline air was very cold. The mountains were breathtaking in fresh snow, impossibly white against a sharp, blue sky. Their stunning presence calmed Is. A winter bird trilled in the stillness and the sound seemed to go into her very bones. Her breath momentarily fogged the scene as she exhaled. She loved this land in a way she loved nothing else. It would be here always. It had a permanence that nothing else had, except death. When she died, that permanence would be hers. She was part of the chain.

The horses had moved down the slope and pawed the snow looking for something to eat. Lark had a layer of white on his wide rump. He seemed content. The mare was hunched against the cold, her belly drawn up and her tail clamped down. She looked miserable. The best thing for her would be to get moving. She'd warm up with activity, and if they got below the snow line there would be grass and water.

The man came out of the tent and Is went to help him pack it up. She avoided meeting his eyes and he seemed only interested in getting under way again.

Chapter 8

After the blizzard they rested the horses two days in the first good grass they came upon. Then they moved on, descending the mountain and crossing the valley floor. They were ascending the next ridge when they noticed the hoof prints of shod horses. The man dismounted to examine them. They looked recent to Is. She glanced around nervously. Shod horses could only be government troopers. When the man remounted and started to follow the trail Is held Lark back. Everything she felt she was starting to know about the man flipped over.

If he meant to take her to the troopers he might use the tool/weapon to keep her from running away. But he hadn't looked back yet. He didn't know she wasn't following.

She reined Lark around hard and drove her heels into his sides. Surprised by her sudden roughness Lark lunged forward into the forest with Is crouched low over his neck. Branches buffeted them as they ran and now Lark had picked up her fear. He plunged down the hillside, dodging trees and ducking low branches.

Suddenly Is was nearly pitched from Lark's back as he stumbled. His neck disappeared from in front of her as he fell, twisting. He was going down on his right shoulder. He would fall on her leg. Possibly roll over her. She kicked her feet free of the stirrups. The ground rushed at her with terrifying speed. The instant before contact the world receded into a spinning dot and . . . came back.

Lark stood, foursquare, under her. She could feel him trembling. She stroked his neck to reassure him although she needed reassurance as badly. She wasn't sure what had happened. Maybe some branch had hit her when Lark was falling and she'd almost blacked out, but he had recovered and she'd stayed on by reflex. That made sense. She'd take good luck like that anytime it was handed to her.

Lark recovered his composure. As he stretched his head down and helped himself to the irresistibly green grass, Is realized they were no longer in the forest but in a meadow.

Funny, it almost looked like spring grass, not the tough mature grass they'd been seeing. Maybe this little meadow was protected somehow.

She'd love to let him eat, but if the man followed her, or if he alerted the troopers, they'd be coming after her. She pressed her legs to Lark's sides to tell him to walk on and a wave of dizziness swept through her. Lark took a few steps and the rolling movement of his walk upset her equilibrium as if she had never sat on a horse before. She had to clutch the saddle and when there were no further signals from her, Lark stopped to eat again.

Is slid from his back. Her knees refused to support her and she ended up sitting on the ground. Pursuit, or no pursuit, she was going to have to rest a moment. Unconsciousness overtook her in a spinning rush.

She woke to the long shadows of late afternoon. Lark grazed near her fully tacked. His reins trailed on the ground between his feet but he had learned not to step on them.

Funny he hadn't gone looking for the mare, but maybe the green grass held him.

There was no sign of pursuit. She'd been really lucky nobody had found her yet, but it was time to get going. Her body felt like dead meat as she got to her feet.

At that moment Lark raised his head and whinnied. He was answered from the other end of the meadow. Is just had time to grab his rein as he went past her. He stopped obediently at her tug. She couldn't yet see what he saw but any company was bad news. She scrambled into the saddle. From that vantage she saw Blueskins, six of them, riding toward her.

She spun Lark around and saw more Blueskins coming from the other direction. They spotted her at the same instant she saw them. One of them shouted and sent his horse into a gallop. He was answered by a shout from someone in the other group and those horses surged forward too. In seconds they would have her surrounded. She dug her heels into Lark and he lunged for the small opening between the groups.

Suddenly a rider barred her way. He flung his arms wide, baring his blue-cast chest and shouting to make Lark turn. Is clenched her heels against Lark's sides. Her voice tore from her throat in a scream of rage. Lark reacted, lunging directly toward the horse and rider in front of him. In an instant he would collide with them. Is was too furious to be afraid.

The collision was not as bad as she'd expected. Lark stumbled but didn't fall. Is felt the impact of hitting the other horse but somehow she never saw the other horse go down. There were no thrashing legs to entangle Lark, no thrown rider trampled underfoot, no horrible scene impressed on her mind, only an open field in front of them. She crouched in her stirrups and let Lark run until he slowed of his own accord. When she looked back there was no sign of anyone.

Had their desperate act convinced the Blueskins to leave them alone? There was no other explanation. Yet Lark was not behaving as though there were other horses nearby. Now that she let him stop he only wanted to eat, and she noticed that the grass was no longer spring green. This was old, dry, winter grass. She felt dizzy again.

For the second time that day Is slid from Lark's back and found her legs unable to hold her. She had no choice but to sit on the ground for a while.

When she stood up she still felt unsteady on her feet. Night was coming and she was dizzy and disoriented. If she let Lark pick the way in the dark he'd take her to the nearest horses. Better to stay here. She got Lark untacked and pitched the fly of her tent, grateful that it was a lot warmer here than it had been on top of the pass.

But when she lay down she couldn't get to sleep. She was constantly listening for Lark. Although he had not shown any desire to go after the mare, Is worried he would leave during the night.

She tried to distract herself by planning what she should do next. But no plan would come. She drifted in and out of a light doze. Dreams and memories intermixed.

.. . It was her first day at the Berserker's Barn. The government rig dropped her off at the front door to the indoor arena. Armed only with a tough yellow folder, which probably told everything she had ever done wrong, and a small satchel of clothes, she entered the ring timidly.

The inside was enormous and quiet except for the exertions of the six horses who were working at that moment. Is closed the door silently behind her and stood transfixed by the beauty of the horses. These were not the older horses, retired brood mares and geldings who hadn't had the quality required of breeding stallions, that Is was used to handling in the Apprentice Barn. These were magnificent, highly bred, proud, powerful stallions in the peak of condition. The riders were so absorbed they hardly spared Is a glance. She stood, pressed to the wall, watching and didn't see or hear the Riding Master approach.

"What are you doing here?" the Riding Master's rough voice demanded, stressing "you" as if she were unworthy to enter the arena with his horses and students.

Too startled to speak, Is just held the folder out toward him.

"Ha," he said brusquely, taking it and flipping it open. "Apprentice!" he bellowed. "Junior apprentice!" As his glance jumped from the folder to Is, she knew he saw a weak frightened child. She forced herself to stand taller and not flinch as he continued. "What are those assholes thinking? An apprentice! A junior apprentice! You'll get killed." Then he paused and his countenance softened as he thought of a possible explanation. "Are you sure they meant to send you?"

Is could only nod. She was terrified of how her voice would sound. Now she understood why Riding Master Masley had sent her here, but she wasn't going to get killed. She was sure of that. These were horses. The most beautiful horses she had ever seen. She wasn't going to be afraid of them, even if they did tower over her, with powerful legs and feet that would crush hers if they ever stepped on her, even if they were stallions and she had never handled a stallion in her life. She would learn how to manage them so they didn't hurt her. They had their instincts and they had to be true to those instincts. She would learn their true nature, their rules and she'd survive - she'd become a rider. With new resolve she raised her eyes to Riding Master Lowbridge, only he wasn't looking at her now. He was reading her file.

"Shit!" he said summing up his disgust with her. Then he turned and roared, "Arimus! Arimus!" in a voice that could have raised the roof if it had not already been so high.

In a moment a tall young man came hustling along the edge of the arena.

"Arimus," the Riding Master said, "this is," he had to consult the file, "Isadora Drey. They sent us a goddamned junior apprentice." His voice had risen again. "Assholes! I can't believe this. You take her. See if you can keep her from getting killed." He stalked off, grumbling loudly.

Arimus looked her over. Dressed in the blue of an intermediate, he was intimidating, but not as much as a senior rider or a master. He wore a dour expression, made more dour by his assignment.

"Junior apprentice?" he asked her.

Is acknowledged what was beginning to seem like a crime.

"What do you know how to do?"

"I can groom, tack up, lead a horse, clean stalls and tack." Her voice didn't sound as bad as she'd feared.

"You can groom, tack up, and lead a school horse," he corrected with disdain, "not a real horse, not one of our stallions, and don't forget it. This is a whole different arena here. You can't mess around here. You've got to keep your mind on what you're doing all the time. You could get killed. Worse, you could get one of the horses hurt." He was looking her over again, but now Is felt he wasn't trying to intimidate her. The warning was real. He couldn't know she hadn't "messed around" in the Apprentice Barn. She had applied herself there, only she had not done what the Riding Master wanted.

"The horses aren't the only danger," Arimus continued. "They told you what we do here?" he asked and didn't wait for an answer. "We train the men who aspire to become the berserkers. They've got to be damn good riders. They aren't completely berserkers yet, and some of them don't make it. Some of them don't pass the riding. Some flunk out physically, or mentally. Sometimes they go crazy." He eyed her closely. "It doesn't happen often, but when it does, it's bad. You've got to be awake. This isn't kindergarten anymore."

Is didn't say anything, but in her heart she swore to learn to handle these "real" horses and one day to ride them. She was not afraid of the horses, nor would she be afraid of the people.

She stirred in her sleeping bag. If her mind must wander into the past at least her memories of the Berserker's Barn were not too bad. She had applied herself and she had won her way, inch by muscle-aching inch, all the way up to senior rider. Surely that had been harder than what she was facing now. At least now she was alone, and if she was alone she could be safe.

When she finally slept, nightmarish dreams plagued her. Involved in them, she didn't wake fast enough. Lark's whinny was part of her dream. The sound of many horses milling about jerked her out of sleep.

She came out of her sleeping bag faster than she'd ever moved in her life. A man was crouched, about to come under the fly with her. She attacked, charging the man with all her might, knocked him down and got past him, only to be tackled from behind by another man as she burst from under the fly.

On her stomach, on the ground, she was very aware of the horses. Their legs were a milling forest in the moonlight, their hooves coming within inches of her prone body.

Unshod. Marauders, not government. Lark was hidden from her view.

The man who had grabbed her had his arms wrapped around her legs. She twisted around and tried to slug him in the face. Only he ducked and her fist just grazed his shoulder. Other men laughed. Someone's feet nearly landed on her as he vaulted from his horse. He grabbed her by the hair and lifted. She swung at him too. She could see him well enough in the moonlight to see the bluish cast to his skin. Until that moment she'd been more furious than scared.

They forced her to her feet by twisting her arm behind her back. She tried to ignore the pain. Keep fighting. They were going to kill her anyway. If they killed her before they raped her so much the better.

Pain from her twisted arm made her start to lose consciousness, and then adrenaline brought her up again. Everything seemed to be happening in jerky little flashes.

Suddenly everything was quiet. She must have been out for a moment. She was lying on the ground and the men had formed a circle around her. No one was moving. She got to her knees. The circle spun. She exerted her will and made the circle be still. The man she was facing was obviously the leader. He exuded a severe dignity Is couldn't ignore. She stood up. The world did one complete rotation, and stopped. She ignored the places her body hurt and focused on the Blueskins, struck by their resemblance to berserkers. They had the same wide chests and thickly muscled arms and legs, but they were shorter than berserkers.

When the leader saw that he had her attention, he beat on his bare chest with the palm of his hand making a surprisingly loud noise. Then he delivered a short guttural speech. Is couldn't understand a word. He would probably be the first to rape her, but all she could do was stare at him. She'd meant to fight as hard as she could, try to get herself killed, or at least knocked out. But now, somehow, it seemed too late. Whatever was happening here was not what she'd expected.

"Chest" finished his speech, turned and gestured and a man led Lark into the circle. Is came alert. She'd kill any one of them before she'd let them harm Lark. She didn't think about how.

They'd put a rope with a slip knot around Lark's neck. He'd never been led that way and didn't know the knot could tighten, strangling him. It would be a very dangerous way to handle a fully trained war horse who would fight anything that hurt him. But Lark followed the man complacently into the circle, confident in the goodwill of all humans toward him.

The leader hit his chest making the loud noise again. Then he gestured to the horse and to Is and asked something in a language Is couldn't understand. She stared defiantly at him. He gave an angry grunt.

Is turned and walked toward Lark. No one made any move to stop her. She reached out and took the rope from the man who was holding Lark as though she expected him to give it to her and he did. She slid it off Lark's neck.

Everyone fell back a few paces, making the circle bigger. For a moment Is hoped they were retreating in fear, but they weren't. The leader hit his chest again, pointed at the horse and said something. Then he too moved back to the edge of the circle. It was obvious what they wanted.

They had not offered her a bridle or saddle. She'd never ridden Lark this way before and wondered if he'd respond to her signals. Without the saddle her aids would feel different to him, and without the bridle there would be no way to make him obey if he didn't feel like it.

She turned him downhill of her. With no stirrups she had to vault all the way onto his back. She experienced a moment of doubt but threw it out harshly. She jumped as high as she could, grabbed his mane, and threw her right leg over. A fairly clean vault. Now she knew for sure where her body was hurt - her left elbow, right hip and leg, left ankle. She put the pain out of her mind.

Is pressed Lark's sides with her calves, asking him to walk and steered him around the circle with her legs and weight. He answered as though they did this all the time.

If he had been fully trained she could have broken through the circle in a moment. But Lark wasn't trained for that sort of fighting and neither was she. If she got out of the circle there would be a high-speed chase on the steep rocky trails in the dark. The Blueskins' weedy little animals would be faster under these conditions. Their riders knew the country and they had weapons. She gave up the idea and turned Lark around the circle.

If Lark had been trained in the battle airs she could have impressed the hell out of the Blueskins. But his training had only gotten as far as the basics that formed the groundwork for the battle skills. The movements he knew were less deadly and more esoteric. But that was all Is had.

She asked Lark for a canter and he moved into that gait with an effortless smooth bound. Using only her seat and legs she brought him into a collected, high canter. They were on a slope, on rocky ground, with only the moonlight, but Lark responded to her aids, bringing his hind legs well under him with each slow-motion bound, balancing as though he had the best footing in the world.

Is felt impressed. But what would her audience of blueskinned barbarians know of the hours of work that had gone into accomplishing this seemingly simple movement, a collected canter on the side of a mountain, with no bridle? They would need to see something flashy.

She turned across the circle and asked Lark for a flying change of lead. He performed it effortlessly, springing into the air and coming down on the opposite leading leg as though he had jumped over a small nonexistent hurdle. Emboldened by the ease of Lark's response, Is asked for another change, and then another in rapid succession. Lark sprang through the air as though he was skipping.

For Is the watchers might as well have disappeared. Lark transported her into heaven. The perfection of his responses made her feel overwhelming love for him. Sitting his bare back, she could feel him use every muscle as though they were her muscles, and in a sense they were. She made a small movement and they responded with a larger one. Hypnotized by their mutual power, she felt their coordination go beyond training and become true communication.

She asked him to halt and he came to a standstill, setting each hoof down once and not moving it again, sitting back into his momentum in such a way that he was able to cease moving instantly and completely.

Without thinking, Is asked for a trot in place. She hadn't taken Lark that far in his training, but he performed it perfectly. Answering her aids to trot but not go forward, he produced the trot in place even though he had never felt her signals applied in that sequence before.

Her heart soared. Lark was giving every bit of his heart, joyously, performing not only for her but for his audience, human and equine. Before he could tire, she asked him to trot forward and he launched himself into the great ground-covering steps of the extended trot with huge, high, joyous strides.

But the circle was too small for such a gait and Is brought him to a halt. She was so filled with joy she had completely forgotten her audience. She slid from Lark's back, intent only on praising him for his gallant effort . . . and then remembered the Blueskins. Sophisticated horsemen would have been impressed by what they had just seen, but she didn't know what the Blueskins would think. For a moment more she didn't care. She had always known Lark had a generous heart, but this night had transcended anything in her wildest dreams. It was the ride of a lifetime, and Lark had given it to her on the rocky steep hillside, with no bridle, surrounded by people who probably meant to harm him. She pressed her cheek against his neck, thanking him silently with all her heart until Chest spoke in harsh grunts.

Immediately a guard appeared at each of her shoulders.

They didn't touch her but it was obvious where they wanted her to go. She let them escort her. What she had just experienced had lifted her above the Blueskins and beyond fear. She had been transported into a place of incredible dignity where any sort of physical struggle was too out of place to be considered and rape was an impossible indignity.

They set off across the little meadow. Is walked on into the night, escorted by mounted Blueskins on either side of her and ahead and behind. In the dark, she could not see the ground but her footsteps were oddly sure. She held her head high, moving among the rocks and roots and steep places, keeping pace with the riders.

Her euphoria lasted for hours. But by morning it was gone. She was hungry and beginning to be very tired. Her hip and ankle hurt with each step, sucking at her attention, draining her energy. By then it was somehow too late to resist. She trudged on through increasing fatigue and refused to let herself think. She also refused to let herself quit. No matter how tired she got she had decided she would keep going. She made that pact with herself, a carryover from Lark's gallantry last night. She was living up to the honor of having been the one he had allowed to train him.

Once Is had made that covenant she never wavered. Walled in by her own fortitude, she was not aware of the changes around her. The first she knew of the approaching riders was when they came galloping, whooping, around the group that was escorting her.

Chest and his warriors sat taller on their horses, making them jig for benefit of the younger warriors. Is caught glimpses of Lark, prancing, neck arched but he didn't try to pull away from the man who was leading him. After a few minutes the other Blueskins departed in a clattering of hooves and great whooping cries.

Within a few more hours of walking, they reached the Blueskin camp. The tents were of an octagonal design Is had never seen before. There were so many that she didn't bother to count.

Is had never thought about the marauders having homes, children and wives. They had always been the enemy – terrifying and savage and unreasoning.

Lark threw his head up and whinnied. He was answered from the camp by a whinny Is recognized. The man's mare stood at the fence of a corral calling to Lark. Is's heart jumped with hope. He was here! And then her hope crashed. He was probably a captive too.

They brought her to the middle of the tents where there was a large clear area for gathering. The people formed a rough circle with her and Chest's group in the middle. Men and boys raced their horses around the edge of the circle, whooping and shouting. Is noticed how the women held back, peeking shyly from huddled groups near the tents.

The men who had brought her in rode tall, especially Chest. Everyone obviously admired Lark. He was excited by being among so many horses. He looked huge beside the Blueskins' stunted animals.

Is was looking around at all the activity when the man to her left tripped her and threw her to her knees in the middle of the circle. Before she could get up, Chest beat on his chest, silencing everyone. As his warriors engaged in a reenactment of capturing her and Lark the leader stood with his chest stuck out. Is had to admit there was a kind of dignity about him. She couldn't understand the words but the acting was very good. She was being credited with nothing. The way the other women held back, and the way she was not even allowed to stand among the men, told her all she needed to know. At best she could hope to become a lesser citizen like the other women, maybe one of Chest's wives. That was if they didn't kill her or make her a slave. At least they would take care of Lark. They would breed him to their weedy little mares and he would improve their herd. He'd be happy enough.

But as tired and defeated as Is felt at that moment she knew she would not submit to the kind of life they'd expect her to lead. She would escape, or be killed trying. She had just reached that decision when she saw the man standing among the Blueskins watching. Her heart leapt with hope. He wasn't a captive. He would help her. But then she wasn't so sure. He was crazy and he had to be some sort of outlaw if he consorted with the Blueskins. He might be her enemy as much as they were.

He didn't look at her but walked into the circle, signifying that he wanted to speak. Like most of the Blueskins he wore no shirt. His skin looked pale and out of place. He was a good head shorter than most of them and still so underweight from his illness that his ribs showed. But there was a confidence about him that Is had never noticed before.

He took center stage and turned slowly around the whole circle, looking at each person in turn. Everyone became silent watching him. Suddenly he beat on his chest the way Chest had done and the noise he made was surprisingly loud in the silence he had created. It startled Is. He didn't speak, but turned and pointed at her and the stallion and beat his chest again. His meaning was clear. She belonged to him.

Is looked to see how Chest was taking that, but he and everyone else just stared impassively.

The man turned and strode over to Is and reached out to grab her by the shoulder as if he were going to make her stand up, but Is had had enough. She came to her feet, swinging at his face as hard as she could. He deflected her punch and caught her by the wrist so effortlessly she felt as if she must have moved slowly. Almost before she could think of hitting him with the other hand he grabbed that wrist too. She let him pull her toward the center of the circle, but when he moved his hand to her shoulder, as though to turn her around, she was having none of it. She meant to spin all the way around and drive her elbow into his gut, but the next instant she was on her knees again. She couldn't figure out how he'd done that to her.

He motioned for Lark to be led into the circle, then stood back, apparently inviting everyone to look at the stallion. Is wondered if he was claiming the horse too. Maybe he was bargaining her for the horse. She got to her feet and no one noticed because just at that moment the man let out a high shriek. The intensity of the sound seemed to penetrate her mind, leaving her stunned and momentarily helpless.

There was a commotion in the corral. The man's mare came out of the herd at a gallop heading straight for the fence. She stretched her neck, eyes fixed on the highest bar as she judged the distance and placed her strides. On the last one, she set her hindquarters well under her and lifted over the fence in beautiful form. No one had much time to admire it as she galloped straight at the circle with no intention of stopping. Everyone was forced to drop their dignity and get out of her way.

Only *he* didn't move. The mare came to a sliding halt right in front of him. It was too much for Lark. He reared, thrashing the air with his front feet, landed, and reared again. Is had a flash of what Chest must be seeing – the small, white-skinned man with the stallion rearing behind him and the mare sliding to a halt in front of him, while he never even turned to see if Lark's hooves would miss him.

The Blueskin who had been leading Lark was not so sanguine. He let go of the rope and jumped out of the way of those thrashing legs.

Is ran forward and caught Lark's rope and he settled.

If Chest was impressed, it didn't show. He was still standing with his perpetual frown and unassailable dignity.

Meanwhile the man stepped back from the mare, inviting everyone to admire her the way he had the stallion. His hands shaped the slope of her shoulder, the way her neck arced out of her chest, the angle of her hindquarters, built for running. Is was struck again by what a good cross she would make with Lark. She didn't think anyone missed the point.

Now the man turned to Chest. He held his arm out and rubbed and pinched at his skin as though showing it was a different color from Chest's. Then he pointed at Is and Lark, and then over the mountains to the northwest. Is thought he was telling Chest that he had a right to her because they were the same skin color and he was taking her to his camp, or village.

Chest was having none of it. He took a step forward, hit his chest a few times and pointed to her and Lark.

The man, in his turn, again acted out how he was taking Is and Lark with him. As soon as he was done, Chest stepped forward and spoke in his own language, at the same time making motions that said the man and the mare had been going one direction, and Is and the stallion had been going the opposite direction.

Hope drained out of Is. She looked around wondering if there was any chance they could make a break for it. It looked impossible, but if the man tried it she'd be ready. Instead he faced Chest in a belligerent pose and hit his own chest, uttering harsh, guttural cries. Is needed no interpretation.

Chest took a step forward and they faced off. Is noticed how strong Chest looked. His pectoral muscles stood out as he displayed his chest. His biceps were huge, and the muscles of his thighs bulged as he sank into a combat stance. Chest would kill the man.

Is couldn't stand to watch someone beaten to death in front of her eyes. She edged back to Lark's shoulder. When the fighting started she would jump on Lark and gallop through the midst of it. Maybe she'd even be able to pull the man up behind her. Maybe Lark would tolerate that. Or maybe she'd be able to create enough distraction that he could mount his own mare. She doubted they'd escape, but she had to do something. Her body tensed with readiness.

Chest chose that moment to charge. Is saw that much. Then she saw Chest flying through the air. He hit the ground hard but was up again in an instant. A murmur of surprise ran through the crowd.

Chest attacked again. This time Is clearly saw Chest grab the man's shoulder with one hand, the other arm cocked back to punch. She saw the punch go wide as the man moved to the side. Then she saw Chest lean over and go down to one knee. She couldn't see what the man had done to make that happen. He seemed hardly to have moved at all. Chest tried to get up and an instant later he was sailing through the air again.

Chest was a little slower to get up this time, more cautious in his attack. The man just stood there seeming unready for another attack. Is wanted to scream at him. Warn him. Something!

Chest pulled a knife from its sheath on his thigh and slashed. Just as Is expected to see the man double over in pain, Chest reversed directions so quickly he lost his footing and sat down heavily. The man stood like nothing much was happening. It took a moment for Is to realize that he was now holding Chest's knife. He held it delicately, as though he didn't know how to use it. Then unbelievably he bent over and placed the knife on the ground near Chest, straightened and walked toward Is and the horses. That was all the signal Is needed. She sprang onto Lark's back with no thought of how tall he was. The man walked on by and the mare turned obediently and followed him. Is let Lark do the same. The circle dispersed to let them pass through.

The man walked to one of the tents and went inside. Is was afraid to get off Lark, afraid someone else would claim her. Now that the man had undisputed right to the stallion, maybe he wouldn't bother to take her along. She waited a nerve-racking eternity until the man came back out with his saddle and bags and unhurriedly tacked the mare. He gave Is no sign as to what she should do, so she just sat and waited. They might have been invisible for all the attention anyone else paid them.

When the man mounted the mare and started out of the village Is let Lark follow. They rode in silence for maybe half an hour while Is debated with herself. Perhaps she should thank him. But she wasn't sure he had rescued her. Maybe he only wanted the stallion. Or maybe she now belonged to him the way she would have belonged to Chest. She might be as much a slave among his people as she would have been among the Blueskins. When she looked at him, trying to determine what her relationship to him was supposed to be she saw that his face was set in a grim expression, as though he was in pain. Is's first thought was that he had been hurt in the fight.

He realized she was looking at him and came to a halt. With a hand signal he told her to stay where she was while he dismounted and walked into the woods on the side of the trail. He moved half bent over as though he was hurt.

Is's instinct was to go after him. He needed help. But his hand motion had definitely told her to stay here. She was dithering over what to do when he returned, walking briskly and upright. She could barely smother laughter when she realized what had happened. He, who had seemed so calm and invincible facing Chest, had had an attack of diarrhea now that it was over. A little sputter of laughter escaped Is. She turned her face away from him, trying to control herself. She didn't mean to laugh at him. It was just relief. She'd been in awe and somewhat afraid of him – if he could handle the Blueskin like that she'd have no hope of fighting him – but now he was just her crazy man again.

She heard the creak of leather as he swung into his saddle. The horses began to walk. Is still couldn't look at him. She couldn't get the grin off her face. And then she was surprised by a little sputtering sound that wasn't her own, quickly cut off. She looked at the man just as he looked to see if she had heard him. That was all it took. He started to giggle, high-pitched with the stress of trying to suppress it, but not the horrible hysterical laughter she had heard him make before. Is couldn't help herself. In a moment they were both out of control, laughing, bent over their horses' manes, trying not to fall off. Gale after gale swept through Is. She had never laughed like this before. Everything seemed funny. Every little thing set them off again. Even after her sides hurt, Is couldn't stop.

For hours, all it took was for one of them to glance at the other, and they would be off again in uncontrollable laughter.

Chapter 9

They followed the trails openly now as though they no longer feared the Blueskins. The day they had laughed together had changed their relationship. The tension Is always felt around the man dissipated and he seemed more relaxed too. They laughed at little things now – a horse's silly spookiness, the antics of the small animals that invaded their camps, each other's mistakes. If the man was crazy it no longer mattered. He treated Is better than any of the people at the government school. He had not tried to claim her as his wife or slave, or dominate her in any way. He was quiet, uncomplicated company. His camping and foraging skills were excellent, and if he couldn't talk, Is didn't miss it.

The only thing she wished she could ask him was where they were going and if he was taking her to his people. But she wasn't worried. She figured that if the man had learned his camping skills from them, they must know how to live as unobtrusively with the land as he did. If he had learned his bridle-less horsemanship from them, they must be great horsemen. Is found herself beginning to want to meet them.

Instead, one day they crested a ridge and in the valley below them Is saw a shabby little town of about twenty wooden shacks. Even from this distance she could see the filth and squalor of the place. Piled behind the buildings were heaps of refuse. Anything that had ever been discarded lay around on the ground.

Is brought Lark to a standstill and her revulsion must have been evident for the man began to explain with his hands. They had to go down there. He tapped his saddle and pointed to Lark's bare back. All of Is's possessions had become the property of the Blueskins the night they had captured her. Sitting Lark bareback for hours on end, day after day was uncomfortable, and Lark was beginning to get rubbed places in his coat that could turn into sores.

So the town was just a place to get supplies. Is felt relieved, but still leery. She was an outlaw riding a stolen war horse. There might be a reward on her. She shook her head at the man, unwilling to take the risk.

He tried to reason with her. Pointing north, he began to count off days on his fingers. They would be traveling many days. He wrapped his arms around himself and shivered. It had been warm enough that Is had not needed a sleeping bag, but she had already had to borrow the man's jacket and he would need it himself as they got higher into the mountains.

He took a wallet from his saddlebag and opened it. Is had never seen so much money. He rifled through it, selected a few bills and put them in his pocket. Then he handed the wallet to Is, motioning for her to put it in the inner pocket of his jacket, which she was wearing. She reached out to take the money, surprised to see her hand shaking.

No one had money like that. He must have stolen it. She remembered how he had handled Chest. She remembered how he had shown her that a tool could be used as a weapon. What if he had killed people to steal their money? Is couldn't put the wallet inside the jacket, next to her body, if that were true.

He watched her, head cocked quizzically.

He couldn't miss how her hand shook. She thrust the wallet back at him. He looked puzzled but took it. Then he shrugged and put it in a different pocket from the one he'd put the other money in. He was still looking at her with a raised eyebrow. She rode past him and started down the ridge ahead of him so he could not see her face. She had to sort out her reaction. Why should she be so upset? She was an outlaw too. She had stolen Lark. If she had stolen as much money as Lark was worth instead, it might have been more than the amount in the man's wallet. She didn't know. Lark was very valuable, but she didn't know exactly how that translated into money. She didn't even know the denominations of the bills she had seen. As a trainer Is had been paid in supplies and credits that had gone toward her retirement. She never handled money and had not been taught how to read it.

Is rode down the hill in turmoil. She had never intended to break the law. She had been forced to do it to save Lark. She wouldn't deliberately harm anyone. But that might be what the man did. Maybe he sought out people and took things from them. Maybe he hurt them and maybe sometimes killed them. If she let him buy her things with his stolen money, what would that make her? She thought of her parents and wanted to weep. She had sunk so far from what they had wanted for her.

She needed to make that right. Maybe she should give herself over to the law. Maybe she should let someone in this town take her in. Her thoughts turned to Lark. Some other trainer would finish his training and he would be sent out with a berserker. He would die fighting in a way horses did not fight if left to themselves. She tried to see the government that did that to horses and people as wrong. But now she couldn't. That government was trying to protect its people. It was not at fault for failing in her parents' case. It had made something better for its people than this stinking outlaw town, or the lawlessness of people like the crazy man she was riding with. She seemed unable to remember any of the things she had felt that had made her steal Lark.

The man caught up and rode beside her into the town. Is was so distressed that she hardly noticed the smell of open garbage. Everything was stained with the red mud of the streets. Nobody had bothered to pick up garbage wherever it had been dropped. They were near the middle of the town before she really looked at the people who were coming out of the houses to stare at her on the war horse and the man on the bridle-less mare.

The men were all of a kind - dirty, with long, greasy hair. They wore filthy, worn clothes and old boots. Their expressions were hard and calculating. Is's instinct for self-preservation started to resurface.

She looked around more carefully. In contrast to the men, the women wore dresses that had once been very fancy and fine but showed signs of wear now. They wore elaborate hairdos like nothing Is had ever seen before and more jewelry than she'd ever imagined. Is was reminded of the way the Imperial Guard bedecked their horses for state occasions. Each service tried to outdo the others, showing off their wealth in jewel-inlaid bridles, saddle blankets of the richest cloth, and saddles so encrusted with precious stones Is had wondered how the horses could carry their weight. She had poured over pictures of such pageantry as a child, and now she saw it dimly reflected in the display these women wore. She wondered if for the men of this town, the women were no more than a means to display ownership and wealth – just like the Guard's horses.

They passed a few dispirited-looking half-starved horses in a corral that was ankle-deep in mud and droppings that no one had bothered to clean in what Is judged must have been years. The horses eyed them listlessly. Is could see where they had chewed the wooden fence in their hunger and she knew then she would not give herself up to anyone in this town.

They came to a building that looked a bit more kept up than the others. This one had an awning and people were sitting under it on old rickety chairs and ancient bales of hay they should have fed to the horses long ago.

The man dismounted and Is followed suit. The men sitting around watched them with shrewd, conniving stares. Is saw one of them get up and saunter off. She wanted to get back on Lark and leave as fast as she could. But the man didn't seem to notice anything, as if he was accustomed to this sort of decadence and danger and implied violence. He walked into the store, leaving Is in a frenzy of doubt. She didn't want to leave the horses but wasn't sure he'd be able to bargain for their supplies without an interpreter.

She heard voices inside the store, and after a while someone came out and trotted off down the street. More people were showing up all the time. Mostly they just hung out in doorways and stared. A few came over and joined the people under the awning. A few went inside. Is wished desperately that the man would come out so they would leave before anything bad happened.

Eventually he did come out carrying an armload of stuff. Is moved to help him pack it in the mare's saddlebags – a sleeping bag for her, food concentrates, and a coat and rain slicker for her. She took the garments without trying them on. They would have to do.

While she was packing things away, he turned and headed back into the store before Is could stop him. A few more people sauntered in after him, making Is very nervous for his safety, and her own. The voices coming from inside the store seemed friendly enough but she couldn't make out the words. More people kept going in. Someone came back out with a bottle in his hand and called to a man across the street. More people went in. Is fretted, while inside the store the men drank and their voices grew louder.

Eventually she saw the man who had left the store earlier, coming back. He was carrying a saddle.

"Try this," he said in a heavy accent Is had never heard before.

She couldn't believe her eyes. The saddle the man was holding out to her was a berserker's saddle, built for a war horse. She couldn't guess how this man had gotten it.

The saddle was old and covered with a thick layer of dust and mildew, but had originally been made with the highest quality workmanship and the best leather. With a little cleaning, and conditioning oil, it would be like new. Other than stiffness from obvious neglect, everything seemed in good repair. The seat would be bigger than Is needed, but the saddle would fit Lark's broad back perfectly.

In the excitement of trying the saddle on Lark, Is forgot about the hostile crowd until one of the men who had been lounging around spoke.

"You gotta pay for the saddle, little lady," he said in a leering tone, and then turned to the others. "Ain't that right?"

Taking their cue from him, other men chimed in. "Yeah." "That right, Gene." "Everybody got to pay their way here." They began to move around her, their voices and actions meant her no good.

She didn't bother to reply. The man who had brought the saddle had gone into the store. He wasn't concerned about being paid.

Is had let herself get caught on Lark's right side and mounting from that side was something she had never seen the need to practice. To mount with the saddle, she needed to jump high enough to stick her foot in the stirrup and then swing the other leg over. It was a coordination her body knew well from the left side of the horse but it might not translate so well to the right. She hesitated a fraction of a second and the men closed the circle around her until it would have been foolhardy for her to turn her back on them to mount.

She thought to swing Lark around so everyone would have to move out of his way. But a man stepped forward and grabbed the lead she had thrown over Lark's neck while she had been fitting the saddle.

"Now, where would you be thinking of going without paying us?" he asked.

The others made similar comments but Is wasn't listening. If Lark had been fully trained she could command him to strike out and the man holding the lead would be dead. Or she could make him kick the men who were standing too close to his hindquarters. But as it was Lark was totally trusting. He didn't know that anyone could hurt him and he couldn't understand what it might mean to him if someone hurt her. These men either did not recognize Lark as a war horse, or they had figured out he was not trained. Lark would be no help to her with whatever happened next and calling for the man's help never entered her mind.

She struck the first man who reached for her, knocking his hand away with an oblique blow. They all laughed and retreated a little but she knew they wouldn't quit now. They were goading one another on, still kind of good-humored among themselves, but very serious for her. "Don't be afraid of the little she-lion." "Hey, Digger, did she scratch you?" "Watch out for her teeth."

She didn't see the man come out of the store. The first she knew he was there was when one of the men surrounding her said, "Ooof," and sat down abruptly. The other men caught on right away though. They turned away from her and now the man was the one who was surrounded.

They still weren't very serious, still razzing each other. "Now, what's this? You suppose the she-cat's his woman?" "Naw, he ain't big enough to knock her down." "Or knock her up." The men laughed and carried on with like comments.

On some signal that Is missed, the whole group charged in and dove on the man. At least she thought that was what happened. An awful lot of people hit the ground. She thought to jump on Lark and try to make him charge into the crowd, but if the man was on the bottom she didn't want to trample him. Instead she raced from Lark's side, grabbed a chair, and was about to wade in swinging as hard as she could when the mare interposed herself between Is and the men. She looked up, and he was sitting on the mare's back, grinning. Is was so totally dumbfounded that she stood, staring stupidly a moment, and that was all the other men needed. They disentangled from the heap, saw Is cut off from Lark and headed toward her. She raised the chair.

Everybody suddenly wasn't in such a hurry.

The man made the next move, causing the mare to pivot her hindquarters toward the men and making an opening for Is to get to Lark. She walked slowly, her muscles tight as springs. No one moved. She made it to Lark, set the chair down and sprang into the saddle.

The mare went by them in a gallop and Lark dug in and went too. A lesser rider than Is would have been left behind in the dust, but Is was too much a part of her horse.

Lark would never catch the mare but he was doing his best. Is crouched over his shoulders and let him run. Whoops and catcalls and whistles trailed them, but no pursuit. For the men of the town the whole thing had just been a little fun to break the boredom. If they had succeeded in raping her, it would have been just the same, a little entertainment for them.

They were out of the town in no time and streaking across the plains, heading for the ridge they had descended earlier. In the name of safety, Is rarely galloped her horses as fast as they could go. Even for an experienced rider such a gallop as this created a rush of adrenaline that was exhilarating. Her body took over the muscular coordination of moving with the galloping horse, her mind free, triumphant, and as wild as the horse's mind.

When they hit the slope the mare slowed. Is let Lark catch her and he was happy to slow to her pace. The man was grinning from ear to ear and Is realized that she was too. It felt good to be able to break and run away from that kind of harassment.

It hadn't been that way in the government school. There had been nowhere to go, and no one to go to for help. Well, that wasn't quite true. If you were "with" the right people no one else would bother you. But Is had never been able to do the things that would have gotten her that sort of protection. She had been fair game for everyone.

They were moving along at a steady trot now. But the day had grown dark for Is. Her mind took her back to the school.

. . . "So you're the peasant?" Phil looked her over with cold appraisal.

Phil was the protector for Beth's group. For some reason Beth had befriended Is and wanted Phil to take Is into the group.

It was after curfew and it was part of the test of Is's mettle to sneak out like this.

Phil walked around her, looking her over. Is glanced at Beth who gave her a little encouraging smile. Beth hadn't told her it would be like this.

"So, what do you know how to do?" Phil asked.

Is knew how to milk cows, cut hay, weed gardens and carry water.

"C'mon, Phil," Beth said. "She's pretty. She'll be fine. I'll watch out for her."

Is already knew enough about Beth to know that assurance wasn't going to help. The next thing she knew, Phil reached right up under her government blouse and took hold of her breast.

"Do you know how to do it?" Phil asked in a lewd voice. "Do you know how to do it real good for a man?"

When she didn't move, Phil let go of her breast as if he were dropping it in disgust.

"She ain't no good to me," he said to Beth, ignoring Is.

Beth was going to protest, Is could see that. Phil saw it too.

"It takes more than a hot cunt, baby," he said sidling over to Beth. Is saw his hand go right up under Beth's skirt as if he owned her. Beth's eyes half-shut as she moved her legs apart and began to push her hips against his hand. But Phil wasn't even looking at Beth. When Is glanced at him, startled from what she'd realized was happening, he was staring right into her eyes. He bared his teeth at her in a wicked smirk.

Is backed off, then caught herself, turned and walked away. At the door she looked back. Beth had both her hands on Phil's chest and her head was bent forward so her forehead was on his shoulder. She was still moving her hips. She never noticed Is leaving. But Phil was watching and his look was triumphant. He controlled both women. One he chose to keep; the other he drove away. She felt as conquered as Beth.

Is shook herself free of the memory. Out here it was different. Surely. But the day seemed darker than before. Maybe the only difference was that there was more room to run.

In the school she had closed the door and gone back to her own ward, but her trouble had only begun. Unprotected by any gang leader, she was harassed by everyone, hated fiercely by the rest of the girls, and blamed for anything that needed a scapegoat.

Early on she had tried to appeal to the authority of the adult attendants. She had quickly learned better. They had treated her as though she was a troublemaker and liar. The other students had gloated and stepped up their harassment of her. Realizing that there would be no help, she had learned to cope on her own.

She glanced sideways at the man who had helped her, twice now. Unaware of her scrutiny he reached forward and stroked the mare's neck and in that simple act of affection Is saw the love that bonded him to the horse.

Aware of her gaze, he smiled at her. Is saw his confidence, good spirits and the love within him – a mixture she could only call joy. But she could not share that with him now, and she looked away. Twice she had been helpless and he had rescued her, facing down bigger and stronger men. Is wondered how it must feel to be able to do that.

Chapter 10

They were making their way north and westward through mostly track-less country. The slopes were thick with forests and the horses found it easier to travel just above the tree line. The view was stupendous.

The mountains showed all their late-summer moods, from cool mornings to hot stultifying afternoons, broken by wind and lightning and sudden downpours.

Sometimes Is hunted in the evenings. Sometimes she hunted without killing anything, just reveling in the beauty of the animals. Sometimes she joined the man in collecting grain for cereal because he did not eat meat. There was always time for sitting, watching the horses graze, watching the streams near their campsites, watching the camp fire, or the stars. It was a leisurely pace, dictated by the land and the needs of the horses.

The man's company had become no more obtrusive than the horse's, which was as high a compliment to Is's way of thinking as she could give anyone. Someone else might have wished for conversation. Is didn't miss it.

From the top of a particularly high ridge the man pointed out land-marks. Behind them was the saddle where they had gotten caught in the blizzard, he mimed. In that valley was the Blueskins' camp. Back that direction was the town where they had gotten supplies. And there, where the perpetually snowcapped mountains towered ahead of them, was where they were going.

Is was considering how impossible it looked to get horses across those mountains when Lark's head swung around to the left. Following his gaze Is saw the smoke of a camp fire rising in one thin column of white straight into the fathomless blue sky. When she pointed it out to the man, he altered their course in that direction.

The next morning they saw the smoke again and by mid-afternoon they had crested the last ridge that separated them from it. A little meadow stretched below them and just at the transition between meadow and forest sat a small cabin.

Is followed as the man started down to it. This looked less dangerous than the town, and that ended safely enough.

When they were almost to the cabin, Lark snorted and shied. What Is had thought was just a bare patch of ground stood up and became a dog. Lark stopped dead, snorting again. The dog was as big as a small pony and its fur matched the tan soil perfectly. It stood with great dignity, eyeing them as though demanding how dared they disturb its nap. Then with odd nobility the dog stretched and yawned, arching its back high in the air. It was thin as a snake, all legs, with a long whip-thin tail. Having finished stretching, it moved off toward the cabin in a ground-covering trot. Lark relaxed and Is urged him forward. The mare had never hesitated so the man was well ahead.

Is saw a man standing in the doorway of the cabin. He had a great mane of white hair and a thick white beard. Is had just time to notice that much when the mare stopped and the man vaulted from her back. He walked forward a few steps, stopped and bowed to the man on the porch.

Is was trying to understand who the old man in the cabin could be to demand such respect from her man, when suddenly her man began to laugh. It was so out of keeping with the respect Is had just witnessed that it took her by surprise. In a moment he completely lost control, his laughter built into the stressed hysterical, insane sound Is hated so much.

He threw his head back and shrieked his laughter to the sky. Then he fell to his knees and beat the ground with his fists, still laughing. Is looked past him to the man in the doorway, who seemed startled, then puzzled. The way he was standing with his right arm hidden by the doorframe he could be holding a weapon in that hand. Is tensed.

At that moment the old man turned and looked directly at her. She saw the wrinkles around his eyes tighten.

"So you are ready to defend him," he said. It wasn't quite a question. His voice carried to her, surprisingly youthful. Is didn't answer.

"A crazy man, who isn't crazy," the old man mused. "Riding without need of a bridle. And a woman riding a berserker's horse."

He seemed to be waiting for Is to say something. She just stared at him, hard, daring him to do anything, while the man knelt on the ground between them, his body wracked with convulsions. It was impossible to tell whether the gasping howling sounds he made were laughing or sobbing.

"Life has brought me many strange things," the old man finally continued, "but this is odd even by my measure." He came out of the doorway and his right hand was empty. He walked over to the man. "Stand up," he said. "Stop making that noise."

To Is's surprise the man stopped. The silence was wonderful.

The old man turned to Is. "I wonder," he said conversationally, "what do they do to someone who steals a berserker's horse? I wonder what do they do with the berserker whose horse this is, eh? That should pose them a pretty problem." He grinned as though the thought pleased him.

There was a feral quality to his smile. He regarded Is with penetrating eyes that held the quick intelligence she had seen in the wild animals she had studied.

"Welcome to my house," he said, sweeping an arm toward his cabin. "Come in. I will feed you and you will tell me your story, eh." He turned and walked into the house without a backward glance.

The man followed. Is hesitated. She did not trust this old man. His observations were too keen. He seemed to know too much. He was not some dumb tough like the men in the town and not an uneducated savage like the Blueskins. The advantage he had over her in knowledge frightened her. She did not want to go into the house, but her man had gone in. She dismounted and followed him.

The first thing she noticed was the books. Floor-to-ceiling bookcases covered two walls and there were books open on the table. Books! Here? For an instant Is was back in the forbidden libraries of the government school where books and reading and the knowledge one could gain were restricted to the very highest ranks. A person like herself should not even be in this room. It took an effort of will not to back out the door.

This was not the government school. She had been invited in.

She was distracted from her turmoil by the man. He had hesitated at the door but now he ran forward.

He took a book off a shelf, hugged it and pressed it to his lips. Is went from being appalled by his behavior to being afraid of him in one heartbeat. He was at ease with books. He had the right to handle them, read them. He could only be some sort of high government official then, not a criminal!

He brought a book to the table, rifled through it, and found a place. He waved the old man to him and pointed to a word in the book.

Is was aghast at his rough treatment of the book and horror-stricken by his presumption toward the old man who must also be a high government scholar, for no one else would have all these books. But the old man appeared more bemused than offended. He walked over and looked at the page.

"John," the old man read, sort of quizzically.

For answer, the man hit his chest and tapped the page imperatively.

"John," the old man repeated, more firmly. Then he extended his hand. "I am pleased to meet you. These days I am known as Amil," he said. The two men clasped each other around the wrists.

Is felt the whole room and everyone in it rushing away from her. Everything she had thought she knew about the man collapsed in her heart, as all she had known about the Blueskins, the Alliance troopers, and the Boundary itself had been collapsing. But this was too much. There shouldn't be scholars here, and books. The air squeezed from her lungs. She must have made a sound for the old man turned and looked at her.

"I am intrigued," he said. "Come, sit down. I will feed you, and you will talk, yes? Come. Wine? I have a little. It will help."

Is had no volition of her own. She walked over to the table and sat down and let him serve her. She was past being appalled. The wine did help.

Amil couldn't be a real scholar, not out here in the wilderness like this. Even if he were, he had no power over her here. And if John were someone even higher than a scholar? That didn't matter here either. Here, he had to obey the rules of the mountains, the same as anyone. But inside, Is felt like crying. Everything had become so strange. Only hours ago John had been as natural a part of her life as the horses and the land. Now he was a million miles away, gone in some weird fashion less explicable than death.

Is didn't try to analyze the betrayal and loss she felt. She needed to get away. She didn't realize she had risen until she heard her chair scrape on the floor. The old man heard it too. He had gone into the part of the room he used for a kitchen, but now he turned and studied her.

"Don't leave us yet, I beg you," he said. "Your story has only begun to ask its questions." He peered at her keenly. "Besides, I am a good cook," he said, turning away. "Why don't you just take their saddles off and let them rest?"

Is went out without answering him. The horses grazed a hundred meters away. The dog came out from under the shade of the house and followed her. He didn't seem unfriendly, but he didn't approach her either.

Being outdoors helped. The smell of warm horseflesh in the sun, the soft sound of the tearing of the grass as the horses grazed, the buzz of insects, the breeze and the birdcalls all soothed her. The mountains rose around her, steadfast and enduring. What seemed like big events to her were nothing to them. To the mountains, scholars were just like other people, inconsequential.

It was quite warm in the sun. The horses' backs would be sweaty under their saddles. Is looked up the valley. She could go somewhere and live alone as she had done before, simple and uncomplicated. Or, she could go back into that house where everything was different from what she had ever suspected.

In the few minutes she'd been inside the cabin her life had changed. If she went back in her world would continue to change. It would never be as simple as it had been these last days. She did not want more change, and yet ... could there be other alternatives than living the life she had run away from, or living the life of running? What were scholars, and books, doing out here far from the government center? And the most unthinkable of all – could she be allowed to learn to read? If she had reached out and touched a book, would they have let her? They had let her see the open books, and Amil had read the name "John" out loud in front of her. What else might they allow? The kind of deep excitement she had learned not to feel at the government school stirred in her and would not be put down. She undid Lark's girth and put his saddle on the ground while she took the mare's off. Then she carried both saddles to the house. The dog followed at a distance, sniffing here and there as though going about his own business and not following her at all.

"Good," Amil said, "you came back." He had stirred up the coals in his stove and steam was already beginning to rise from a pot on top of it. He had been busy cutting up tubers, keeping his end of the bargain.

John was standing at the bookshelf with his back to her. He didn't turn around. His forehead rested against the books on one shelf as his fingers traced the writing on the spines of one book after another on a lower shelf. Pain and loss emanated from him.

Is sat at the table where she had sat before. She didn't even try to lie. She told Amil why she had stolen Lark. John turned around and leaned his back against the bookshelves, watching her. This was the first time he'd heard any of this too. To keep from looking at him, Is watched Amil. He continued to keep himself busy in the kitchen, but she knew he was listening intently. Somehow it was easier to talk to him while he worked than it would have been if he were sitting looking at her. When she paused, he asked, "How did you meet John?"

So she told him how she had found John. How sick he had been and how she had come to believe someone had tried to poison him. When Amil glanced at John for confirmation, John nodded.

Is went on with the story, telling about the Blueskins and the outlaw town. It gave her a funny feeling to realize how differently John might tell the same tale.

Amil was a good cook. He knew how to use wild herbs and spices to make the simple grains and vegetables he'd prepared taste completely different from the fare on which Is had been living. The plates he served it on were finer than anything Is had ever used and oddly out of place with the rather crude workmanship of the table and chairs.

She was content to eat silently. John came to the table but did not touch his dinner. He pushed his plate aside and set a book in front of him, turning the pages slowly, running his fingers lovingly over the words. Suddenly his finger stopped at a word. He tapped it imperatively. Amil, who had been watching, unhurriedly set down the odd polished sticks with which he was eating, wiped his mouth and pulled a blank piece of paper and a pencil to him. Then he wrote down a word that didn't look like the word John had pointed out. But John seemed happy with it. He was off again, turning pages, running his fingers down them, looking for another word.

Is's heart beat fast with excitement. They were allowing her to stay in the same room where reading and writing were going on! They were breaking the law so nonchalantly.

She was so intrigued she forgot to eat. John and Amil managed to get a few words written down that way, but Is could see that John was struggling.

He squinted hard at the words as though it was hard for him to see them. His hand shook as he traced his finger across the page. When his finger paused at a word, Is couldn't tell if he was tapping it for Amil or if he was getting so out of control he couldn't proceed. She was afraid that he would tear the page if he tried to turn it.

Amil noticed too. He reached over and slid the book away.

John convulsed as if an electric current had run through him. He grabbed wildly after the book, but his movement was ill coordinated and without aim. His face twisted. His throat worked as though he were swallowing repeatedly.

Suddenly he stood up, pushing his chair away from the table with such force it went over backward. He started to bend, as though to right it, but then he just folded up on the floor beside it. He wrapped his arms around himself and began to rock. The muscles of his arms stood out as he gripped himself. He rocked faster and began to make a sound like a high-pitched animal keening. It made the hair on Is's arms stand up. A moment later the high hysterical laughter she hated so much filled the room. Suddenly John threw his head back and screamed, breaking free of the laughter for a moment, but only for a moment. It came back, wracking his body, and filling the room.

Is jerked to her feet and then stood undecided. Amil remained unperturbed. He continued to eat, watching John with one eyebrow raised, inquisitively, as he might watch an interesting insect crawling on the floor.

Is couldn't take any more. She went around the table and knelt by John, talking quietly as she might soothe a hurt horse. But it only seemed to make John worse. He jerked away, putting his back to her and laughing louder.

"Why don't you do something?" Is shouted at Amil. "He stopped when you told him to before."

Amil set down his eating sticks, wiped his mouth and sat looking at her for a time before he spoke.

"Perhaps he needs to laugh."

"He's not laughing. He's in pain. Can't you see that?" Is screamed. Her nerves were frayed beyond caring who Amil was.

"What else is laughter, but the release of pain?" Amil said easily, but when Is turned angrily away he spoke more gently. "Let him release it. He has something he wants to tell us. He will return to that when he is able."

Is wavered. She could see the truth of what Amil said, but she was disturbed on some deep level by the uncontrolled release of anguish that John's noise expressed.

"Come, sit down," Amil said, motioning to her chair. "We will talk, you and I."

So Is returned to the table and sat, answering Amil's questions as if they were having a perfectly reasonable conversation and it was not at all strange to have to shout over the noise of a man convulsing on the floor. But while her body behaved, her mind was completely unable to concentrate. She had no idea what she was telling Amil.

As abruptly as it had started, it was over. Silence filled the room. John got up, righted his chair and sat down. Amil slid the book to him. John began paging through it again and Amil went back to writing down words.

Is drew her shattered nerves together. She was no longer in awe of the old man.

"You're no proper scholar," she told him. "What are you doing with all these books?"

Instead of being offended, Amil smiled. "I thought you would never ask. You might say I have stolen them." He paused and watched for her reaction. His eyes sparkled under arched brows. "Or you could say I have rescued them. Much the same as your horse."

Stealing books, taking things of such power and significance, affected Is as the desecration of a holy shrine would affect someone who was deeply religious. Books, and the knowledge and power they contained, were something the government held. Citizens received the information they needed in order to achieve the purposes of their lives. Her purpose had been to train war horses. She did not need to know how to read or write, or the denominations of money. Wanting more knowledge than that was improper. Taking it was wrong in some way Is had never contemplated.

Amil's chuckle brought her whirling thoughts up sharply.

"So I have fallen from being a god, to being the worst sort of criminal," he said good-naturedly. "You might want to look at a belief system that allows that to happen."

Is couldn't make any sense of his words.

"You did me the honor of telling me why you stole the war horse. You wanted to rescue him. I wanted to rescue the books. You see, within the Alliance there are different factions. One or another gain more power and they decide what things will be known and what forgotten.

"Yes," he said to her expression of wonder. "It is not just the citizens who are not allowed to know things. Even within the upper levels it is sometimes better for the people holding the most power if certain things are forgotten."

"What sort of things?"

"Oh, history mostly. The way things really came to be the way they are. These," Amil waved his hand at the bookshelves, "are the old books. In many cases they are the original chronicles of an event, a discovery, or an experiment. From time to time the old books are copied. At those times they are shortened and condensed, which I suppose is necessary, but they are also changed. Sometimes quite on purpose, so the next generation will believe things were different than they really were. The Alliance would have us think it is a small thing. Not all knowledge can be retained." He sighed. "I suppose they are right. A bias always creeps into history. I just hate to see it done deliberately.

"So I took the books. I couldn't see them burned. But their fate here is no better. They will rot eventually."

John had been watching the exchange keenly. He started to say something. For a moment Is believed he would succeed. Some rational sentence would come out of his mouth. Instead, at the last instant, his lips drew back and the sound he made was a scream like a hunting hawk.

He jerked to his feet, turned abruptly on his heel and began to pace with sharp staccato steps punctuated by an occasional peal of high laughter. He covered the small room in three strides, spun, three more steps, a pivot, three steps. He looked like a caged animal desperate for its freedom. Is couldn't watch.

Amil reached out calmly, pulled John's untouched plate to him, and began to eat with the delicate unhurried precision with which he had eaten his own supper. Is thought she would go crazy. John's unbearable tension and Amil's calm seemed equally insane to her.

Then John reseated himself, opened the book, and pointed to a word. Amil put down his sticks, picked up his pencil and wrote with the same calm lack of haste with which he had been eating. Everything was back to normal – as normal as it was going to get.

When every grain was gone, Amil took the dishes to the kitchen. He dipped hot water from a bucket sitting on the stove, poured it over the dishes and scrubbed as meticulously as he had done everything else, interrupting his work to write down a word whenever John rapped on the table to get his attention.

When no one was watching, Is slid her hand out and touched one of the books John had pushed aside still open. She could feel the texture of the paper and smell the slightly musty smell, almost like old leaves. She had taken too long. John noticed. Is snatched her hand away guiltily. But instead of being mad John slid the book toward her. Surprised, Is raised her eyes to his. He nodded at the book. Is took it in her hands, lifted it, felt the weight of it, smelled its scent, felt the texture of its binding.

The sounds from the kitchen had stopped. Amil watched her too. Defiantly Is ignored him. She took her time, turning the pages and looking at the incomprehensible words. When she handed the book back to John, she did so boldly. He went right back to work and Is wondered if the message he was trying so hard to finish was going to make any sense.

Amil returned to the table with a kettle of steaming water and three cups. Cups and kettle were made of the finest porcelain and at odds with the rough cabin. When he poured the water into the cups it was not clear but reddish and sweet smelling.

John suddenly pushed the book away and sat back. Amil finished taking a sip of tea, put his teacup back in its saucer and set the whole thing away from him. Then he wiped his mouth one last time with his napkin, folded it, and set it with the cup.

"Well," he said, "shall we see what John has written?"

Is could barely believe he would decipher the writing with her sitting there, but Amil was already studying the paper.

"Ahhmm, well, this is difficult. This is an old language," he explained. "It was a root language from which the language we speak today was developed. We all studied this as young men, but my knowledge has grown old. Well, let us see.

"'I,' and a verb that means 'to have existence,' but with the ending that denotes duty or obligation. 'I am obliged,' I suppose. Then, 'belonging to my family,' no, larger, 'my tribe or people.'" He glanced to John for confirmation.

John motioned impatiently at the paper and Amil continued. "'I am under duty or obligation to my people to make information of a secret nature openly available.'"

Amil's gaze jumped from the paper to John. "You are a spy?"

John nodded quickly and vigorously as though yes, wasn't that obvious, and he was trying to hurry the old man on. But Amil sat back from the paper, a thoughtful look in his eyes.

"You inform on the Alliance to your people?" It was only half question. John stopped nodding. He was watching Amil with a keen alertness that made Is think John was ready to defend himself, but Amil went on calmly. "There wouldn't be anything worth finding out unless you had posed as a scholar. That means you would have lived at Court?" Amil paused to watch the hand signs John was making, a collecting-in motion, the center of something.

"Court Center?" The old man seemed impressed. He had named the highest seat of government research. "Who trained you? To pass as a scholar there would not be easy. That degree of knowledge is hard to come by outside the government schools, and even within them unless you are specially picked. I would have said it was impossible. But you were not trained in the government schools?

"No," to the quick shake of John's head, "I thought not."

"So your people trained you. They have that level of knowledge? The rumors were true, then, about 'outside' spies. But I could never figure out where those spies would come from. You are not a Blueskin. And the people in the outlaw village are too uneducated. Your own people then? Whoever they are, on the far side of the Boundary. They trained you." It wasn't a question. John met Amil's gaze steadily.

Is felt the hair on her arms stir like the ruff of a frightened dog. To her the government was an all-powerful and very distant being, like a god. It was not something one could question, let alone spy on! If people were spying on it, what were they doing with what they learned? Because didn't the fact that John's people spied on the government imply they meant to do something? Not only John, but all his people were criminals of a sort Is had never imagined. She wasn't sure how she felt about that. She had hated the government school, but she had considered that to be her own failing. It was her inability to fit in and do what other students did that had caused the problem. Later, she had come to hate having to let the government take her stallions, and now she had accepted that she had to hide from the government because of what she had done. But she had never considered herself in opposition to it. It was hard to accept that there was a whole group of people who opposed the Alliance government.

Amil's voice brought her back. "Let us see." He was studying the paper again. "It is hard to get the sense of this next part. The first word means captured. The ending signifies great force, or perhaps torture. This word," he said, pointing to it, "means 'mind' and in its placement in the sentence it receives the force of the torture." He raised his eyes from the paper.

"You were caught and tortured?" he asked John. "And they did something to your mind?" Their eyes met and a depth of understanding passed between them. Sobered, Amil went back to the words.

"This word means literally, 'divorced.' It is followed by the word for reproducing, but in an asexual form, and 'spoken language.'" He looked up, his eyes bright and serious.

"Divorced from reproducing spoken language," he repeated with dawning understanding. "They caught you. They tortured you, and then they took away your ability to speak."

"No!" Is blurted out and froze, surprised she'd spoken. "John can speak. He spoke some words once," she said, hesitating. "They just didn't make sense," she faltered to a stop.

Amil studied her before speaking. "So what they did to John was even more sophisticated. They 'divorced' a critical connection in his mind. He can speak, but he can't communicate with words. He can't even write them, or he would have written this note himself. And we saw, just trying to organize the words for me to write was almost too hard."

He appraised John for a long moment. "If you were at Court Center, you would have been in Research. I was at Court South, in Records. I thought I followed the research closely. But I had no idea that what they have done to you was even possible.

"More hidden knowledge," he growled, his tone deep with anger. "More research that didn't get recorded. Or if it did, it was kept from the general records. I can only guess how much else they have hidden from us."

He turned to Is. "That is why I took the books. They would erase so much of this research." He waved at the bookshelves. "They hide it even from the scholars, as they hide everything from the citizens." His voice trembled with rage. He paused to collect himself, then took another very precise and unhurried sip of tea before he returned to deciphering the message.

"The next sentence begins with the imperative form of deliver and is followed by the most respectful form of the word for lady. This message is to be delivered to a very important lady," he explained to Is. But they were interrupted as John slammed his fist against the table and gestured at Is.

"This is for you?" Amil asked. "Does he not know your name?"

Is realized she had never told it to him. She shook her head, embarrassed. It seemed so rude now not to have told him, but she had not done it out of rudeness, or even on purpose. She had just fallen into the habit of not speaking to him because he did not speak to her. She was too accustomed to being with the horses. One doesn't tell a horse one's name. To a horse you are a certain collection of smells that the horse names in his own fashion. Besides, at first Is had thought John might be an agent of the law. Why would she tell him her name? She missed Amil's hesitation that was an invitation to tell them her name now. After a few seconds' pause Amil continued.

"The next word denotes thanks in a very heartfelt way. The whole structure of this sentence conveys gratitude in a very personal mode, followed by an apology, also of deep feeling." He paused again, but Is made no comment. She didn't understand why John would apologize to her.

"The next paragraph begins with 'deliver' again," Amil said. "This time directed to, ahh, 'the possessive of people.' Oh, his people. This is for his people." He glanced up as though seeking John's permission to continue. John waved him on.

"'Extreme,' let me see, 'all-encompassing activities' - ahh, 'circumstances.'" He paused and tried again. "'Extreme circumstances have led me to undertake an extreme action.'" He looked to John as though for help, but John just gestured at the paper.

"This action has something to do with a mirror." Again he glanced at John for confirmation. "The word mirror is followed by the suffix that means opposite." Amil shrugged. "A mirror that is not a mirror only, mmmm? Well, this mirror has possession of some sort of opening . . . oh, a key. A key to 'the connection of mind and language.' And the whole thing ends with a word that means 'promise,' but is in a hopeful, almost wistful form.

"I can only conclude he thinks, or hopes, this mirror thing can help restore his ability to speak."

He studied the page a bit. "Evidentially there is some risk involved. There is a sentence here about 'sudden, involuntary action of great power' in regard to this mirror. But 'some knowledge possessed by John may make possible a different dialog with it.'" Amil glanced at Is. "There is also something about a relationship that is somehow related to the mirror's key, but has to do with a man of great strength ..."

"Berserker," Is said.

"Yes. Also an animal of great strength." Neither of them bothered to say "horse." "And also," Amil added, "a ghost of great power."

"No?" Amil questioned as John thumped the table and shook his head. "Well, something amorphous but of great power." He looked at Is but she had no idea what that could be.

"Let me see, there is also something here about 'a system of long standing,' the Alliance, I would guess. And a word for misunderstanding that implies a deliberateness and bad spirit in this action. This is all couched in terms of gravest warning.

"This is followed by the strongest imperative that understanding must not be lost." The old man looked at John. "I'm sorry I can't do better with this. If I were to study it more . . ."

John shook his head.

"I hope your people will translate it better than I." Amil studied the paper again.

"The next paragraph begins 'Lady' in the most honored form – the one he used for you before. This is followed by a verb of being, in the near future tense, connected to the action of going or traveling somewhere. Then, 'people' of his 'possession,' and the word for guest in a form of highest honor. Reassurance is intended."

"He is taking me to his people," Is said. It was a relief to know her status among them would be as an honored guest, not a slave.

"So you will continue with him?" Amil said, and there was something wistful in his voice that set Is on alert. She thought for a moment that Amil might ask her to stay with him. She thought about the books. Maybe he would teach her to read! She would have knowledge. But he didn't ask, and if she had heard longing in his voice, it was probably because he was lonely and wanted to bed with her, not teach her to read. She thought about John's people who trained their horses to go without bridles. They would have much to teach her too and that was the sort of thing she was suited to learn. But she felt sad and would not let herself understand why.

When she looked up, she caught John quickly looking away from her.

Chapter 11

The next day, as they rode away from of Amil's place, the dog appeared and followed them. Is spent the first half of the day trying to chase it back. The dog was probably the only company the old man had and she did not want it to leave him. John watched her attempts with a quizzical expression and did not offer any help. Eventually Is gave up.

The going continued to get steeper and rockier. They swung west to cross a saddle in the last ridge before they would have to cross the snow-capped giants of the range. Is no longer worried about how they were going to get the horses across that sheer forbidding wall. A scholar would know how to do it.

They camped high in the saddle near a little stream. Is could feel the altitude in muscles that cramped in her legs and feet; and in her mind, which wanted to wander aimlessly from her tasks. It seemed to take forever for the water to get hot and it never did really boil. The leaves John put into the tea sieve made the water taste bitter and after one sip Is thought she wouldn't drink the rest. But her body craved the liquid, and making her way to the stream for more water seemed like too much effort.

She had pretty well learned to ignore the tricks her eyes liked to play when her mind was like this. So she was ignoring the man shapes visible among the shadows cast by the bushes when the dog came in. He had stayed back from them all day, but now he came right up to the fire, slinking with his skinny tail pressed under his belly. He made a sound between growling and whining. Is snapped out of her trance.

John was already standing, facing the shadow shapes. Now Is recalled that there had been no bushes around big enough to cast man-tall shadows. All the tales she had ever heard of the supernatural horrors of these mountains crowded her mind.

Is edged backward. The packs were behind her and the tool in John's pack might stop the shadow men if they attacked him.

But John didn't seem afraid. In fact he got down on his knees, moving slowly, like a man trying to coax some wild animal closer. Is heard the breeze blowing through the leaves of the bushes, until she remembered that the bushes didn't exist. Then she heard voices instead. They talked rapidly and softly, one overlaying another and another. She didn't know how anyone could make sense of such speech. Sometimes there were little crackling sounds like sticks breaking. She had to keep reminding herself that there were no bushes, no breeze, no cracking sticks.

Nothing else seemed to happen for a long time. She might have dozed off, although that seemed unlikely given how scared she was, but the next thing she knew John was surrounded by the shadow men and she couldn't remember having seen them move.

She was determined to be more alert, but it was hard to keep the shadow men focused. Her mind kept telling her they were bushes and shadows cast by the fire, not men. Now they seemed to be stroking John. They weren't using hands, but gliding against him, weaving from side to side and slipping down the length of his body. He was standing again. When had that happened? Other than the shush-shush talking there was no sound.

The dog had stopped growl-whining sometime back. He was lying flat out on his side, not a posture a frightened dog would assume. There was a ghostly darkness in the air over him. Is knew he was dead. The shadow men had somehow sucked the life out of him.

She thought they were taking something vital from John too. They might deplete him. He would lie dead like the dog when they were done with him. Despite her fear of the shadow men, Is was more afraid to let them kill John. She stood up and moved toward them in a rush, shouting and waving her arms before she could lose her nerve. Somehow she knew to push them back with her voice, and not just her voice, but the release of energy, angry energy. She could almost feel the force of her voice, her energy pushing them. Then suddenly John caught hold of her. He pulled her against him and wrapped his arms around her. Is could feel the tremors running through his body.

She stood still, making herself solid, letting him feel her solidness because that was what she felt he needed.

When he let her go, she saw the dog. He was curled by the coals, not flat out as she'd seen him before. Careful not to disturb him, she went close enough to see that he was breathing. The hair on her arms stood up and goose bumps ran down her back. She felt a strong presence, but could not say if it was benign or harmful. Her own system of superstitions made her react with fear. She desperately needed to ask John what had happened, but that was impossible.

John curled up by the fire and soon fell asleep. Is got his sleeping bag and tucked it around him. That gave her an excuse to be close to him, to touch him. After a while she got into her own bag and sat awake the rest of the night listening to John breathing. It became a vigil, something she had to do to protect him. She didn't know from what. She kept thinking about the "ghost of great power" in Amil's translation of John's note.

John seemed fine in the morning. Is watched him for any strangeness and really wished she could talk to him.

Little gusty breezes accompanied them as they rode. Whenever Is heard the wind she turned to look, but saw nothing unusual.

By mid-afternoon they had reached the top of the saddle. There was a light dusting of snow here. The air rising from it was cold, but the air above them was hot with the moisture-sucking stillness that only a summer afternoon at high altitude has.

Facing them was a sheer wall of mountains. The crystalline air made the mountains seem close enough to touch. Exposed rock showed in vertical stretches shining with melt water like the black bones of the earth itself. A man with a rope might make it up there; no horse would. Above them rose peaks so white the air seemed to vibrate off their color. Below them the mountains' flanks were covered with green forests, inviting and cool.

John pointed east, where the highest of the mountains ran a long white shoulder down into the valley. His hand motions said they would ride down into the valley, around that shoulder, and up over something. Is supposed through a pass that was hidden from their view by the height of the long ridge of that shoulder. She calculated two days to get down to the bottom of the valley, two or three days to get around that shoulder, and perhaps another few days to get over the hidden pass. She wished it would be longer.

They camped below the tree line, sheltered from a storm that blew through. Is woke several times to the sound of low branches scraping against the tent in the wind. In the morning she knew there could have been no branches. Neither of them would pitch a tent where branches could possibly puncture its waterproof fly. Again she longed to talk to John.

The air was cool after the rain. The horses felt frisky, shying and snorting at the dark rocks like foolish youngsters instead of horses who had trekked this land for weeks already. Is laughed when John's mare refused to pass an especially big wet rock, and then they both laughed when Is tried to ride Lark past it first and he behaved as badly as the mare.

It was dark under the tall trees as they descended, and though the rain had stopped, the branches dripped big wet drops on them as they worked their way downward. Instead of getting lighter, the day grew darker and soon they were riding in a thick fog from which the massive boles of trees would appear and disappear, sinister and dark.

The gay mood of the morning slipped away. The horses shied more often and more seriously. Is could feel Lark's tension along with her own mounting sense of unease.

Lark snorted, sidestepping hard, and came to a halt. The creature sat on the rock regarding them with baleful red eyes. It blinked and disappeared. Lark snorted a loud blast, his legs braced wide, ready to run in any direction. Is stroked his neck. "Some trick of the light," she told him, her voice sounding less reassuring than she'd intended.

Lark continued to snort. He refused her aids to go forward even though the mare had passed that way in front of him. Is turned him to go around the rock since he wouldn't pass by it.

Lark sidled sideways, snorting and tense. Is didn't feel so brave herself. The back side of the rock seemed bigger than the front side. Going around it took them more off track than she had thought it would. She'd been depending on Lark to pick up the mare's trail again, but he seemed more interested in shying from every tree and rock he saw.

Is tried to deal with Lark's foolishness, keep her sense of direction, and look for the mare's trail at the same time. When she couldn't find it, she wanted to zigzag back and forth over the area looking for it but Lark wouldn't cooperate. He continually shied off the line Is would have ridden. Knowing how well the trees could muffle sound, she decided to call out before John got too far away.

Her voice sounded muted even to her own ears, as though swallowed by the fog. She heard no answer of any sort, but she still wasn't worried. She would keep riding downhill and find her own way around the shoulder and over the pass if she had to. Surely she'd meet up with John somewhere en route.

As the fog grew thicker, Lark was more reluctant to go down into it. He snorted and shied and moved sideways. Is could feel his heart beating between her legs and tried to soothe him with her voice. He kept managing to turn aside from the deepest fog, which lay below them. They were traversing the slope rather than descending it.

Finally Is slipped from his back, took the reins and led him into the fog. He followed reluctantly, snorting and hesitating, right on her heels. With his head up, Lark towered over her and Is hoped he wouldn't forget she was there and jump on her if he shied. She talked to him and kept contact with him through the reins.

All of a sudden, Is was spun around as Lark bolted backward dragging her with him. Unable to resist him, she was forced to run after him, trying desperately not to let go of the reins. Her commands of "Whoa!" had no effect. If he got turned, he would take off at a gallop and she would not be able to hold him or keep up. Though she was determined not to let that happen, there was nothing she could do to prevent it. He outweighed and outmuscled her many times over and all of his training was now completely overridden by fear.

Is was jerked to the side as Lark turned. The dark bole of a tree appeared in front of her the instant before she slammed into it. Her hand let go of the reins involuntarily.

She hit the tree with such force she was thrown backward, landing on her backside. At first even hitting the tree didn't hurt. For a few seconds more she could hear Lark crashing away, then silence. The arm that had held the reins had wrapped around the tree so fast that the bark had taken her skin off. Her arm was beginning to bleed now, stinging like crazy. As she had been pulled around the tree the side of her face had smashed against the rough bark, and then her body had been slammed against the tree with enough force to fling her on her backside three feet away. When she tried to turn her head she felt dizzy and pain lanced down her spine. She had no choice but to sit still a moment. That helped. Wherever the pain had come from it retreated and waited. Good. Let it wait. She didn't need to move just yet. She was distracted by the warm creeping feeling of blood beginning to run down her neck. When she raised her hand to touch her face, she saw that her hand was covered with blood too. She stared at it. The two outside fingers stood out at an angle that didn't look right. She tried to flex her hand. Pain returned with a vengeance and relocated itself in her hand, shooting up her arm until it nearly made her sick.

She looked away from the blood. *The pain will only get worse*, she thought. *Do it now!*

Before she could think better of it, she took hold of the two dislocated fingers with her good hand and twisted them back into place. She'd been braced for pain, but it didn't come. Shock, she thought. Thank you. Best to get moving before it wore off.

It felt as if something heavy were sitting on her neck. She couldn't turn her head to the right at all. If she kept her head tilted down and left she could walk. She started to ascend, bearing off to the left all the time. Lark would have gone up to get out of the fog. Once he'd outrun his fear, he'd turn back. He'd want his companions, but Is doubted he'd descend into the fog again. With luck she'd find him wandering above the fog line.

Her arm and hand throbbed with her heartbeat and the stiff neck made her whole back hurt as she leaned forward to climb the slope. She felt nauseated and weak. It took an act of major concentration to keep putting one foot above the other.

She found herself skirting the deepest patches of fog, reluctant to enter them, which was ridiculous. But every time she'd tried going straight into the fog, there'd be a rock or something she'd have to go around anyway.

She was not ascending enough.

Stupid to avoid the worst fog. She couldn't see farther than her own feet anyway. The slope of the ground was her guide.

She was not ascending.

No smarter than the horse to be afraid of the fog. Look at her feet. One step, the next. Keep going.

Still, she was not ascending.

The fog was a wall above her. She turned around, slowly so she wouldn't lose her balance. The lack of visual references didn't help her dizziness.

The fog was definitely thinner below her. She could make out the trunks of trees.

Maybe down was the right direction to go. Follow the original plan she'd had with Lark. When she found the pass, she'd find John. Together they'd come back looking for Lark. Or maybe Lark would find them. Yes, it made more sense to look for John than for the horse. She turned downhill.

The fog was herding her now. She'd given up resisting it some time back. She'd given up thinking, and her mind was too numb for fear.

She had to sit down.

A breeze came gusting over her and was gone. Seemed strange, a breeze at ground level in a forest this thick. Besides, when there was fog the air was still, usually.

The breeze came again in little fits and starts. The fog swirled and shredded when the breeze blew, only to resettle as thick as ever when it stopped. Is sat and watched this little contest. If the breeze cleared the fog away maybe she'd have more energy. Maybe she'd be able to make her feet go where she wanted them to go.

She could hear leaves rustling with the breeze. It was some time before she thought, leaves! In a pine forest?

If she listened just right she could hear the voices instead, one over the other in a quick shush-shush whisper. She couldn't begin to understand them.

She got up and moved with the breeze, downhill and left, which was the direction she'd need to go to get around the shoulder. Sometimes her mind seemed to wake up, or clear, or something. Then she'd check with herself that she was still going the direction she wanted to go. The rest of the time she might as well have been sleepwalking.

When she had to stop, she lay down and slept. Let whatever was going to happen to her happen.

... In the dream she was riding Lark, following the mare.

Lark's left front hoof came down jarringly on a rock. The jolt traveled up Is's spine into her sore neck. She put her hand up to rub her neck. The fingers were stiff. The pain of flexing them to squeeze her neck was worse than the pain in her neck. She gave up trying to massage herself. They'd be stopping for the horses' afternoon break soon. She'd lie flat on the ground then. That would feel good. If she relaxed enough, maybe the muscles in her neck would un-kink.

The mare stopped. John twisted around in his saddle and looked at her. He seemed to stare at her and past her at the same time. Is began to worry that he would start one of his fits. She made Lark walk past him. Then she heard John say, "Hast thou dreamed a life, or lived a dream," in a completely ordinary voice.

Shocked, Is turned to stare at him. Was there some message in his riddle, or were the words only the wandering of a disturbed mind.

"Be thou not confused of reflections that guidest thee astray, or true. Thine own heart knowest not."

"You're not real, are you?" Is challenged him. "This is just a dream isn't it?" When John didn't answer, or respond to her in any way, she concluded, "Really, I'm lost in the fog, and dreaming."

Then she saw what she had somehow failed to notice before, Lark standing beside John. She forgot everything else and said, "Lark," and walked toward him.

When she reached out her hand to touch him, her neck was stiff and her hand was swollen and wouldn't open all the way. She was surprised by that, until she stroked Lark's soft coat. Then everything seemed alright again.

The saddle had a scrape along one side where he'd cut too close to a tree or something in his panic, but other than that everything seemed fine. She started to ask John how he had found Lark and realized John wasn't there. Only Lark was real.

She wasn't going to fight with Lark about going into the fog, but now the fog was gone. She mounted and let him pick their course. Once he whinnied and broke into a trot. She let him go and in a few minutes she heard the mare's answering call.

John welcomed her with a smile. He looked relieved and happy, which made Is feel good. Then he turned and rode on, just as if nothing had happened. Is followed and began to doubt what had really happened.

Chapter 12

Is could tell they were getting close. John was tense with excitement. He turned often to smile at her. His mood was infectious and she began to lose her apprehension.

At one point, John stopped his horse and waved in the direction of a wooded hillside. Is could see no one there. They continued on, descending the final pass and wending their way through a labyrinth of boulders. Eventually they came out into a land of rolling meadows where the grass was thick and tall. The mare picked up her pace, either because she felt John's excitement or because she knew where they were.

Suddenly the horses threw up their heads and stopped. The mare whinnied. Four horsemen erupted into view, galloping dead at them. Lark tossed his head and began to prance. The mare whinnied and went forward at a high springy trot. Lark followed immediately, his trot thrusting him high off the ground with each extravagant stride. Is needed all her skill to keep from bouncing in the saddle.

Just as a collision seemed imminent, the four approaching horses sat back into their haunches and slid to a stop. Their hooves gouged the ground. The riders were already vaulting off their horses backs as John threw himself from his mare. Lark reared, unable to contain himself, then came into a trot in place. Is could feel the suppressed power running through his body, about to erupt in some fashion. At the same time she took in the refined bridle-less heads of the horses, their sleek coats and well-muscled bodies. All the men ran together, embracing, laughing, and shouting John's name.

As John's mare moved to touch noses with the other horses, Lark sprang to cut her off. Is knew better than to try to control him. He kept his position between his mare and the other horses, prancing and snorting, until the lead mare of that group came forward to touch noses.

The other horses started to come too but one of the men gave a shrill whistle. The horses halted as if anchored to the ground. Is realized she and Lark were the center of attention. She hoped he wouldn't do anything too disorderly. John's people would not think much of her horsemanship - she who was an expert among her own people.

At least none of the other horses seemed to be stallions. Apparently Is and John had been seen and this contingent of riders had come out to meet them. Since Lark was obviously a berserker's horse, and all war horses were stallions, the people had known better than to ride stallions to meet them. Even so, Lark's presence could get the mares squealing, kicking, and running around, and it would be dangerous to be on his back. John motioned for her to come to him. Well, she could no more control Lark from where she was than she could from down there and it would be safer to be out of the way. Is vaulted from Lark's back, and careful to stay out of range of the nearest mare's feet, went to stand beside John.

Left on his own, Lark circled the mares in an exaggerated high trot. The mares began to mill around and there was a lot of squealing, striking, and kicking as the horses sorted one another out.

The men made no further attempt to control their mounts. They laughed good-naturedly and made short comments on the mares' behavior or admiring remarks about Lark as they withdrew a distance to let the horses have room for their displays.

They watched the horses until it seemed they were going to settle down to grazing. Then everyone's attention came to focus on Is, making it impossible for her to ignore her fear. Every time she had been thrust into a new place with new people it had not gone well. They had not liked her or wanted her.

Suddenly John caught her arm and pulling her to him he hugged her hard.

Is was too surprised to react. When he released her, he turned her so she was facing the man who seemed to be the leader of the band. Is stood awkwardly, but knew that John had presented her as best he could without words. His hands rested on her shoulders and Is could feel him trembling. In a moment he could lose control.

"He can't talk," Is blurted. "The Alliance did something to him, tortured him and made it so he can't say anything he wants to say. And sometimes he goes crazy, but he isn't really. He can't help it. He's trying to help you. You've got to give him a chance." She stopped in embarrassment. Here she was frantically defending John to his own people who obviously knew more about all this stuff with the Alliance than she did. They would think her some sort of imbecile. She couldn't even take refuge in her superior ability with horses here. Not with these people.

All four men were looking at her very curiously. The leader took a step forward. "Thank you for telling us this."

He had such an aura of poise and control about him that Is settled immediately.

"John is my brother." His voice was sensual, like the sounds of nature. Compassion radiated from him. The way he pronounced "John" sounded like "Hon."

"We are the Hluit," he said. "My name is Ondre. You would say Andrew." He looked at John with his hands still on Is's shoulders. Then he said something in a language that sounded like birdcalls. Is heard one of the other men draw in his breath, obviously surprised.

"I have pledged to value you as my brother values you, even should my tribe turn me aside. This I have said before warriors of my people."

Is knew she had been accorded a very high honor but she didn't know what to do or say. Ondre rescued her again.

"Come," he said to everyone in general, "let's go home." He turned to Is. "Then you can tell us your story, if you will."

One of the other men laughed, breaking what was left of the tension. "If the horses are ready to allow us to catch them," he said, which gave the others an opening to comment on his lack of horsemanship.

Is felt her insides tighten, waiting for the cruelty behind their seemingly easy words. Instead the man grinned and said his mare had very good taste in stallions and he wouldn't blame her a bit if she wasn't ready to be caught. He gave Is a big wink and she saw how his eyes danced and that he was not hurt at all by the other men's words. But the mares were easily caught and mounted and Is wondered if, having seen her lack of control of Lark, they would be willing to accept her as they would an apprentice and teach her their horsemanship.

As they rode, the one who had been kidded came to ride beside her. He had a round face that looked as if it should always be smiling, and his body was soft-looking compared to the sinewy toughness of the other men. But his horsemanship looked excellent to Is. He introduced himself as Petre.

"Peter," she repeated his name, trying to soften the second syllable into a soft "trrr" the way he had said it.

"Close enough," he smiled at her and introduced the others as Don - which they pronounced with an "h" like Dhon - and Phol. They all bantered in a friendly manner as they rode, teasing one another about their mares' behavior, and even teasing John about not being able to talk and thus defend himself from their humor.

Is felt totally adrift. She had never been around people who treated one another as these did. They seemed to include her so naturally, yet she couldn't trust it. She kept waiting for the cruelty behind their humor.

John was grinning like a fox. He loved these people, and was loved by them. *He is home,* Is thought, and tried to understand what that meant in terms of what "home" had been to her – the farm with her parents. But that had been a long time ago and she never let herself remember too much because the memories could only bring pain.

She was not allowed much time to reflect. The men were chattering on, telling John all kinds of news. Someone had married. Someone had had a child. Someone had died. And other stuff that made no sense to Is.

The teasing took a new turn as they began kidding John about the condition of his mare.

"Celeste, he's been mistreating you," one of the men addressed the mare directly. "You ought to come live with my herd." It was true that next to the people's sleek well-rounded animals John's mare appeared underfed. But John just grinned even bigger and sent Celeste into a canter that quickly escalated into a gallop as everyone followed suit. Is had no choice but to let Lark run with them. Soon they were flying over the ground in a dead run with John's mare well out in front. Is guessed that was his answer to the teasing.

When the village came into sight they slowed to a respectable trot. A crowd was gathering at the outskirts of the tents. Horses grazed around the edges and there were herds farther out on the hills. Kids came cantering out to meet them, drumming their heels on the sides of thick-bellied brood mares who obviously had no desire to gallop. Lark arched and danced but seemed willing to let Is control him.

Suddenly a woman broke from the crowd and rushed at them on foot. John jumped from Celeste's back and ran to her. They came together and John lifted her off the ground and spun around and around with her in his arms. Then the other people rushed forward to surround him. Is noticed the way John kissed the woman before he released her, and she felt the odd twisting sensation of pain she had come to associate with the departure of one of her horses. Then the people were on top of John, everyone hugging him and talking at once. And Is saw that the way these people kissed him, and the way he kissed them, was different from the way he had kissed the one woman.

Is was angry with herself. She should have known John was married. That would explain why he had never tried to touch her. That, and the fact that she wasn't pretty like his tribe's women with their light hair. Nor was she cultured like the women that a high Alliance official must know. She was just a rude country seed. And not only had John had other women, he'd had great women. Of course he had not been interested in her. Is tried to put her foolishness away. These were to be her people now. She should not start by resenting them.

She looked around and met Petre's eyes. He had stayed at her side. He leaned toward her now so she would hear him and said softly, "Welcome to our village. I hope your stay here will be happy, and long."

She found herself smiling. It was good to have someone talk to her.

Chapter 13

The council was made up of men and women, some of them quite young, some very old. They all sat on the ground in an informal circle. Anyone else who wanted to hear sat outside the circle. Ondre's wife, Ellie, escorted Is to the circle and showed her where to sit. Everyone was sitting in the same manner, on their knees with their buttocks resting on their heels, so Is sat that way too. It wasn't uncomfortable and it gave her a feeling of stability which helped her find some sense of calm.

Ellie took a place beside her. John sat directly across from her. He smiled at her but it wasn't a real smile. He was very tense and Is realized how important this meeting was to him. He had given the council the note Amil had written, but there were a lot of things Is could tell them that might help. There were also countless things she could possibly do wrong without even knowing.

They had gotten Lark situated with Celeste and one of Ondre's wise old mares in a gorge far from the other herds. He would not get into trouble with the other stallions and even if the herders could not control Lark they could keep the mares in the canyon and Lark would not leave without them.

An old woman opened the meeting, addressing Is directly.

"We have seen you ride with John. We have heard that Ondre has extended family rites to you. On the strength of our trust in these two men, we wish also to welcome you. We have read the note John brought us, but much has happened that he cannot tell us. It would be a great help if you would tell us what you know."

Is glanced at Ondre who sat next to the woman, but his expression remained serious and remote.

Is was not sure of the protocol here. She was not sure whom she was addressing, but the woman seemed to be some sort of leader.

"I'm glad to help if I can," she said honestly and then thought how rude her words sounded after the woman's. Embarrassed she looked at John and he gave her another tense smile and made a small go-ahead hand motion.

Is started by explaining how she'd found John, which led her to telling why she had been in the Boundary, which led her to explaining why she had stolen the war horse in the first place. Then she realized she was going backward. What they wanted to know about was John. Flustered, she took up the tale again and tried to tell it all in order and coherently.

She was aware of John watching her acutely while she spoke. She had the feeling he was dying to say something, perhaps to disagree with some of her memories. She couldn't look at him at all. She tried to emulate Ondre's poise and calm while speaking in front of all these strangers, but she didn't know if she succeeded. They gave her virtually no feedback, their expressions remaining composed to the point of being unreadable. Some of the old people especially seemed to stare into the space around her without looking directly at her. No one made any comments or asked any questions. When she was done there was a long period of silence. Then one of the elders thanked her.

Is thought the meeting was over. She would be escorted away and the real talking would begin. Instead, a kind of free-for-all discussion began. Within the circle people spoke to their neighbors in quick, low voices that reminded Is of the almost-voices of the wind. She caught the words "herd fog" and "Dark Bodies" and "Mirror" passed around. The people beyond the circle remained silent.

One of the elders leaned over and spoke to John. Suddenly everyone was quiet again. Is had missed whatever signal had silenced them.

Everyone's attention focused on the elder. He looked older than anyone Is had ever seen before. His head was entirely bare of hair. The flesh of his face stretched tight across his prominent cheekbones and hooked nose. His eyes were sunken, giving his head a death skull's appearance. The top of his head was freckled with age spots. His hands, also spotted with age, rested on his thighs. There was no flesh left on those hands at all, just the bones and sinews, crisscrossed by protruding blue veins.

The elder dipped his head slightly in acknowledgement of the respect the people showed by their silence.

"What they have done to John is very sophisticated." His voice creaked with age. "They have not taken away his ability to speak. As Isadora testified, he can speak. What he cannot do is form what he wants to say into words. They have disconnected that one ability without, apparently, harming anything else about his mind or body. That is extremely skillful tampering." The elder fell silent.

People began to speak quietly among themselves again.

Is found herself trying to understand what this must be like for John. She had lived years with only her animals and no real need for speech. But for John it was different. He had something very important to say to his people. But now that Is had seen his people, she suspected that even if there had been no message to deliver, John would not have been happy without speech. Speech was a part of who he was, and how he related to all these people. Also, he had been a scholar. Words and books, poetry and songs must be to him like her riding was to her - art, the essence of what his life was about. Unexpectedly tears welled up in her eyes. If suddenly she could not ride again it would be more than the loss of something she liked to do. It would be the loss of who she was, and of what was important about her, and to her. It would not be like the loss of an arm or a leg; it would be the loss of what was inside her. For John, what he had lost must feel like that.

Is missed whatever signal was given to end the meeting. People were getting up. Ellie stood beside her waiting. Is scrambled to her feet and nearly fell over. Two men caught her as she almost careened into them. For a wild moment she couldn't understand what was happening to her. She had lost control of her legs and there was no feeling in her feet. Through her own rising panic she realized that everyone was looking at her. But their eyes were shining and a few of them laughed out loud.

"Your feet have gone to sleep," said one of the men holding her.

"Happens when you're not used to sitting that way," the other man explained.

"You could have sat cross-legged," a woman offered. "It would have been all right." But Is had not seen anyone else sitting that way.

The feeling was coming back into her feet with a sensation like a million hot needles being jabbed into her skin.

"You should walk," one of the men instructed and he began to walk her around.

Is tried to make her legs work. Her knees wanted to buckle at odd moments and her feet couldn't feel the ground. Without feedback from them it was hard to keep her balance. She didn't want to lean against this strange man but she had no choice. He seemed to be enjoying himself immensely.

Fortunately it only took a few minutes before she could navigate on her own again. Ellie took her in charge.

They walked through the village which was made up of about eighty dome-shaped tents. They were similar to John's tent, but larger. Is had lost track of John. She supposed he had gone with the woman who had kissed him.

The inside of Ellie's tent was warm and glowed with a reddish cast from a small wood stove in the center. It smelled of a delicious sweet tea Ondre was brewing for them. Is had not realized how tense she was until she had a moment to sit in that warm quiet place. The tea seemed to be a mild stimulant and with Ondre's gentle prodding Is found herself recounting her story all over again.

Unlike the people at the council, Ondre kept stopping her and making her back up and remember details. All the things she had not thought the council wanted to hear began to come out.

When she told Ondre about riding Lark for the Blueskins, she said, "I wanted them to think he was a dangerous war horse and I was their only way of controlling him, but he isn't, and they must have seen that. They treated me like dirt. I guess I would have been a slave, or something, if John hadn't rescued me."

"My god, child," Ellie interrupted. "If they didn't rape you, they must have thought you were the next thing to a god!"

"And you kept up with them walking all night," Ondre said. "That's not easy." But his eyes said something different to his wife and Is felt a little shudder of warning run through her as she went on with her tale.

Ondre laughed when she told him how John had beaten Chest. He made her recount every detail of that odd fight. But Is couldn't tell him much.

"It was like magic. John barely seemed to touch the Blueskin. But he must have done something I couldn't see." Her description sparked an animated discussion between Ondre and his wife and eventually Is understood that they were discussing what "techniques" John had used to throw and disarm Chest.

"You know what he did?" she asked Ondre. "You know how to fight like that too?"

"Yes," Ondre assured her. "We all know how to fight like that."

Is wondered if she might be able to learn too, but she was too well trained in Alliance protocol to ask, or to even dare hope for it.

Ondre laughed gleefully when she told him about the outlaws who had attacked John. She could see that he loved and admired his brother. Some place in her heart woke and hurt. She would never have family like this.

They were intensely interested in the old man, Amil, and the whip-thin dog that had followed them but must have shied away when the other men appeared. No one had seen the dog since. Again she felt that something passed between Ondre and his wife, a question from one and an answer from the other, all without words or overt looks.

When Is came to the part about how she'd gotten separated from John in the fog - which she had barely mentioned to the council because it seemed so confusing and unlikely - Ondre was fascinated. This time she saw him openly catch his wife's eye.

"A herd fog? In the first valley? I've never heard of one that close before."

Then Is found herself telling them about the dark figures that had come around John that one night by the fire.

"You heard them speak?" Ellie asked, implying that she believed Is had seen something. "You heard words?"

"Yes, but I couldn't understand them. They all talked at once, over each other."

"They touched John?" Ondre asked. "You're sure?"

"Yes. Was that bad?"

"Not necessarily. They can be frightening. But there have been times when they seem to have acted to help someone too."

"When you were lost, you said the fog was blown away. That could have been them," Ellie put in. "The fog sometimes takes travelers miles off their route. Some people have died because of it."

Is felt the stirring of a very deep fear. "I thought it was all a dream. Inside the fog I was on foot. Then suddenly, I was with John again like nothing had happened. And he spoke, but in a riddle, and then he was gone, but Lark was there. I thought it was all a dream, but . . ." She held out her arm, showing the long, partially healed scrapes. Ondre took her hand and examined the arm carefully. Is knew what he was thinking. Those cuts were too well healed to be only three days old, the three days it had taken them to ride from what he called the first valley to the village. He exchanged a glance with Ellie. Neither one said anything.

"I don't know what really happened." It was the first time Is had confessed that, even to herself. She saw Ondre meet his wife's eyes again before he answered.

"If you want to find out, we probably can help," Ondre said. But Is saw the look of alarm in Ellie's eyes.

Is felt the hair stir on her arms. "Is it important to know?"

"It might be," Ondre said, "especially if you go with John."

"Why would I do that?" Is blurted, surprised by the idea. She had understood that John was going to look for the Mirror/non-mirror thing, but that had not seemed to concern her. As far as Amil had understood the message, John seemed to expect her to stay with his people.

"You might be able to help John."

"Ond . . ." his wife rebuked him.

"No, Ellie, she needs to know."

"Yes, but Ondre, she is Alliance trained." Ellie's voice sank to an urgent whisper, intensely uncomfortable talking about Is in front of her.

"I'm sorry," Ondre said. "I understand some of what the Alliance does to its people. But she's here now. She'll have to learn to make decisions and take responsibility for herself." There was a touch of surliness in his voice Is hadn't heard before. People had always been angry with her for wanting to know too much. Now it seemed that he was getting mad because she didn't know enough.

They were interrupted by a girl's voice outside the tent. Ellie answered and the tent flap lifted and a young woman entered. She smiled shyly at Is. She had the beautiful blond hair and blue eyes of many of John's people. She acknowledged Ondre with a smile and spoke to Ellie.

"Mother wanted me to tell you, we are going to have a feast. You will bring Isadora?"

Ellie laughed. "Of course," she said as though she should have expected this. "Of course we will come."

Is felt her heart sink. She dreaded facing so many people but she tried to tell herself it couldn't be worse than being thrown into the government school. In fact, it was bound to be better.

Ondre left with the girl and Is was alone with Ellie.

Is was suddenly aware of how dirty she was. She had only her patched-together part-cloth part-animal-skin clothing and although she had washed in streams whenever she could tolerate the cold water, the dirt and smoke from the cook fires was ingrained in her clothes, skin, and hair.

Ellie chatted pleasantly while she brought out soap and shampoo. Water was heated by dropping the hot stones that lined the stove into a bucket. It made the water a degree more bearable than the snow-melt streams Is had been using.

"There is a hot spring we often use," Ellie said apologetically. "But it is a two-hour ride."

Ellie's clothes fit Is well enough. The coolcloth onesuit was undoubtedly stolen. Only people high in the government wore coolcloth. It molded to Is's body but without binding. She could move in any direction without hindrance. It felt wonderful. But she was shy to wear it in front of people until she saw what Ellie was going to wear.

Ellie's skirt hung low on her ample hips and reached to her ankles. It was also coolcloth, but patterned like a field in flower where Is's onesuit was all one shade of deep blue. Ellie's breasts were bare. Her blond hair was pulled to the side and braided so it fell over one shoulder. She had woven a string of black polished river stones into it. Her feet were bare. Is thought Ellie was the most beautiful woman she had ever seen.

She began to feel less conspicuous in her onesuit. It covered her breasts quite modestly and was in no way interesting to look at.

She allowed Ellie to braid her thick dark hair and tie it up in an intricate knot on top of her head, until only a few wisps fell about her ears and neck. She didn't see Ellie braid a string of glistening white shells into it.

They were walking toward the area where the feast would be held when John came out of a tent. The moment he saw Is he hurried to her. She was unprepared for the leap of joy her heart felt. He came right up to her, clasped her arms to her sides and looked deep into her eyes. Feeling overwhelmed by everything, she was afraid she would cry. When he pulled her against him she didn't resist. Instead, she wrapped her arms around him. She stood feeling his body against hers, amazed at how her body responded. She smelled the clean male smell of him, different from the sweat and smoke smell she'd known. For a long moment everyone else might as well have ceased to exist.

When John let go of her, he took Ellie in his arms and hugged her too. Is felt confused and disappointed. It was just his way of greeting people.

He seemed to have his own direction to go. Is let Ellie lead her away.

Somewhere ahead drums began beating like a pulse. People had collected around a big pit full of coals. Meat was being roasted on spits and tubers were cooking in the ashes. People sat gossiping while they tended their cooking. Children raced around chasing each other and playing with hoops they rolled on the ground and tossed through the air.

The drumbeat drew Is.

Ellie excused herself to go help with the cooking and Is went closer to the musicians. Some people were already dancing on the bare hard-packed ground where the drummers played. Is was fascinated by the sound. The drum players moved their hands in sensuous and delightful ways producing an amazing variation in sound by using the heels of their hands, the flat, or the fingers. The beats interwove with one another in impossibly intricate patterns. Is couldn't imagine being so in tune with other people as to be able to make music like that with them. She imagined it to be like the magic that could happen between a horse and rider, only with other people. She had never thought about the possibility. She looked from one player to the next and thought, *they must love each other in a special way to play together like this.*

One of the women began to sing. Sustained, mournful vowel sounds issued from her open throat, startling, and yet perfect. A man's voice joined hers, working a pattern of deeper, shorter notes through her song. Enraptured by the music, Is didn't see Petre approach.

He stood with her awhile, watching her enjoy the music. He didn't speak until she noticed him.

"It's beautiful, isn't it?"

Is felt suddenly flushed and confused as though she had been caught doing something too private to be shared.

Petre's words somehow cheapened the music. Beautiful? It was so much more than that. But Is also recognized that he was trying to be friendly. He was trying to reach out to her the way people did, through words.

"Yes." She had to clear her throat. "Yes. It is."

His smile said more than any words.

"I hope you will let me show you around. This must be very different from what you are used to. I would like to help you feel at home."

Is's mind whirled. Was he offering her protection? He was much more polite than the boys at the government school, or the men at the Equestrienne, but it could be the same thing. Was he claiming her? If she went with him, what was she agreeing to? She meant to confront him but there was such an earnest hopefulness in his face, Is hesitated. There was no trace of the calculating, victorious, demeaning things she was expecting to see.

He took her eye contact for consent and a smile came up from deep within him, joy-filled.

She went with him, despite feeling more unsure and off balance than ever. He introduced her to his friends, fielded questions whenever she didn't know how to answer, and made her feel . . . protected.

She studied the interactions between people. There were obvious couples. Yet they were different from the couples Is was used to. There was no blatant possessiveness. The men did not dominate the encounters. The women were as likely to speak to her as the men were, and without jealousy or any obvious attempt to show her up.

Not everyone was coupled. There were groups of unattached men. Is felt them looking at her, obviously sizing her up in sexual terms not unlike the boys at the government school.

What surprised her were the groups of unclaimed women. In the government school they would have belonged to one man or another. Perhaps it was just more subtle here, but Is couldn't see it.

No one seemed to be making a serious challenge to Petre's claim on her. That could only mean he was very powerful and feared. If that were the case, he must have other women and maybe men under his "protection." Is tried to discover who else belonged to Petre, but again she couldn't tell.

No one seemed afraid of him. In fact there was much humor at his expense. But Petre never seemed to take offense. Is was becoming more perplexed by the minute. Nothing she had learned about people seemed to apply.

The Hluit wore a great variety of clothing. Most people went bare above the waist, but not all. Some had painted themselves, or wore polished stones, shells, or feathers for decoration. Others seemed not to have bothered to change from clothes they had worked in that day. There was an intermixing of everything from tanned animal hides, to woven plant fiber cloth, to the expensive exotic Alliance coolcloth. Most of the men wore their hair as long as most of the women did, and some of the women wore theirs short. Many of the men had taken as much care with their dressing and body ornaments as the women had.

Petre had covered himself more than most men his age, who seemed to delight in displaying their bodies. Is felt shy, scared and fascinated all at the same time by the nudity of their upper bodies. She was glad Petre was more covered.

She caught people looking her over when they didn't think she was noticing. Her dark skin and hair must seem exotic to them. Perhaps no one contested Petre's claim because they found her ugly. But in the government schools that wouldn't have mattered. Ugly or not, fighting over her would have been a way for someone to prove, or lose, their power. The more beautiful or sexy a girl was, the more power could be had by owning her. But even an ugly or flat-chested girl could make herself an item in the power struggle if she played the game right. Other than Is, the only people who hadn't been worth anything to anyone were a few kids who were too retarded, mentally or physically, to fit in. But Petre did not seem to be like those rejected ones, and the way some of the men looked at her, Is knew she hadn't been immediately dumped into that category either.

One of Petre's friends offered her a juice fruit with a hollow stick stuck into it. Is had noticed that other people were sucking on them. It had a strangely bitter aftertaste. When Is made a face, Petre explained it had alcohol in it. Is had never drunk alcohol before. In the government schools you had to be highly connected to get such a contraband substance.

Food was set out on blankets and everyone helped themselves. If there was any order or etiquette Is couldn't detect it. Somehow Petre was always near, unobtrusively guiding her.

Through it all, the drums continued like a heartbeat. People began to gravitate over to the players. Is watched them dance. Dances taught in the government schools had intricate footwork, but people held their bodies stiffly. Here the steps could be as simple as a shuffling of the feet, but the body movements were fluid and gorgeous. Some people were elegant dancers. While they hardly appeared to move, they somehow conveyed the music through their bodies so gracefully Is was fascinated. Other people moved energetically, spinning around, jumping in the air, doing back bends and splits and hand stands that seemed impossible.

Some couples danced together, bringing their bodies close with sensual movements that made Is feel funny inside. In the government school, half that amount of touching would have brought swift punishment.

Not everyone danced in couples. Groups formed, dancing together and then drifting apart. Sometimes one person or group would seem to take center stage. Others might stop dancing to watch. The drummers seemed to understand what kind of beat was wanted and then a special thing would happen between the dancer and the drummers.

In all their various styles the people seemed exotic to Is. She was intimidated by their grace and freedom and even by their good spirits. She felt overwhelmingly out of place.

She saw John dancing with the woman he had kissed. He motioned to her as though she should come and join them. But she could not do that.

Ondre and Ellie tried to get her to dance with them too.

Now that the cooking was done, people had built the fire up. It cast an orange glow on the dancers. Blond hair turned to burnished gold, set off by deepening violet shadows.

"May I have the honor of dancing with you?" Petre asked, startling Is. She had forgotten him standing beside her.

"I don't know how," she stammered.

His eyebrows went up. She had surprised him, but in a second he recovered.

"There's nothing to know. You let the music come into your body and go out again."

Is shook her head, too afraid to speak.

"Look, I will show you."

Is wanted to bolt away from him.

"Look, look," he called to her. "See, the music comes into my foot through the ground." His foot began to tap and then to flop about in a most comical way. Several people stopped to watch. They laughed.

Is did not want to be the center of attention. She felt more intimidated than ever.

"Look," Petre insisted. "It starts in my foot and goes up my leg." His leg began to bounce as if it had a life of its own. More people were stopping to watch.

"Now the other foot is getting it," Petre said, and while his right foot was bouncing and hopping most energetically, his left somehow began to twitch and give an occasional hop. People were forming a circle around them now, laughing and calling encouragement to his backward left foot.

"And the music gets into my right arm," he informed Is, while his right arm began to jerk and wave about.

"Come on, left arm," he said, and with his right hand he picked up his limp left arm and shook it, all the while dancing with his right foot and giving strange little awkward jumps and taps with his left. Slowly, his left arm seemed to get the idea. But when he let go of it, it immediately fell limply to his side. The crowd that had gathered let out a collective "ahhh" of disappointment.

Petre picked up his left arm again and made it dance. This time when he let it go, it danced on a moment before falling to his side. Once more an "ahhh" rose from the watchers and now a much bigger crowd had gathered. So again Petre picked up his arm, and this time it responded. So now he was dancing energetically with his right leg and arm and awkwardly with his left leg and arm. Is couldn't help but laugh. But aside from Petre's clowning she was aware of how athletic he must be.

"And then the music gets into my center," he said, and slapped his belly. Instantly he was transformed. His whole body knew how to dance. He leapt and spun, and the drums went faster and faster. Most of the dancers had stopped to watch. Some called encouragement. Some clapped their hands faster and faster with the music. Finally, throwing his arms wide,

Petre gave one last magnificent spinning jump into the air and landed, arms and legs thrown wide, in front of Is. The drums rolled to a stop and then began again, slower.

Petre stood in front of her, grinning and panting for breath. The people applauded by slapping their hands on their thighs. Petre acknowledged them with a funny bow. Then he looked at Is, head cocked to the side.

He began to tap his right foot again pointedly. The people were still surrounding her, watching. The pressure of their eyes made her try.

She tapped her right foot, following Petre's lead. Encouraged, he began with the left foot. She imitated the best she could. He began waving one arm. She followed suit. He added the other arm. So did she. He began to weave and dance with his body. She tried to imitate and felt awkward and stiff. People laughed and clapped, calling encouragement. She tried to jump the way Petre jumped. It was much harder than he had made it look but now she was having fun. She tried one of his spins and nearly fell down. Hands caught her and set her back on her feet in the circle. She laughed, surprising herself. Petre baited her with all kinds of exotic jumps and spins. Is tried them. Other people tried them too and added their own flourishes. Soon everyone was dancing.

Is found herself dancing with another man and then another woman. Where had Petre gone? And then she was in a line, holding hands with strangers, snaking through the other dancers. Then that formation fell apart and she was coupled with someone else, and then someone else. Sometimes she saw Petre dancing with other people. He always caught her eye and smiled at her.

Is danced until she was exhausted and too out of breath to go on.

Petre reappeared at her side, breathing hard, but grinning. Without warning he threw his arms around her and pulled her against him. The feeling that went through her body was like an electric shock. Her heart got all out of time. Her arms and legs were instantly weak. Her mind tried to tell her several contradictory things at once: He was claiming her. No, it wasn't like that here. He expected her to "pay" him for his protection. No, it wasn't that sort of hug. She couldn't tell, the reaction of her own body was so intense and unexpected. Part of her mind was trying to tell her it was okay to do what Petre wanted. She should try to get along better here than she had in the schools. She should do whatever that took. But she couldn't. She knew she couldn't!

Petre released her as unexpectedly as he had hugged her. She tried to walk away from him. Her legs felt funny and she stumbled. Petre put his arm around her waist and steadied her against his side as she walked. She surprised herself by allowing his support.

"The alcohol," he said. "It creeps up on you." He was sweaty, but Is was enthralled by his smell and touch.

He got her a cup of water from a bucket and they sat on a little rise overlooking what was left of the fire. There were only a few dancers still going, dark silhouettes moving around the glowing coals. Petre didn't touch her any more and Is began to relax. She could feel the beat of the drums as though it were the pulse of the mountains. Half-formed thoughts and small hopes chased through her mind riding that beat. She wouldn't let any of them stay.

They sat while the coals burned down to a dim red glow and one drummer after another dropped out until the last drum fell silent. Only a few people sat around the coals now, their still forms dark against its shimmer-rippling warmth. Where had everyone gone? Is had not noticed them leaving. Had she dozed?

Petre was still sitting beside her. What would he think? What was she supposed to do now?

"May I walk you home?"

Petre's words startled Is into realizing she didn't know where "home" was. Ondre had said she could live with him and Ellie, but Is didn't remember how to get to their tent. She didn't think she could distinguish it from all the others, especially in the dark and it was only one room. They wouldn't want her there, not really.

"I think I'll just pitch my own tent."

"I'll show you where Ondre put your things."

Is was suddenly afraid that Petre had invited himself to spend the night with her. He insisted on carrying some of her stuff. He showed her which one was Ellie and Ondre's tent and suggested she might want to be close to them. He hesitated a little.

"Would you like help putting it up?"

"Oh, no thanks," she answered quickly, wanting him to know he was not to stay and also not wanting him to see the crude tent she had made for herself.

"Well, good night."

"Good night." She wondered if the relief she felt showed in her voice.

"I hope you feel welcome here," he said. "I hope you like us."

She wondered if he had wanted to say, "I hope you like me."

In a sudden rush of gratitude, she said, "I do," and added, "Thank you."

He laughed softly. "Thank you," he said and walked away.

Chapter 14

Is had thought she would sleep late after having been up half the night, but she woke early, strangely alert. She crawled out of her bag and stood still, testing the air for what had awakened her. There were many footprints in the dew, all going in the same direction. She followed them.

On the top of a little rise, in an open field, she saw a group of people. They were all moving in unison lined up more or less in rows, with one man leading them. They did a fast spinning turn with arms outstretched. Stopped suddenly. Then turned back the other way. Again and again. The movement was beautiful. The sun was not yet above the mountains. Fog lay in streamers on the plains below the knoll where the people exercised. The people spun and stopped, spun and stopped. Except for the swish of clothing they were silent.

Then they all knelt down. The man who had been leading the movement stood in front of them. A young man walked toward him, seeming to glide over the ground, fit and strong. He picked up a long stick, like a stave, from a pile at the outskirts of the exercise area and advanced menacingly on the leader, carrying the stick behind him. Abruptly he ran forward and swung with all his might.

Is shuddered, expecting to see the leader slammed to the ground with a broken skull. Instead the stick whistled by him and the attacker flew through the air as though launched. She expected the young man to land hard and not get up. Instead he did a flip in the air, straightened his body out parallel to the ground and landed all in one piece. In an instant he was on his feet again, but the leader was now holding the stick. He held it out to the attacker who took it and without an instant's hesitation swung again and went flying through the air. This time Is knew what to expect. There was a beauty to their movements, timing and unity somewhat like the best dancers the night before.

After a few more fast throws, the two men went through the attack in slow motion. Is observed exactly how the leader moved out of the way, how he used the attacker's momentum while twisting the stick for leverage. It made so much sense she wanted to cry out with understanding. A deep excitement took her. This was what John had used against Chest and the men in the town. Maybe they would teach it to her. There were as many women out there practicing as there were men. If she could learn this she would never have to be afraid of a man again.

All the people who had been kneeling stood up. They paired off, one with a stick, one without and began to imitate the movements of the teacher. Some of them were very good, but some were not. From them Is got an idea of how hard the movement really was. Getting the timing right would take experience. Is was dying to try it. She thought her years of riding would surely help with the timing. But she noticed that the partners always switched roles after a few throws so that whoever had been throwing would now be the attacker and have to fly through the air. She wondered if she could learn to fall like that. In riding falling was bad, always to be avoided, and Is had never thought of it as something that could be beautiful, or fun.

A young girl came walking across the field toward Is. The child smiled at her in a shy way and said good morning softly.

"Good morning, Chandra," Is replied, amazed that she had remembered the girl's name after being introduced to so many people.

The child went from shy to beaming. They watched the practice together. John was working out with a stout man who looked as if he could break the stick over John's head if he ever connected. John was having no trouble with him. He was grinning.

"He's really good," Chandra said.

"He looks good to me," Is admitted.

"He is. Is it true he can't talk?"

"He can talk, but only sometimes, and then his words don't make any sense."

"Are you going to marry him?" the child asked. "I wish you would."

Is felt as if someone had kicked her. She took a moment to seem nonchalant.

"I thought he was already married."

"No. He's been 'sposed to marry Alene. But I wish you'd marry him."

"It's not that easy."

"Why not?"

Is didn't know the answer to that herself. She caught at the first thought that came. "He may not want to marry me."

"He does," the girl asserted.

Is decided she'd better discount everything the child said. She probably just had a good imagination. They watched awhile longer in silence. More children collected around them.

"I have to go now," Chandra said. "It's almost our turn." She and the other children filed over to the knoll.

The people had lined up again. They kneeled and bowed to the man who had taught. Then they began drifting away. They were laughing and talking together and they all seemed relaxed and happy after their workout. Is could almost see the energy sparkling in the air around them.

But not everybody left. John and some of the other adults stayed to work with the children. Is watched John correcting the way one child was moving during the warm-up exercises. He did it all with mime. Is understood him perfectly. The child laughed at his rendition of the mistake he'd made. Others stopped to watch and laughed too. Is could see that the children loved John. She loved him too. All of a sudden it was easy to admit that. She wondered if Chandra was right about his not being married.

The children's practice looked different from the adults'. They did a lot of tumbling. Is watched intently and tried to learn how the falls were done. Some of the children were fearless. They would dive over each other and roll to their feet. Others were more timid, but the adults who had stayed to help were patient. Although the children were having fun, there was an undertone of discipline, but it was different from the dry hateful strictness of the government schools. Loving strictness. She wondered how that balance was achieved.

The children didn't work with the sticks. They practiced throwing someone who had grabbed them. Is was amazed at how even the small children could throw someone bigger. It seemed to be a trick of leverage and timing rather than strength. Again she was struck by the feeling that the moves made so much sense it was a wonder she had not thought of them herself. But she had never thought about defending herself at all. How could she? She would have had to fight everyone in the school. And how could she have defended herself from the teachers, like Riding Master Masley, who had so much power over her? And the berserkers? She felt certain that even the best of these people would not be able to handle a berserker.

When the class ended, Is went over to the children, intending to walk with Chandra. But John saw her and came to her immediately. He put his hands on her shoulders and looked deep into her eyes as he had last night. Is thought her heart would stop. Her whole body felt strange, hot and weak. After a moment he let her go and she walked with him back toward the camp. Other people surrounded them, talking. They asked her what she thought of what she had seen.

"It was stunning," she said and they laughed

Everyone seemed to radiate energy and good spirits and Is found herself feeling good just to be around these people. The children chattered and laughed and rough-played their way back to camp.

The talk switched from practice to breakfast and the day's work. Breakfast was a communal affair featuring large pots of slowly bubbling cereal. Petre saw Is and came over to her. He had overslept, he said, which caused a number of people to start kidded him. He seemed to take the razzing good-naturedly.

"Someone has to stay here and cook," he said. But no one believed him.

"Cook!" they said. "Only if you've learned to do it in your sleep." And they wouldn't allow him to argue. Is watched the exchange carefully and could detect no malice - so unlike the government school.

People sat in informal groups. Is sat with Ondre, Ellie and Petre. John seemed to be a guest of honor in a group nearby - if by teasing him they were honoring him. He had no way to defend himself. Watching him, Is saw how much he loved and was loved by his people. She was aware of how Ondre never took his eyes off his brother and aware of how Ellie watched Ondre as closely. She would have to be blind to miss the love that connected those three.

Surreptitiously she also watched Alene, John's girlfriend, trying to see if that special connection extended to her. But Is could not tell and realized she was not an impartial judge.

As people finished eating they wandered off in informal groups to get the day's work done. Ellie and Ondre asked Is to come and talk with them some more.

They rolled back the roof of the tent so it was basically a roofless wall encircling them. The mid-morning sun shone in. The sky was blue and birds sang, but Is felt sudden trepidation.

Ellie prepared tea and Ondre opened by saying.

"I hope you understood, the feast last night was to thank you for what you've done for John, as much as it was to celebrate his return."

Is had not understood that, any more than Ondre's people had understood that a big public gathering was the absolute last thing she would have wanted. When she didn't say anything, Ondre sighed. She was not making whatever he wanted to say easy for him, but she was not doing it on purpose. Ellie stepped in.

"Is, we love John. We thought he was dead. We're so glad he's back, and we thank you for helping him. Nothing would make us happier than for both of you to stay here forever. But that isn't what John's going to do. It is important that you understand your options. You could stay with us, or go with him. What he is going to try will be quite dangerous. We think that you might be a help to him but it is important that you understand as much as possible about the risk involved; and it is important we understand you." She looked directly into Is's eyes and Is felt dread sink into her stomach. She did not want more danger or more odd occurrences. But she made herself nod so Ellie would continue.

Ellie backed off from the intensity of what she had been trying to express. She glanced at her husband and Ondre spoke.

"The Mirror thing that was in John's letter . . . we don't know what it really is or why the Alliance is so interested in it. That's part of what John was trying to find out.

"You must realize that, most of what your government has taught you about our side of the Boundary is simply not true. They don't send the berserkers against the Blueskins. They send them against the Mirror."

They were both watching for her reaction. Is wished they would stop referring to it as "her" government. She was an outlaw too.

Ondre took up the tale. "The Alliance has a certain vested interest in keeping its citizens on its side of the Boundary, and therefore a certain interest in keeping them ignorant and misinformed. The Alliance doesn't want people to know anything about the Mirror, or about us. And what you have been taught about the Blueskins is also false."

Is could see Ondre was getting wound up into real anger.

She didn't understand what he was trying to tell her and she was glad when Ellie interrupted him.

"The Alliance has an 'arrangement' with the Blueskins. It doesn't send the berserkers to hunt them down because of the farmers they kill, or the goods they steal the way you have been taught. The Alliance wants the Blueskins to attack a certain percentage of farmers every year. That way the people believe there is a real threat and that the berserkers are necessary." Ellie stopped because she could see Is had gone pale.

"What's wrong?"

"Blueskins killed my mother and father and that was part of the . . . the arrangement!" Her voice shook. "That's why the men came and took me away the very next day. They knew it was going to happen."

Ondre slapped his thigh with a loud report and turned angrily away. No one said anything for a few minutes.

"I'm very sorry," Ellie said. Her voice was filled with such compassion that Is had trouble believing a woman who hardly knew her could care so much.

"She still has to know," Ondre said to his wife. His voice was gentle and without anger now.

Ellie didn't say anything but Is had the feeling she agreed with her husband. Is did not want to be treated like a child. She tried to think of something to say that would show her toughness and let them know she wanted the truth.

"Why do they send the berserkers against the Mirror?" she asked.

"The Alliance would have us believe it is their way of studying the Mirror," Ondre answered. "Only, they created the Mirror in the first place so we're not sure what they're doing. It kills everyone who approaches it. The berserkers are designed to be unafraid of death, to fight hard and not be killed too quickly. They are the government's eyes and ears. When they fight the Mirror, the government can see and hear what happens. It's transmitted to them, as when people 'fast' their talk." He was watching her acutely and Is felt he was trying to simplify down to her level what he was describing. It embarrassed her to be so ignorant.

"If it kills everyone, then it will kill John," she said, sounding a lot more calm and impersonal than she felt.

"He seems to think he has learned something that will make a difference," Ondre said. Is could tell Ondre didn't want his brother going anywhere near the thing.

"We don't actually know what the Mirror is. We gave it that name because it has some of the properties of a mirror. It reflects anything that approaches it. But it isn't just a surface projection. It seems to somehow reflect what's inside a person's mind. We know of no one who has lived through a direct encounter with the Mirror, but people sometimes live through encounters with the herd fogs, which can do similar things to a person's mind. We think the herd fogs are part of the Mirror. They may be like its hands, appendages with which it can reach out and manipulate things. People who have gone through experiences with the fogs are often very confused."

He looked at her closely and Is could tell he was holding back something. But her years of training in the government school had led her to accept having information withheld from her. It never occurred to her that she could simply ask and he would tell her.

"It's important to us to know about your experience in the fog so that we can learn to understand the herd fogs better," Ellie said.

"I may have imagined it," Is said.

Ondre and Ellie exchanged a look.

"In a sense, all our experiences of the herd fog and the Dark Bodies and the Mirror are imagined," Ondre said. "None of them is exactly 'real' in the way that, say, a horse is 'real.'"

Dark Bodies, Is thought that was a perfect name for the shadowy apparitions that had surrounded John that night.

"You may have caused the Dark Bodies to come in order to help you when you were stuck in the fog," Ellie tried to explain. "If we can find out how you did that, you may be able to call them or send them away at will."

"Why would I want to do that?"

"Because, if you go with John, you may be able to help him find the Mirror, and you may help him have the right dialogue with it." Ondre's voice was serious. "John seems to think he can get the Mirror to reflect something that won't kill him. He seems to think it can cure what the Alliance did to him."

Ellie took Is's hand. "John desperately needs to talk again. You know he was posing as a scholar and spying on the Alliance for us. We try to keep a few spies in the government all the time so we will know if they are planning anything concerning us. For years they have just let us live here in peace, but we know there will be a time when that will change. So we keep our spies watching.

"John had a special task. He was trying to learn about the Mirror and the berserkers. Our people have kept a record of the changes the Alliance has made in the berserkers and their horses over the years. It seemed the Alliance was trying to perfect something, using the Mirror like a mirror, to reflect their flaws. What we have never been able to understand is what they are trying to perfect. Years ago, we thought it was the physical perfection of the fighting team of horse and rider the Alliance was after. But they have taken man and beast as far as they can in that direction, and still they send them." Ellie paused, and Ondre took up the story.

"A whole network of industry has grown up around developing and supporting the berserkers and their horses. You were part of it. You saw all the levels of training, the different Barns, the Equestrienne schools, the elaborate apprentice program. Of course not all of it is aimed at producing berserkers - there are the Breeding Barns, the Troop Barns, the Training Barns - but the berserkers and their horses are the ultimate achievement. The whole thing is too complex for the explanations the Alliance offers its citizens especially since we know the berserkers do not fight the Blueskins.

"John had worked his way up in the research branch of the Alliance dealing specifically with the berserkers. He must have learned something very important."

"All we know is he is willing to risk facing the Mirror and the possibility of being killed for the chance to regain his speech," Ellie said bluntly.

"He may have a better chance to succeed if you help him," Ondre added.

Is looked away, giving herself a moment to think. She could see how much these two loved John. She wanted to help them, and she certainly wanted to help John. But she didn't know what they thought she could do, and she was afraid. Deep in her soul she didn't want to go anywhere near the Mirror, or the herd fogs or Dark Bodies again, ever.

"There is another reason you might want to go," Ondre said. He sounded tentative. Is met his eyes feeling more scared than ever. "Have you thought about what you'll do when your stallion reaches maturity?" His voice was grave, his eyes compassionate.

He could only mean when Lark was old enough for his berserker. But there would be no berserker for Lark. He would never feel the man coming. He would not change, the way the other horses had changed. Is had never believed it would be otherwise. But now Ondre was looking at her with such concern and sadness he could only mean she'd been wrong.

"You didn't know?" Ellie asked compassionately.

"But his berserker won't come," Is cried out. "Lark won't change."

"He came from the Castle Stud, didn't he?" Ondre asked. "He had the brand on his forehead, didn't he?"

Is could only nod. Lark had arrived at her place as a leggy yearling, his coat still fuzzy like a colt's, and his tail the short flag of a baby. He had been so friendly, making up to her immediately, as if she were some long lost friend. She had rubbed his forehead where the scar was and he had loved it because it was itchy with new healing.

"He's about seven or eight now, isn't he?" Ondre asked.

"Seven," Is confirmed.

Ellie spoke to Ondre. "He's too old. We can't remove the chip."

"It gets too integrated into their brains," Ondre explained. "It controls the chemical output of the pituitary and other systems. Among other things it tells his body when to make the hormones of fear, or anger, or aggression. So far it has only regulated his hormones for maximum growth and development. He is as strong and fast and smart as his biochemical makeup and his breeding, and your training, can make him. But when the chip determines that he is fully developed, it will switch its message. It will make him as aggressive and as fearless as it is possible for a horse to be.

"Each chip has a frequency all its own. It is set to resonate with the chip implanted in the berserker they prepare for that particular horse. That is why the horse and the berserker do not fight each other. Their brains recognize each other."

"Even if his berserker doesn't come," Ellie continued, "Lark will become too aggressive to handle. His training and his love for you will not be able to override the hormones his system will be pumping out. I'm sorry."

Is did not want to believe them, but she had seen too many of her beloved stallions change. There would be no way to control Lark when that happened to him. She grasped at the small hope they had mentioned earlier.

"But if I go with John, that could make a difference?"

Now Ondre came over and put his arm around his wife and took Is's other hand. "We don't know," he said honestly. "John seems to believe he has found a new way to approach the Mirror. He seems to think he can undo what the Alliance has done to him. But even if he can, it may be totally different from undoing what was done to Lark. There may be some sophisticated answers to a lot of things about the mind there, but I do not want to mislead you. We simply don't know if any of it will help Lark."

"If you decide to go with John," Ellie said gently, "I think you should base that decision on reasons other than the hope of saving Lark."

"I still don't see what you think I can do that will help John," Is said.

"We don't know that for sure either," Ondre said. "But don't you realize? Some of the things you've experienced! Seeing the Dark Bodies.

Hearing them! Not many people can hear them speak, even if you couldn't understand their words then, you heard them and there is a place in your mind that remembers exactly what you heard. And then there was the way the Blueskins treated you! Not raping and killing you. And the house, the house where you met the old man, Amil – it doesn't exist. But where you saw that house is the ruin of an old chimney. There used to be a house there. But now there is no such house, and no such person living there."

"Stop, Ondre. You're scaring her," Ellie interrupted.

Is felt the hair standing up on her arms. "But John saw it too," she objected. "He was there, and you have the note Amil wrote."

"Yes, we have the note," Ondre said solemnly. "And we have sent scouts to see if they can find the house. Maybe someone moved in there and rebuilt. But it would have to have been very recently."

"How can that be?" Is asked, trying to keep a feeling of mounting horror at bay. The cabin she had seen had been well worn, as lived in as an old shoe.

"For the same reason the Blueskins have a legend about you. Well, about a girl who roams the mountains on a war horse the color of the earth. In fact they believe he is made out of the ground, and the girl's hair is the color of shadow, and her skin dark like the soil. That is how they disappear, those two. They go back into the ground and shadow from which they were made. But it is very strong medicine to see them, and even stronger medicine to capture them, although it is impossible to detain them for long."

Is shook her head. She couldn't begin to find the words to refute Ondre. He saw her expression and smiled.

"Hard to understand, huh? Hard to explain." His eyes met hers searchingly. "Have you ever looked into two mirrors at an angle to each other? Your reflection repeats itself into infinity. It is a property of mirrors."

Ellie squeezed Is's hand. "Enough," she told Ondre.

"No, Ellie, she needs to know."

"But it's only your theory, Ondre."

"Theory!" Ondre laughed and there was a little bit of his brother's hysterical quality to the sound. "It's not even that," he said. "It's a bunch of things that don't make sense, all lumped together. How could the Blueskins have a legend about you? How could an old man and his cabin be there when you go there, but we know it only as a ruin? The only thing I can think is that the Mirror is involved. Lark was intended to take his berserker to the Mirror but you're riding him instead. Is he somehow connected to the Mirror's weird ability to manipulate time but since you don't want to go to the Mirror he's taking you to all sorts of other places instead . . . places in the past? We know the Mirror makes hallucinations and we know that people who have any dealing with its herd fogs experience time differently.

People who have been lost in a herd fog may think they have been gone only hours and yet they have been gone for days or longer. Could the Mirror be throwing reflections of you back in time?"

"But I've never been near it!" Is cried out.

Ondre and Ellie waited for her to grasp what she'd heard.

"If I go with John," Is started hesitantly, "the Mirror is going to get my reflection . . . and . . . but it already has it, and I haven't gone there yet. Can it do things all backwards like that?"

"Yes," Ondre answered. "That seems to be part of what drives a lot of people crazy in the herd fogs. Things get out of order. Some people don't ever recover."

"Lark was lost in the fog," Is said thoughtfully. "But then John was with him. And John spoke to me." She met Ondre's eyes. "Am I crazy? Did it drive me crazy?"

"No." He met her eyes steadily until she looked away.

"If the herd fog can do that, what will the Mirror be like?" Her voice sounded small and timid even to her own ears.

"It will be even more confusing and frightening," Ondre answered.

"Ond . . ." Ellie reproved him.

"No," he said to her, "Is needs to know everything any one of us knows, or thinks, or guesses about the Mirror. She might be the one to tie all this together."

"But Amil wasn't a reflection," Is objected. "We ate food he cooked, and the note he wrote is real. You saw it. You held it in your hand.'

"Is," Ellie said in a calming voice. "We don't have the answers, we need them."

Is could see that they were desperate for her help. It was not just that they wanted to help John, whom they loved. They needed something from him, and from her. She sat back stunned. She had never been needed like this before and it frightened her in a way she had never been frightened before.

Ellie spoke to Ondre. "You should tell her about the troopers too. It's her right to know."

Is froze.

"They came here twice," Ondre said. "The first time must have been just shortly after you disappeared with their stallion. They were just looking around, just wondering if we'd seen you. They only wanted to recover the horse. Seemed he was something special they wanted for their breeding program. No mention of killing him off with a berserker. Would we let them know if we saw you? They were friendly and polite, and ever so casual." He gave a crooked little grin. "This, you realize, after having not made contact with our people, in our homeland, for..." he glanced at Ellie for confirmation, "fifty years."

"At least," Ellie agreed. "It was much too casual. We were suspicious. But we had not seen you then. We couldn't tell them anything but that. We didn't immediately notice that your description matched one of the Blueskins' legends. We wouldn't have bothered to mention it anyway. They can talk to the Blueskins for themselves."

"They brought a whole troop when they came back in the spring," Ondre continued. "They weren't quite so polite. They seemed absolutely certain the horse was still alive. They were sure the only way you could have made it through the winter was if you'd come here. They demanded that we turn the stallion over to them. They demanded the right to search our herds, which of course they don't have, and we denied it to them on principle. They reminded us the horse was near maturity and would become unmanageable. They tried to make us believe they would know if we killed him, and they said they would be back with his berserker. Either he will call the horse out of our herds, or wreck our village. Or both."

Is felt as if Lark had landed a kick in her stomach. "You should have told me immediately. I'll leave right away." If she concentrated on the fear and the urgency, she wouldn't have to feel the pain and disappointment.

"That's not necessary," Ellie said. "It will not matter what you do - go or stay. The Alliance believes what it will, and we will not let them search our herds whether you are here or not. That is a larger issue. The Blueskins also have their own reasoning and will act on it whether you approve or not. We believe they will not let the Alliance take you back if they can stop them. Each group is autonomous. You are not responsible for our actions. You are responsible only to yourself, and those you have included within that self."

Is met Ellie's eyes to see if she really believed that. Ellie's gaze didn't waver.

"If all people lived that way," Ondre said, "each one taking responsibility for his or her own self, and allowing all others to take responsibility for themselves, we would have true freedom."

Is had never had the luxury to consider freedom in the sense that they meant it. She had been trying too hard not to get noticed, not to get hurt. Even when she'd been a trainer at the Border Station, although she had lived alone and made all her own decisions concerning the horses' training, she had not been free. She had trained those horses to be taken by the berserkers and killed. When she had run away, she had had no one to answer to, and yet she had not been free, not in the sense she thought Ellie and Ondre were talking about. Freedom to make real decisions, not decisions based on fear.

Freedom from fear. Freedom from the coercion of a corrupt government. Responsible only to herself, and those she had included within her self.

They would have her believe she could decide to run away, or go with John, or stay here. For a moment she could see that they were really extending that freedom to her. But she could not accept it. In her mind there was very little choice. She had never meant for anyone else to become involved in the consequences of her decision to steal the stallion. She could not just stay and see how many people got killed over her.

But she would not run away, not this time. She would go with John. She did not believe she would be any help with the Mirror, but there was a small chance it would not kill him. What he had learned could be important to his people. There was the even smaller chance he would be able to help Lark. Is found she didn't believe that either, but it was the only chance Lark had. And John . . . John, who wanted to have a "dialogue" with the Mirror. John who couldn't speak. What if he tried and the Mirror cast his insane hysterical laughter back at him?

She did not want to be a part of any of this. She wanted to train horses and deal with things that were "real" the way horses were "real." But she could not stay here now. There was one other option: She could go back to the Alliance. She rejected that idea almost before it was formed. Better to die.

"I'll go with John," she told them. "But I don't know how to help."

"Maybe you do," Ellie said. "You just don't know how to access that information."

"It's like riding," Ondre tried to explain. "It is your body that knows how to ride. You can't possibly use your conscious mind to instruct your body to move with a horse, any more than you can consciously instruct your body to walk. The motor skills are too complex. You have to let your body-brain do the work, not your thought-brain. The kind of knowledge you need for this may be somewhat like that. It's too complex or too confusing for your thought-brain, your conscious mind. But the Dark Bodies may have given you some information that resides somewhere in you. You may be able to access it through your body-brain, or some other way we don't fully understand. But we have ways of bringing those experiences up to the conscious level, if you are willing to try."

"What do I have to do?"

"Just listen to my voice," Ondre said. "Do what I tell you. I want to get your conscious mind to relax so I can talk to another part of your mind."

Is had her doubts, but agreed. Ondre had her sit in a comfortable position, then he began talking to her, telling her to relax her face, her neck, her arms.

His voice was like a caress on her skin. Muscles she hadn't been aware of holding tight let go. Her whole body seemed to sigh and something inside her mind became calm. She was aware of Ondre's words manipulating her body. She could feel his voice as though it was touching her in long stroking motions, in a way no man had ever touched her with his hands. She could feel her body responding, releasing everything - tension, fear, desire. In some distant part of herself she was amazed. Ondre was the first man since her father who didn't threaten her.

She was watching like that, from a great distance it seemed, when Ondre said, "You are back on the hillside with the fog. What do you see?"

Instantly, Is was surrounded by the thickly shrouded trees. She was alone. Lark was gone. John and his mare were gone.

The breeze was doing battle with the fog. She could see that so clearly it didn't occur to her to question it. She was trying to get to a clear place so the breeze would have an advantage. Her arm hurt and she could barely turn her head. Walking was strangely difficult. John came riding out of the fog. He seemed relieved when he saw her. He opened his mouth and was going to speak, just as ordinarily as anyone ever spoke. But the voice Is heard was Ondre's.

"What are you seeing inside the fog?" And instantly she was back inside the fog. John and Lark were gone. The voice became more insistent.

"Tell us what you are seeing."

Is wanted to answer that voice, but other voices were saying something else, very fast, on many tracks at once.

"Can you hear me?" the voice outside the fog asked. "Tell me what you are hearing?"

Is tried to repeat what she was hearing.

The next thing she knew Ondre was gripping her shoulders. "Wake up. You are safe now. Wake up." She seemed to remember that he had been saying that for a long time.

She stared about her frantically. The fog was gone. She was inside the tent wall. The sun shone through the open roof. Insects buzzed. She tried to move, but there was a weight on her legs. She looked down and saw Ellie's face red with exertion. Her hair was tousled and her pupils were big. She moved off Is's legs. Ondre was still gripping her arms so hard they hurt. She wanted to tell him to stop, but her throat was dry and sore.

Ondre moved back from her. Ellie brought her some water. No one said anything. Is tried to remember what had happened. The other two looked as shaken as she felt.

Ondre started to speak. His voice creaked, and he had to clear it. "I'm sorry. I didn't know ..."

Ellie made a harsh noise to interrupt him.

"Are you all right?" she asked Is.

"Yes. What happened?"

"I asked you to do something you weren't able to do, when you were in a state of mind in which you had to try," Ondre said.

"Oh." Is felt better. If that's all that had happened . . . She was used to being in the position of having to try to do something that seemed impossible - training the young horses, dealing with the berserkers. "Did you learn what you wanted to learn?"

Ondre shook his head. "No, but you might have."

Is tried to remember what she was supposed to have learned - something that might help John survive his encounter with the Mirror. "I don't think so. We better try again."

Ondre drew in his breath, surprised. Ellie's eyes got even bigger.

"Not on your life," Ellie said heatedly.

"You're very brave to want to try again," Ondre explained. "But you could be hurt. We won't do it."

"Not brave," Is said. "It wasn't anything to me."

Ondre shook his head. "If information was given to you, it was given in a way you cannot repeat."

Is was swept with disappointment. She would be no help to John, or his people, or Lark.

Chapter 15

Is was filled with urgency to leave, but no one else seemed to share her feeling. Ondre thought John needed time with his people to heal as much as he could before facing the Mirror. Is thought Ondre just wanted to keep his brother around as long as possible, and normally she would have agreed except that the troopers would be coming back for her.

Ellie tried to reassure Is that the Alliance troopers could not surprise them. The Hluit had put out extra scouts, plus everyone seemed to think the Blueskins would interfere with troop movement.

Is objected, but she was told again that the Hluit could not control the Blueskins. They could not even be sure what the Blueskins would do. Is began to realize that the relationship between the two peoples was more complex and subtle than she could hope to understand quickly.

Meanwhile, Petre became her almost constant companion. He loved to talk and his ceaseless chatter was a great source of information for Is, as she was trying desperately to figure out her new people.

Petre took her out to see the herd they had given Lark.

Boys and girls around ten to fifteen years stayed with the breeding herds and kept them separated. For the young people it was training in independence. They were completely responsible for the horses. They rode trusted geldings that the stallions would tolerate.

These people revered their horses in a much more natural way than the way the Alliance treated theirs. Even the youngest children seemed to know how to ride. They learned to care for the needs of their horses as they were learning to take care of their own needs. Is had seen small children lugging manure away from the camp, and toddlers tagging along to help spread it where the grass would reclaim it for nourishment. It was part of life, like dressing oneself, or taking care of one's own hygiene.

They had given Lark a herd of six mares. Is visited the stallion while Petre chatted with the kids who were in charge of the herd. It was good to have Lark's soft brown nose snuffling over her hands and arms, good to see his big intelligent eyes and the familiar way he twitched his ears, to have his scent and the big reassuring bulk of him next to her.

Inevitably Is thought of what Ondre and Ellie had said about Lark going crazy. Her fingers ran through his mane, absently untangling it. If she rode him to the Mirror, would it trigger him as the coming of his berserker would? Would it kill him? If she left him here and he went crazy, the Hluit would have to kill him. If the Alliance got him back, they would send him against the Mirror and that would be the end of him. Was there really some chance the Mirror wouldn't kill John? Was there a chance it would heal him? Was there any chance he would learn something that would save

Lark? It seemed an impossibly small hope, but it was the only one Lark had.

The days began to take on a routine. First thing in the morning nearly everyone would turn out for martial arts practice. Petre had formally invited Is to practice but everyone taught her. First she had to learn to fall so she wouldn't be hurt when someone threw her. Then she had to learn how to make the movements work so she could throw someone no matter how big or strong they were, or no matter how fast they attacked. At least that was the theory. In practice everyone moved very slowly and carefully with her. She understood that it was important to do things correctly from the beginning. As in learning to ride, it would be harder to break bad habits later on than to develop the right habits in the beginning.

The practice was extremely taxing both physically and mentally but Is loved it. She soon overcame her fear of falling and everyone was so nice about teaching her that she even overcame her fear of making mistakes and being ridiculed. Also during practice she could interact with John without the need for words and there was no time to worry about the future. Sometimes Petre practiced with her, sometimes he practiced with John and that was a treat to watch. They made it look like play as one or the other of them went sailing through the air, obviously enjoying each other.

When either of them practiced with Ondre it looked more like a struggle – at least for Petre or John. Ondre was very fast and apparently inexhaustible. His movements were so minimal it was hard to see what he had done to cause the other person to fall. And when it was his turn to be thrown, no matter how he landed, he seemed to bounce off the ground, attacking again before either John or Petre was ready.

There was nothing mean spirited about it. At the end Ondre always thanked them sincerely for helping him to improve, while they stood trying not to be obvious about being out of breath. But with Is, Ondre always worked slowly and carefully, correcting her every mistake with such gentleness she never felt put down.

After practice and breakfast came the daily chores. At this time of year the people were busy harvesting crops they had cultivated in outlying plots. At breakfast someone would stand up and say something like, "The roots are ready to harvest in High Plot." Or, "The harnuts are ripe in Blue Forest." The people seemed to be free to decide which jobs to assign themselves, and as far as Is could tell all the work was getting done. It was so different from the government school where everyone was assigned to tasks and proctors stood over the students to make sure they kept working. Since Is had been unwilling to do the things that would have kept her in the proctors' good graces, she'd had to do a lot of the work while other students loafed, and she was considered stupid for getting herself into that position.

But here the attitude was different. People talked and kidded one another. The only competitiveness Is could discern was a friendly try at being the one to get the most work done. As in the martial arts class, anyone who was near her was willing to teach her a more efficient way to shell harnuts or dig bigroots.

Is tried to put away old reflexes and relax. But sometimes the tension of just being around so many people was too much for her. So in the evenings when the work was done and people were resting, gossiping and just being together, Is would often slip off by herself.

No one ever said anything to her about it, or followed her, or tried to prevent her from going, but she knew people noticed, especially Petre. He seemed to have appointed himself her special guardian. She was aware that she shouldn't really need one - everyone looked out for her - but sometimes she felt unsure. Whenever that happened, Petre always seemed to materialize to guide her unobtrusively through the situation.

John often chose to be in her work group too. Sometimes Alene was with him, sometimes not. Is did not understand their relationship and didn't dare allow herself to hope that it might be breaking up. The people apparently had a very special love for John. Is began to feel that she was just one more person who loved him and it could never be anything more than that. Since he was already a hero in their eyes and would soon do something even more dangerous than anything he had previously survived, Is felt that all she could hope for was to help him, if possible. She was terrified of what they were planning to do and she did not know how she would find the courage to be any use.

The day the Big Rain began, all harvesting came to a stop.

"It'll rain for days now," Petre told her. "Possibly weeks."

The people constructed a huge communal tent and sat around drinking tea and talking, smoking whatever foods and meats they could, or just catching up on their rest.

Is was unaware of how it began, but sometime during that first day the talk had gone from idle conversation to something more structured. Ondre was sitting cross legged on one of the rugs. As he spoke, people began to collect around him. His words became simple, his sentences cadenced, as if he were reciting something. The people fell silent, listening to Ondre with rapt attention, and something else. Satisfaction. They were like people who were thirsty and had found a well. Something powerful was happening here, without fanfare, without introduction, and all the people were participating in it deeply. Everyone except Is.

Slowly, she realized that Ondre was reciting the history of the Hluit. ". . . We were scholars of the Privileged class, highest in the hierarchy, but we were dissatisfied. We presented our ideas and were rebuffed. We moved to outlying villages and they brought us back. We petitioned for change and went unheard.

"Then Hluit came to be governor of the Grand Council. He proposed an experiment. 'Let them have their own land. Let them try to make a different society.' The ones who said man's nature must be controlled said we would fail. We would end up in chaos or with a more restrictive government than the Alliance. Hluit said, 'Let them try. If they fail, it is no difference to us because they will be isolated beyond the Boundary. Whether they succeed or fail they will never again be a problem to us.

"We became the Hluit. We are an experiment.

"Our forbearers numbered one hundred and eighty. We honor them all. Among them were William Demansc, the great philosopher who set the tone of our constitution; Annette Aneet, who brought us the science of ecology; Lis Mistome, the great mathematician; Bihl Ahmanhet and Ondre Dreel, who brought us knowledge of medicine . . ." The list went on and on.

Is could not believe anyone could memorize so much. But Ondre must have been getting it right because everyone was watching and some were nodding to themselves. Some were mouthing the sentences silently along with him. Even the children seemed to know it.

Ondre began to catalog the differences between the Hluit and the Alliance.

"We do not build houses or cities. We do not rape the land. We do not set one person above another. We do not withhold knowledge of any sort from any person." As the list went on Is began to recognize the things she had only sensed as "wrongness" in the government school.

These people had made a study of what was amiss in the Alliance and they had tried to change those things. They had purposefully formed their society to be as different from the Alliance as possible.

"To say, 'This will be the way,'" Ondre went on, "is only a first step. People must have a road to walk. The road must have a map. Intention was the beginning. The map was the second step. But the map is not the road. Each person walks the real road. Sweat, blood, tears, laughter, frustration, joy - these are the real road. Horsemanship and martial arts are the map. Love is the destination."

Is didn't hear the rest. Love is the destination. Not control. Not power over someone else.

She had seen the women taking an equal part in Hluit society. She thought of the fearlessness of the children. She thought of the bridle-less horses. The Hluit would not even coerce their horses!

Even their martial arts could only be used effectively in self-defense. The success of the throws depended on the aggression of the attacker. Lost in her own thoughts, Is mostly missed the rest of Ondre's recitation. A whole new world of thoughts and questions opened for her. She was surprised that she had never thought to ask Petre about his people's history. The government school had taught her well. Don't ask questions. No, something even deeper than that - don't want to know.

That was the biggest wrong the Alliance perpetrated against their people, not just the withholding of knowledge, but their attempt to kill the desire to learn.

Set above those uneducated, unawakened masses were the privileged few - the scholars. They had all the knowledge, the books, and other resources with which to learn. For the first time Is wanted to know, not just what the scholars knew, but what the Alliance did not want its people to know. Now she understood why the Hluit had spies, and why John's need to tell the people what he had learned was so urgent that he would risk his life to do it. She understood why his brother, who loved him, would back him in taking that risk.

She couldn't listen to any more. She had to think about what she had already understood. She was sitting on the edge of the crowd so it was easy enough to slip out from under the tent.

The rain was like ice water. She pulled her coat up around her neck and began to walk. A few steps away she made the mistake of looking back, and met Petre's eyes. No one else had noticed. Everyone's attention was focused on Ondre.

Is turned away, walking quickly, against the chill of the rain. This time she wished Petre would follow her. She wished she could talk to him as easily as he talked to her. She would tell him all the things that were happening inside her head. She would tell him about all the changes – as though the ground beneath her feet was shaking, as though her heart was filled with sky one moment and heavy stone the next, as though her brain would explode like the sun. And the only thing she had to hold on to was something from the government school, dark and heavy and bitter.

But that past horror and its lingering effects had no place here. Here people were trying to be good in their hearts, trying to make something good of their lives. She could choose to cling to what the government school had done to her. She could be the person they had tried to mold – dark, scared and suspicious. Or she could put that behind her and open new doors.

She sat with her back against a tree, cold and damp, and watched the rain. She felt it finding its way into her clothing but she would not move. The physical misery matched her internal turmoil. She wanted so much to tell someone what was happening to her. Feeling this way made her realize how much more intensely John must want to tell his people something much more important than what was happening to her. For the first time she understood that there was a good and positive reason to go with John to the

Mirror, not just because she could not stay here with the troopers coming. For the first time she felt that she might be able to gather the courage to do what was right. She could do more than just run away. She could embrace this bigger cause.

The rain continued for days. Instead of the martial arts practice, Ondre led meditation sessions. Is learned to still her thoughts and find a place of inner peace. The problems she faced and the decisions she had to make could be handled if she didn't limit herself to a single part of her being. Rational thought and logic would do her very little good facing something like the Mirror or the herd fogs. The courage she needed to find would not come from the part of her mind that wanted to yammer with fear.

So Is attended all of Ondre's sessions. When he saw she was interested, he helped her with special postures, different methods of breathing, fasting and purification rituals.

Is was not the only one. Many people seemed to use this time of confinement to work on their inner selves. She often saw John or Petre in meditation. Chanting and drumming were sometimes part of the rituals.

Finally the rain broke. The clouds parted enough to let the sun shine through. Then a breeze came and the clouds began to move. The people rejoiced like children. It was time for the feast of the Splitting of the Ways.

Each year, when the harvests were in, and the good summer grazing was depleted, the Hluit split into smaller groups and traveled slowly outward letting the horses graze in outlying places where they had not eaten all summer. While the horses ate some of the grass, the people would cut most of it for hay. Later in winter, when all the grass was gone, they would retrace their steps, moving from haystack to haystack as needed, until they all came together again when the spring grass was full.

The feast of the Splitting of the Ways was similar to the feast they'd had in celebration of John's return but much more elaborate. The final harvests had been brought in and whatever couldn't be preserved must be eaten. After the fasting and deprivations and inner strictures of the last weeks it was good to let go.

There was food, drink and dancing. Is thrilled to the drums and for a while she forgot herself in dancing. She danced with Petre, John, Ondre, Ellie and practically everyone else at one time or another. She felt as if she loved everyone and everyone loved her. This was how it was to be Hluit.

For a time she forgot that she was not Hluit, that she would not be staying here, that she had no future with these people. Eventually the fire burned low and most everyone had gone home, but Is was not ready to let go of this night. She lay back on the hillside where she and Petre had sat that first night, which seemed so long ago, and Petre found her there.

He had brought some of his people's excellent mead.

They lay side by side, speaking very little, watching the coals shimmer below them and stars shimmer above them. Is wanted to stay there forever but the night chill began to penetrate her clothes. For a while longer her mind held it at bay but eventually she sat up and hugged her knees.

Petre immediately took off his own jacket and put it around her shoulders.

"But you'll be cold," she protested.

"I think I drank too much to notice."

She laughed at that. She never wanted this night to end and she suspected Petre felt the same. She knew he wouldn't mind being a little cold in order to prolong their time together.

"Is . . ." there was a softness in his voice, a little catch Is had never heard before. She was afraid he was going to say something about the future, about leaving. She did not want that. She turned to face him, ready to say anything to stop him and saw how he was looking at her.

She was caught in an upwelling of her own emotions, pinned. He reached out and so lightly touched her face, stroking the hair back from her cheek. Her whole body reacted to his touch as though his fingers had stroked every nerve. She could not move.

She looked into his eyes and saw into his heart. This was not her Petre who was always there, always her friend, talkative, joking, but always carefully in his place. He had let that distance go. He was stripped of everything. Open, vulnerable.

He was in love with her. She had known this, but she had never believed it.

He leaned toward her slowly. She knew what he was asking. He was going to kiss her. She knew that she should draw away. What she saw in his eyes was too much. For him this was not a simple kiss, a little too much to drink and a little slip across the bounds that usually held him. But she was held, fascinated by what his touch was doing to her.

His lips were almost touching hers. She could taste the sweet mead on his breath. She didn't know how to stop him when she really did want to feel more of the way his touch was making her feel.

When his lips touched hers the pleasure that rushed through her body was almost painful in its intensity. His lips were moist and soft, not at all the hard and needy things of the boys at the school who had tried to force themselves on her. She let her mouth open to his. Her body was filled with heat and exquisite, almost painful rushes of pleasure.

Suddenly he pulled away from her and in the next instant he was on his feet. Is jerked in response. She heard her own breath pant harshly a few times before she controlled it.

"I'm sorry." Petre's voice was husky in a way Is had never expected to hear. "I'm way out of line. I'm sorry." He looked scared, confused and deeply sorry.

Is was fighting her own battle with fear and confusion and shame. In the government school such behavior would be punished if adults caught them. But she was not afraid of that here.

In the school a kiss would have been for any reason except that the person actually cared about her. Sexual advances were all wrapped up in issues of power, ownership, and runaway need - games that Is would not play. There Is would not have cared if she hurt anyone who tried to kiss her.

But this was different. What Petre wanted was more subtle, more complicated and much more frightening.

Petre was still looking at her. For once he didn't seem to have anything to say. Is felt more vulnerable sitting down so she stood up. Petre tried to give her an encouraging little smile. It didn't quite work.

"Are you all right?" he asked her.

She nodded. He seemed more like the familiar brotherly Petre now and the fear and confusion Is felt had taken care of her other bodily reactions.

"Will you forgive me?"

His question surprised her. "I . . . wanted it too."

Petre looked away.

"I don't know how it is for you but for me it wouldn't be what I wanted if we just ..." A vague hand motion said what he meant.

"I apologize," he said, speaking softly again. "I didn't mean to . . ." and he stopped himself, searching for the truth of what he hadn't meant to do. "I didn't mean to fall in love with you."

Touched by the sense of wonder in his voice, Is couldn't speak

"I know you are in love with John," Petre continued. "I know he loves you. I wouldn't do anything to hurt him. Or you." He tried a little grin. "I was . . ."

The boyish shrug of his shoulders expressed the way he had been helpless, the way Is had been helpless too.

She didn't know why Petre thought she loved John. She never spoke about John. As for John loving her, he couldn't have told Petre that. But Is couldn't ignore the hope she felt, even as she was telling herself it was all false.

"I'd uh . . . I'll walk you home," Petre said.

She nodded. She knew he would not touch her, would not lose himself again. What she had seen was the truth in his heart.

That made her sad. A precious thing had been offered to her and would never be offered again.

She would go away and never again feel the way he had made her feel, not just his touch but the way he had looked at her - to be loved like that. She would like to feel that, again and forever. She would like to live in that kind of embrace.

Instead she would hurt him by the simple fact that she did not have the same depth of feeling for him that he had for her. It was scary to have that kind of power over him.

She did not want it.

And she did want it. She wanted to be loved by him even if she didn't love him as much. She wanted to have that power over him, and she loathed the part of herself that felt that way.

They were almost to her tent. She stopped walking.

"Petre. . ."

She was keenly aware of his presence. She did not know what she could say. She did love him but not the way he felt about her.

"Thank you."

She felt his surprise. "For what?" he asked, and since the question seemed real she gave him a real answer.

"For being such a good friend. For looking out for me when it wasn't in your best interests. For showing me things. For *talking* to me." But those were things that all of his people did for her. What Petre offered was more important to her. And much more dangerous for him. "Thank you for . . . loving me."

The smile he gave her was genuine and the spring was back in his step.

"I will always . . . be your friend," he said.

"Yes," she said. He was telling her he would still be here if she came back from the Mirror, and whether he could have her or not, he would still love her no matter what happened. It gave her strength.

Chapter 16

Is rode Lark ahead of the creaking wagons. John rode on her right, and Ondre drove the first wagon. A young couple drove the second wagon, and the others of their group followed behind with more wagons and extra horses.

The Splitting of the Ways had begun. Is occasionally looked back. The plains were covered with similar parties heading out in all the directions of the compass.

Petre had gone out with a group of scouts. The Hluit were putting out more scouts than usual to keep an eye on any Alliance troop movement.

"Everyone trains at scouting," Petre had told her. "It's a good way for young adults to earn status. You have to be able to survive on the land alone or in small groups for extended periods. There are dangers. The Blueskins are always ready to pick off an unwary scout or at least give him a good beating. And of course wild animals and the elements are a challenge. We like to feel that any one of us can survive on his or her own under any conditions. We like to think that everyone can find their way around and avoid trouble."

He had told her that scouting and infiltrating the Alliance were the two biggest tests that young people routinely put themselves through. He had done both. Although he had not been a spy exactly he had learned to pass as an Alliance citizen, get through the gates, meet at a certain point with other "infiltrators" and get out again. It was training in the "courageous use of skills," as he had put it, and it was one of the ways the Hluit got information out of the Alliance.

But Is knew that his decision to go away now was complicated. Of course he wanted to help his people, and he had told her he was a good scout. But she suspected he also needed to be away from her and doing something dangerous to keep from thinking about her too much. Although it might not match the danger that she and John were riding into, at least it would relieve some of the pressure he must feel. If he could not take this risk with her, he could take another risk and contribute something rather than sit and wait.

There was something else too, though Petre was not going to say it. Even if Is and John lived through whatever happened at the Mirror, Petre would still lose her to John. So Is suspected that going away on scouting duty was Petre's way of beginning to make the separation. He was too close to her, too much in love with her. He was trying to do the honorable thing.

"You know if there was anything I could do to help I would be going with you," he had told her and she had known it was true. "But John thinks it should be just the two of you, and Lark and Celeste."

They had explained to her how the Mirror wasn't exactly a solid "thing" in a solid location. Each berserker had to take a different path to find it. If Petre, or Ondre, or anyone tried to come with her and John they might keep them from finding it. Or, at the very least, they would change the complexion of what they did find.

There had been several sessions between Ondre and John, and between Petre and John where both men had tried to persuade John that they should go with him. John had used his best body language to show them that he loved them and appreciated their offers but no, they could not go with him. That was clear.

When Is asked John if she should go with him he had gotten tears in his eyes and come close to one of his hysterical outbursts. It was obvious that he did not want to expose her to risk but he needed her for something he could not explain. He would not ask her to go, but he did not forbid it as he'd done with the others.

Ondre had tried to explain it to Is. "Lark may be the key to finding the Mirror and we know Lark has taken Celeste with him to Amil's cabin so he may take her to the Mirror. Because you're riding Lark and because he's not fully trained he may not fight the Mirror, and John may have his chance to do whatever he is going to do. The two of you belong together in some way on this. I think you were given some information John needs. Hopefully, when the time comes, it will fit in somehow." But Is didn't feel as though she knew anything that would help.

For the first few days, while she and John traveled with this splinter group, there was much work to do. There was hay to cut, turn for drying, or stack for winter caches. The work was hard, and in the evenings everyone sat around the campfire talking, or just staring, until they rolled out their sleeping bags and slept.

Alene had not come with them. People said she and John had broken up.

In their group there was a young couple who was deeply in love but not yet married. They would live the winter together before they decided whether to marry or not. Then they would need at least one couple, and one elder, to stand up for them before the clan would accept their marriage. The girl, Bonice, explained all this to Is. They had come with Ondre and Ellie's group because theirs was one of the most envied marriages. The couple hoped to learn from them, and it seemed to Is, they thought if Ondre and Ellie gave their approval, the success of their own marriage would be guaranteed.

Is asked Bonice what they would do if they didn't get that approval.

"We'll go on living with each other as long as we want.

"No one cares?"

Bonice gave her a funny look. "Of course they care."

Is was struggling with her upbringing in the government schools, where sex was a tool to advance oneself, a weapon to hold over others, or a means of winning favor with someone you feared or whose protection you needed. Love was something uncontrollable that sometimes happened and had to be hidden from all adults or they would surely separate the couple completely. Students caught at sex, or suspected of being in love, were punished equally severely. Of course, punishment didn't stop them, just forced the behavior underground and gave it even more power.

Is had never imagined a society in which a sexual relationship between two young people would be openly tolerated by adults. She was often present when Bonice discussed her relationship with Ellie, and there didn't seem to be anything Bonice couldn't talk about. The couple practiced contraception with lady's root and a careful accounting of the days of the month.

One of the other people in the group was an old lady. She had family of her own, but she had opted to come with Ondre's group for some reason Is didn't understand and was too inhibited to question. The woman was too old to be much help at anything except taking care of a baby that belonged to one of the other married couples. Surely she would be a burden to the group. Is watched carefully, but she could detect no animosity toward the old woman for her helplessness.

There was also a teenage girl, Ahl, who had a crush on Ondre. This worried Is. It was obvious to her, so it must be apparent to Ellie and Ondre. Ellie treated the girl as though she were fully adult and her equal in every way. Ondre treated her with a beautiful balance of love and discipline that Is admired. She sometimes compared his response to the way Riding Master Masley would have acted. To have had that kind of power over a young girl's emotions would have brought out the worst in the Riding Master. He would have either taken advantage of her, or blatantly and hurtfully rejected her. Is found herself loving Ondre for the way he was behaving.

She watched John most carefully, but as discreetly as possible. She did not want people to think she was like Ahl, with a crush on John. She didn't want to bother him, and most certainly didn't want him treating her the way Ondre treated Ahl. She wasn't sure what she did want.

She missed Petre a lot. She thought about how he had said good-bye and worried all sorts of interpretations into it.

"You know my heart will be with you, Is. And when you get back I will come see you." His words had been casual but he'd held her in a hug such a long time Is believed that Petre thought, one way or another, he would never hold her again.

The ground began to get steeper and the grass less thick. Then came the day that the wagons turned aside. Ondre accompanied Is and John another two days.

Is was filled with doubt and fear. She thought Ondre had placed false trust in her. She had tried to tell him so several times. On their last night together, she tried again.

"Ondre, I don't know anything. I can't help John. I wish I could, but I can't. You're sending him with false hope. I don't know anything."

"I'm not sending him," Ondre said softly. He was sitting cross legged by the fire, his boots lying beside him. He glanced at this brother. "And as for false hope, if I were in his shoes, I'd probably have to go too. And if he were in mine, he'd understand how much I don't want him to go."

John met Ondre's words with a look of desperate pleading.

"It's okay," Ondre said. "I'm not trying to stop you. I just want you to know, I love you."

John's answer was to clasp hands with his brother, and a moment later they moved together and embraced. There were tears in John's eyes when he faced Is and that made her less ashamed of her own tears. When she looked into his eyes she seemed to be falling forever and ever into somewhere very beautiful, very important. She couldn't tell if the love she felt was something John was feeling for her, or only something precious within him he let her glimpse.

As always he released her without making any further move that would confirm his feelings. She felt confused and embarrassed.

"Please, try to have faith in yourself." Ondre's voice was so kind, Is couldn't resist looking at him even though he would see her tears.

In the morning she was crying again as they packed up their camp. Without a word, Ondre took her in his arms for a long time. Then he touched his brother's hand, just that one small touch, no words. They were that much at peace with each other's decisions. Then Ondre mounted his mare and headed back the way they had come.

Is watched his back and knew she had been entrusted with an enormous gift, Ondre's love for his brother.

They rode the morning in silence. Sometimes Is's tears ran freely, sometimes they cleared. She didn't realize John was crying too until they stopped for lunch and she rode up beside him. He touched her hand and she was quick to return his grip.

The night was colder than it had been on the plains. They huddled close to their small fire. Is wondered if John felt as lonely as she did. She wished he would touch her.

In the morning John was gone.

Is had never heard a thing. Lark was tied to keep him from following. It seemed strange that he had not whinnied a farewell to the mare. Is felt totally adrift. Why would John leave? There was no sign of anything having taken him against his will. In fact there were no signs at all. His sleeping bag was gone from its place next to hers without so much as a smooth place in the dirt. All of his equipment was gone. She could find no tracks to tell her which direction he had chosen. It was as though he had never been there at all.

Lark wasn't behaving right either. He was not anxious to be off after the mare the way he had been when he'd been left before.

Is had a vague, disquieting feeling, as if she had been here before and knew what to do. But she could not bring it into focus.

Instead of concentrating she sat staring blankly. The air was crisp and still, too cold for insects. Bird songs began slowly. A meadowlark trilled in the distance. After a while it was simply time to go.

Her feet had gone to sleep and she walked around a bit to restart the circulation. She began packing up the camp. She should probably go back to the meadow before the people left, and tell Ondre what had happened.

But when she thought of Ondre, she knew she wouldn't do that. She would try to find John. She tacked Lark and headed out in the general direction they'd been going last night. Lark picked his way leisurely. He gave no sign of knowing which way the mare had gone, or caring to find her.

Their course took them down into a deep cut. It didn't seem odd to run into fog down there, but Lark snorted and hesitated. They moved along to the soft clop of his hooves on the gravelly ground and the rhythmic wuffling of his nostrils, betraying his tension with every step. A crow called harshly once, twice, and the third time sounded too distant for it to have flown that far so quickly. A horse and rider appeared out of the fog, twenty meters to her left.

Lark hadn't seen them yet. Is turned him in their direction, but he still didn't see them. By now Is was certain of who they were. The mare's finely chiseled head was turned toward her and Lark, ears pricked. The man was wrapped in his coat, looking away from them.

Lark continued to edge along, snorting to himself, while Is waited for him to see the mare. John turned and saw her, raising his hand in greeting. Is kept waiting for Lark to snap his head up, pause in surprise, whinny – anything.

He never showed any signs that he was aware of the mare. John was looking in her direction but seemed focused on a spot a distance behind her. The mare also seemed intent on something beyond Is. She did not act as though her best horse friend had come to stand right in front of her. Is's skin began to crawl.

John was undeniably real. "Hello," Is said. But of course he didn't respond.

"Why did you leave?" she asked.

He seemed to be listening intently, looking at something distant, right where she was.

She started to twist around in the saddle, to see what had his attention.

"No. Don't!"

The desperation in his command, as much as the fact that he had spoken, spun Is back around.

"You can speak?" she stammered.

"You have to come back," he said in a perfectly normal voice. "There is only one path. You must make the horse follow that path."

Confused, Is glanced around for the path.

"No!"

The sudden distance of John's voice startled Is into looking at him again. The mare was bearing him away at a rapid pace, but Lark didn't react. There was something wrong with the mare's movement, not in any gait Is recognized. Instead, she appeared to be floating, or sliding, not trotting.

"Take the left turns," John called back to her. "All of them, except the third one . . ." His voice faded and a crow cried over his last words, obliterating them.

"Wait!" But it was too late.

Is sat a moment and tried to collect herself. She could sleep, or blink, or look aside, or a crow would call, and the whole world would be different.

She looked around at the meadow they had been traveling through. There was no path, only a narrow rut that was more of a spring runoff than a trail.

When they came to a fork, she guided Lark left.

The third time the path forked, Is went right. Why not? She had no other clue as to what she should do.

She didn't sleep well that night. She kept sensing a presence nearby. She'd catch herself thinking John was in camp, just down at the river or something, and have to remind herself that he had left.

The morning was crisp and cold, no fog, and Is hit the trail early. It wasn't long before she saw smoke, one thin strand of white rising straight into a sky so blue and so distant it didn't look real. The trail seemed to be leading her to the campfire so she stayed with it. Lark picked up the pace on his own and Is began to hope they would find John and the mare.

The man sat at the fire with his back to her, but Is would never mistake him for John. He was slumped forward, sleeping. But even in that position Is could see the width of his shoulders and imagine his height if he were standing. Her heart wanted to stop. The bright morning threatened to go dark. Perhaps he was just a very large man. She glanced around the camp, searching for clues. No tent. No packs. Traveling light.

She spotted the horse grazing downhill of the camp. War horse. There was no mistaking his massive hindquarters.

At that instant Lark whinnied.

The horse's head came up. He turned on ponderous legs. His bridle hung from the saddle he wore, as though the berserker had stopped here only for a short rest to let the horse graze.

Is glanced at the man, but he had not moved.

The horse came toward them. He lifted his knees and hocks high. His huge feet flattened the shrubby bush-like covering that grew on the rocky soil. He carried his head high. His neck rose out of a chest as broad as a small building. His nostrils flared and his ears were pricked as he tried to make out the nature of what he was approaching. He was taller than Lark and a lot heavier - a mature, fully trained war horse. Is's heart rushed. He was gorgeous, and deadly.

But he wasn't behaving right. He raised and ducked his head as though trying to focus something he was unsure of. Instead of displaying the aggressive posturing Is had expected, he stopped uncertainly like he was having trouble seeing Lark.

Lark wasn't acting right either. He stood alert, head high and ears forward, yet he seemed unaware of another horse. He showed no signs of challenge or intimidation.

The other horse trumpeted a blast through his nostrils. The berserker came out of his doze and onto his feet with impossible speed. Lark never reacted to the abrupt movement, as though he couldn't see the man at all.

Standing, the man was well over seven feet tall and as gigantic as his war horse. His biceps bulged as he gripped a knife that had appeared in his hand. He was looking in the same direction as his horse, but seemed unable to see Is or Lark.

Is began to back Lark down the trail. The other horse snorted and trotted forward a few steps. Is was on the verge of turning Lark to make a run for it when the berserker spoke. His horse halted on the spot.

Is pivoted Lark on his hindquarters and started to walk him quickly away. She watched over her shoulder as the berserker reached his horse and began to put the bridle on, then she pressed Lark with her calves and sent him into a trot. The other horse whinnied once, not as a challenge, but more of a "where are you?" sort of query.

When they had gone a short distance, Is turned Lark off the trail and up among the trees. Before long, she heard the war horse's hooves crunching the gravel as he trotted by below. She gave them a few minutes then dropped down to the trail and continued in the direction she had been going.

She didn't know which way the berserker had been traveling before she found him. When she got to his campfire, she'd stop and check for hoof prints that might tell her.

They rounded the last curve at a trot. There was no sign of the berserker's fire. Is didn't think he had taken the time to put it out. Anyway there should still have been signs of it. There was nothing. Maybe it was around the next bend?

Nothing.

She slowed Lark to a walk. No sense risking his stepping on a rock and laming himself when there was no one chasing them. They were as likely to run into the berserker ahead of them again as they were to have him overtake them from behind.

With that thought, Is lost her calm and began to shake, not because she didn't know *where* the berserker was, but because she didn't know *when* he was.

He could have been as long ago as Amil's cabin. But Amil had seen them, and the berserker hadn't. Although his horse had sensed Lark, neither horse had seen the other well. Is was sure of that. Did that mean the berserker was from longer ago than Amil's cabin, which even the oldest of John's people knew only as a ruin?

She acknowledged then what she had been hiding from herself about John. They were separated, not by distance, but by time. Somewhere - somewhen - had he awakened and found her gone? But when she had seen him again, or some image of him, he had spoken. Did that mean he had found or would find the Mirror and be cured? Is was suddenly lightheaded. If she never caught up to John again, she could at least believe he had been successful.

That thought sustained her for several hours.

Chapter 17

Is was jarred from her thoughts by the trumpeted challenge of a horse. She had heard that sound too many times not to recognize it for what it was – a berserker's horse. The echoes rolled around the valley, confusing the direction of the sound. Lark snapped to a halt, his head up. His ears flicked this way and that uncertainly.

The whinny came again while they were both standing undecided. Lark's head came around to the right and he set off in that direction. For a moment Is considered stopping him. She didn't want to be anywhere near a berserker or his fully trained horse and she didn't want such a horse seeing Lark. But there was something else at work in her mind. What if the berserker had found John? What if he had found the Mirror? She would learn nothing wandering around in the fog. If she was too timid to investigate, she should probably go back to Ondre's people and admit her defeat. They might want to send someone else.

Is let Lark have his head, but when the meadow funneled them into a ravine she pulled him back from the entrance and made him go along the ridge top instead. She didn't want to get trapped in a narrow space with a berserker. From up here they could look down on him and he wouldn't be able to get at them quickly.

She spotted the berserker and stopped Lark. All she could see was horse and rider in a bare spot in the ravine, their attention riveted on the empty air in front of them. The horse was in his most aggressive posture, neck arched, nostrils flared, stepping high as he advanced on the empty air. The berserker had drawn his long saber. He appeared ready to strike. That was all Is could see. She wondered what Lark was picking up with his keener senses.

Lark's head was up and his ears pricked but he did not seem aggressively inclined or frightened. He was merely interested. Is was glad he hadn't whinnied. Suddenly the berserker's horse reared. Lashing out with his front hooves, he plunged forward exactly like a horse fighting another horse. The berserker slashed to the left with his saber. Slashed again. Is couldn't see what they were fighting, but they were definitely fighting something. The horse plunged, wheeled, kicked, wheeled again. The rider struck first to his left, then to his right, parried and stabbed repeatedly.

The hair on Is's arms stood up. She had never seen a war horse or a berserker in full action. The horse was magnificent. There was a beauty to it, yet there was something in her that responded positively to the violence, surprising her.

For several minutes the horse lunged, struck, and kicked with all his might while the rider was equally busy. Then the horse began to tire. His dark bay coat became black with sweat. White foam formed between his hind legs. The whites of his eyes showed. The red lining of his nose was visible as his nostrils stretched wide with his exertions. The man was becoming tired too. His strikes had less power in them, his parries sometimes collapsing in the face of a force Is couldn't see. When that happened, he called on the horse to wheel him away and attack again from a new angle.

The horse reared, lifting his rider clear of some blow Is couldn't see. His hindquarters gave way and he collapsed to a sitting position. In an instant he had righted himself. The rider drove his spurs into the horse's ribs. The horse lunged frantically against the unseen force. The rider swung with his saber and dropped it as though he had hit something so hard he could not hold onto it. Is had expected to hear the clang of metal. All she heard was the harsh breathing of horse and rider.

The rider wheeled the horse away and drew a shorter blade. Is saw him dig his spurs into the horse again. The horse leapt forward, but now his movements were desperate and ill coordinated. She saw the rider's exaggerated aids with bit and spurs to make the horse rear. Before, the signals between the two had been invisible as though they saw and reacted to the same thing with one accord.

Where the beauty of the horse's movements had drawn awe from Is, now she felt awe for the gallantry of the animal. Where the violence had elicited a response in her gut, now it drew sharp pity. Where she had felt an unfocused anger, now that anger was focused against the rider who was going to push his horse to its death.

The horse reared and lost control again, going down on his hindquarters and this time over onto his side. The rider jumped clear. Ignoring his horse's struggle to rise, the berserker attacked the invisible foe on foot. He had lost his blade in the horse's fall and now he struck with his hands and feet.

Is had enough training in Hluit self-defense to appreciate the skill the berserker showed in his attacks. Meanwhile the horse got to his feet. His sides heaved and his nostrils expanded with each breath. Is expected him to stand, head low, legs wide and wait to recover. Instead he charged viciously biting the air to the left of the berserker.

A cold shiver shook Is's body. Horses shouldn't behave like that!

A stallion would fight another stallion, but when beaten he would retreat. But the war horses were crazy. Whatever had been turned on in their brains could not be turned off. She had been feeling sorry for the horse, thinking she should somehow try to rescue it. Now she saw the proof of all her years of training in the Berserker's Barn and the Last Station: you could not handle a berserker's horse after it had connected to its berserker.

The horse fell again. This time he thrashed on the ground and could not get up. It was terrible to see the massive animal down like that. Whatever force the berserker battled, it had moved away from the dying horse. Is felt a deep sorrow for the animal. It had not wanted to be a berserker's horse. Its destiny had been determined by people and Is was as guilty as anyone. In her mind's eye that horse represented all the horses she had ever trained and sent to their deaths. In her heart she knew that horse was also Lark. There was no way to save him from his fate.

To avoid watching the horse die, she watched the man fight. She could not let herself get lost in grief and guilt. She had to stay focused on the danger here and now. The man had grown so tired he could barely lift his arm to deliver another blow. Kicks were out of the question for him now. His technique had vanished. He was a drunken street brawler, staggering, striking wildly without focus and without force. He fell more and more often and took longer to get up, but he could no more quit than the horse could have.

Is locked all emotion away in cold storage. She watched the berserker dispassionately and she began to see something. Whatever he was fighting never struck him. When he fell it was from his own exhaustion.

She had seen him counter blows, and seen his arm give under the impact of those blows as he tired, but he had not been cut. There was no sign of bleeding.

Is could only conclude that he wasn't fighting anything. He struggled to get up off the ground again, looking around for his adversary. Now he saw it. But the adversary didn't take advantage of him. It could have knocked him flat. She could have. Why didn't it? Was it exhausted too? Was it hurt? Or was it nonexistent?

With that final thought, a berserker appeared in front of her up on the ledge, fully armed, rested, and mounted on a horse that seemed equally fresh. Fear raced through Is. She started to wheel Lark to run away.

Lark didn't respond right. That broke through to her. If Lark saw what she saw, he should either be aggressive or scared. At least he would be attentive. Instead he was still staring at the man and horse down in the ravine.

The berserker in front of her advanced, saber drawn. His horse, poised for action, snorted its challenge with every breath. Lark didn't even notice.

Is forced herself to sit still. The berserker's horse reared and came forward on its hind legs. Its front hooves thrashed the air. In an instant it would crash into Lark, sending both of them sprawling into the ravine. Is froze.

Just as the horse should hit her, a strange tingling sensation rushed over her skin and the image disappeared. A moment later Lark shook himself like a dog, waggling his ears, as though he too had felt something strange.

Is glanced into the ravine again. The horse lay flat out on his side now. His hind legs were still kicking, but feebly. She looked away, keeping her emotions frozen.

The berserker was down too. He rolled onto his side to stare up at her. He raised a hand toward her, obviously at great effort.

"Help me."

She could barely hear him. Her skin crawled. She would never have expected to hear a berserker plead like that.

"Help me." It had to be a trap. He sagged back onto the ground, his sides heaving as though breathing were an effort.

For a moment Is felt pity Then all the fear she had ever known broke loose of the control she had slapped on it. She could not go near that man.

Immediately a berserker appeared at her side, unmounted. He reached to pull her from Lark. She felt the heat of his hands on her thigh as he grabbed her. He could easily drag her from the horse. She could smell him and hear the grunting sound he made as he breathed, excited and violent. She swung at his head with all her might, nearly throwing herself from the saddle when the berserker dodged, and startling the heck out of Lark. Until that moment she had sort of forgotten Lark, but now he spooked and snorted, rearranging his legs to balance a rider who was doing crazy, unexpected things.

In spite of her fear, Is realized that Lark did not see, feel, smell, or hear the berserker who was still at her side, ready to pull her from his back. Although Lark wasn't a fully trained war horse, he would respond to anyone suddenly appearing beside him exuding such bad intentions.

Is sat still. The berserker grabbed for her, grinning wickedly. For a moment her mind replayed scenes that were intermixed and inseparable from the memories of watching her mother being raped and killed. It took every bit of her willpower to not move. As the berserker's hand touched her, he disappeared.

Is breathed a shaky sigh of relief and stroked Lark's neck. Twice Lark had saved her from believing in the illusions that had seemed so real to her.

She looked into the ravine again. The horse had stopped kicking, but his hind legs stuck stiffly out from his body, vibrating with quick little jerks. As a fully trained, fully augmented, mature, switched-on war horse, he had seen what his rider had seen: An enemy, probably another berserker mounted on another war horse. Feeding on each other's emotions, horse and rider were connected to a degree that was unreachable by Is's unaugmented senses. They lacked the cognitive powers to realize that what they were fighting wasn't real.

She wondered if the horse could feel or think anything now. Maybe he was already dead. The twitching of his legs could be some leftover reflex that would die away in a few minutes.

Her gaze went to the man. She could see his lips move. "Help me," he whispered. A strange fear took her, not of him exactly, but of his death.

A strangling sound practically at Lark's feet brought her back. John lay there convulsing and vomiting. All the fear she had felt when she had first rescued him came back, tangled with all the love she felt for him now. She picked up the reins, closed her calves against Lark's sides and guided him to step on John.

Lark went without hesitation. He never even picked his foot high, just set it right in the middle of John's chest. The vision vanished as the others had.

Now Is was curious. Purposefully she thought about something nice, her memory of how John had looked that first time he had opened his eyes and seen her - a look full of joy and rapture and love - and how she had felt.

Mistake! Instantly she was so lonely and bereaved she could hardly stand it. The pain racked her body. Her mouth twisted in a silent scream. She slid from the saddle and clung to Lark's neck. There was no image for her to make him step on this time. She had to handle this one on her own.

Ignoring the emotion was impossible. Turning it off, like a water faucet, didn't work. Covering it with other thought - impossible. Balance, she thought, balance it with something else. Without conscious choice she found herself thinking about the people's martial arts.

"Never meet an attack head-on," they had told her. "Do not take the attacker's force into yourself. Turn with it, deflect it around you, return it to the attacker."

The overpowering emotions vanished, replaced by a small sense of triumph. Careful, Is cautioned herself. "To vanquish the enemy is not the goal. Even if you 'win' such an encounter, it is only temporary." She heard Ondre's voice instructing everyone in one of the classes. "You have done nothing to diminish the overall aggression, or the need to place one person over another, or the need to win or lose." His words had seemed so esoteric. Is had just wanted to know how to move, where to place her foot or her arm, how to turn her body to throw someone who was attacking her. She had waited through Ondre's lectures, impatient for practice to begin. But now there was no one to throw, possibly no one to beat, no one to place herself above or below, no need to win or lose.

No more visions and no more exaggerated emotions came. She had not given her attacker anything to work with. Good.

She looked at the berserker again. He was still watching her but he had stopped begging. She turned Lark and rode back to the entrance to the ravine. To the berserker it must have seemed that she was riding away.

She turned Lark up the ravine and when they could see the berserker and his horse again, the horse lay still, no longer twitching. Lark snorted distrustfully and sidled by it. The berserker had collapsed onto his face. Is wondered if he was dead. It took a lot of willpower for her to get off Lark. It took more to kneel down by the man. Surely she did not fear his death. He meant nothing to her. And surely she did not fear he could hurt her. He was too spent for that. Even so, Is was afraid.

Suddenly the man leapt up. He wasn't hurt at all.

No! No! Is cried in her mind. He's nearly dead! Desperately she tried to make that be the reality she saw. Lark snorted and pulled back. Is could not take her eyes from the berserker but she heard Lark gallop away. He had seen this. This was real!

She was desperate enough to think that even though her self-defense wasn't very good yet, she would try. Maybe there was some small chance she'd defend herself. She threw out all doubt and waited.

The berserker seemed to sense the change in her from easy victim to composed prepared defender. He hesitated. Is heard a sound she shouldn't have heard, the slurpy sound of a horse opening his mouth to graze. She laughed. If she turned around she would see Lark right behind her trying to pick the few sparse bits of grass that grew nearby. He had not run away, that was just part of the illusion.

The image of the menacing berserker vanished. Is knelt and touched the real man's neck, trying to find his pulse. It was quick and fluttery. His skin felt clammy. With considerable effort she rolled him onto his back. His eyelids fluttered, but only white showed behind them.

Shock, she thought. What was wrong with him? Exhaustion? He didn't have a cut anywhere. Could a person die of exhaustion? Maybe his heart was damaged. But as long as he was alive, he'd be susceptible to hypothermia, pneumonia, and dehydration. Those things Is understood.

She got her jacket from Lark's saddle and put it over the man's chest. He didn't look comfortable lying on his back. She brought over other pieces of her clothing and pillowed his head.

What if he lived? Would he still be crazy? Was she doing him any favor helping him?

But if she walked away, would it be because she feared him and didn't want him to recover? Or would it be because she believed that leaving was the best thing for him?

She sat back on her heels and observed him. He was the nightmare she'd had when she was treating John, come true.

If she made a decision there was no way to know what motivated it - fear or logic. There was no way to know what was best to do.

She found herself just sitting, staring at nothing, thinking nothing. After a while she stood and stretched. It would be cold when night came on. She should have a fire. She began to search for firewood and realized that the decision had been made, for now.

While Is collected kindling she looked for grazing for Lark. After they had brought the wood back to "camp" Is untacked Lark and took him up the ravine to a place with some grass. He could graze there all night while she sat with the dying man. For a few minutes Is just stood with Lark, watching him attack the grass. She was afraid to leave him. She was afraid of losing him. Her logical mind told her there wasn't much chance of that. The ravine ended not much farther ahead. Lark wouldn't climb up its steep sides. If he went looking for more grass, he'd have to come back by her camp. The ravine was narrow there and she'd see him by the light of the fire. Yet another part of her mind told her that wasn't the only way to lose him. She had awakened from what had seemed like a night's sleep and John had been gone. She wondered if she could lose Lark the same way, maybe even without sleeping. She didn't know what she would do without him. She loved him, and once again he was the only companion she had. He was also her transportation. And how would she tell real from unreal without the horse to guide her?

She was becoming angry and frustrated and scared. How could she make the right decision when she didn't know the rules? She didn't know if Lark could disappear. She didn't know if the man could recover.

Just in time Is recognized what was happening. She calmed herself before her emotions could be used against her again. With sudden clarity she realized that the issue wasn't about making a right decision. It wasn't about whether staying with Lark or the man was more important. It wasn't even about what would give her the best chance to survive. It was about something more important, more subtle, more difficult to define. It was about what was "right." And it was about being brave enough to do what was right.

She left Lark and went back to the camp. It was easy while she could occupy her mind with building the fire. When she checked on the man he seemed to be having trouble breathing. She thought he would be better off sitting up more. She could use her saddle and sleeping bag to prop him up.

He was awfully heavy. There was no gentle or graceful way to do what she had to do. His skin felt cold and clammy as if he were already dead. It took a lot of nerve for her to touch him. To grab hold of him and pull and push to get him situated was almost too much for her.

Finally he looked more comfortable and his breathing sounded less labored. Then Is was glad she'd made the effort.

She took a long time heating water and making a soup of the provisions Ondre had sent with her.

Then it was time to wait. Wait for the man to die or recover enough to give her trouble. Wait for some sort of renewed attack from whatever had attacked her before. Wait for morning. Wait to find out if Lark had disappeared. Wait to become too afraid to go on.

She slipped into the non-waiting mode she used when she hunted and sat a long time without thought. She was in touch with the night and its many small presences. That worked until the man began to snore.

The sound was not an ordinary sort of snoring. It was an unbelievably loud rattling, punctuated by snorts, gasps, and sudden seconds of unnerving silence.

Is tried to reposition him so he could breathe better. His body was even colder than before. She couldn't think of any way to make him warmer. The night was not very cold. The fire was putting out good heat. He was insulated from the ground by her sleeping bag and Lark's saddle.

She was sure he was dying. Well, that should be a relief really, and she could feel good about herself for having tried to help him. She tried to sit and not think again but it was impossible with all the noise the man was making.

She became aware of a new sound within the snoring, sort of like a breeze in the bushes. She'd better cover him more, she thought, if there was a breeze. She was staring at the fire, and the flames were going straight up, as they had all night. There was no breeze. There were no bushes nearby. Then she knew where she had heard that sound before.

She turned slowly to look at the berserker. He was lying, propped against Lark's saddle just as he had been before. She watched the flickering flames make the shadows dance in the background and let her eyes see anything they wanted to see.

The dark man-shapes were all around the berserker, talking in that quick shush-shushing way that sounded like a breeze. They were in constant motion, as though the heat from the fire buffeted them.

One of them was sitting on the berserker's chest. He seemed more stable than the others. Is thought he was sitting cross legged, then she realized that she couldn't see his legs because they were somehow inside the berserker's body. The other man-shapes moved about constantly. They seemed to be caressing the berserker all over.

After a very long time the man stopped breathing. The night was suddenly very quiet. Is could no longer see the dark bodies.

Chapter 18

Hours passed. Is had slipped into her comfortable state of non-thought, non-emotion, when she heard the horse coming. She looked up from the coals, startled that it was close enough to dawn to see shapes away from the fire. The rider's silhouette was very familiar.

John and his mare, Celeste. Is stood up and moved around the fire toward them. John looked at her, at the dark hump the dead horse made, and at the dead man propped up by the fire - equally and without reaction or recognition.

"John," she called. "It's me."

John glanced at her and away again. His mare was looking intently down the ravine. No doubt she could hear Lark down there. John seemed to take his cue from that. He turned her away from Is and headed into the ravine. They were going to pass right by.

Is stepped in front of the mare and Celeste halted, extending her head for Is to scratch. Only then did John believe she was real. He leapt from his horse's back and grabbed Is in a bear hug. She laughed and hugged him hard, trying not to let him crack her ribs.

"It's so good to see you." She thought he would say something in return. The last time she had seen him he could talk perfectly. But he could barely see her then, and she couldn't have touched him at all. Now he was obviously glad to see her, but he didn't speak.

"What's wrong?" she asked. "Can't you talk?"

He shook his head, puzzled that she would think he could.

"The last time I saw you, you could talk."

He shook his head, more mystified. He clearly didn't remember it. It hadn't happened to him yet. Or else it had only been a reflection of him, sent to her by whatever had sent the illusion that had killed the berserker. Why? To lead her here? She saw John's gaze go to the dead horse and the dead man.

"They're real," she told him.

The mare whinnied and a moment later they heard the hoof beats of a trotting horse as Lark approached. Is's heart jumped. Lark had not disappeared during the night. She had to restrain herself from running to hug him. She and John stood back and watched the horses greeting each other. It seemed to Is they were giving each other a thorough investigation. It reminded her of the way dogs sniff their owners to learn where they've been and what they've been doing. She wondered what the horses were learning. Did running into illusions, as they both obviously had, leave some sort of odor?

Is went over to the coals and dug some breakfast mix out of her food pack. Seeing what she was doing, John picked up the water can and headed for the canteen on the mare's saddle. As he passed the dead man, he stopped and looked at him a long time.

The man's eyes had come open. They stared lifelessly into the lightening gray sky. His mouth hung slack and a string of spittle had run from one corner and dried on his face. He looked unloved and uncared for. He had been used and discarded. Is felt slightly ashamed of herself. She should have taken better care of him. John's face registered a deep sorrow. Is imagined he would look that way if he were looking at a child who had died without having had a chance to live. Tears flooded her vision. She had never expected to feel such compassion for a berserker.

While breakfast heated, Is told John about everything she had seen and felt. She told him that what she had learned of his people's martial art seemed to help control the illusions. He nodded often, as though agreeing with the conclusions she had drawn. Sometimes he gave her hand a squeeze of encouragement and, she thought, praise. Until she told him about the dark bodies.

"I think they took what life the berserker had left," she said. "Maybe I should have tried to chase them away. I guess they killed him." She stopped because John caught her hand and shook his head. He desperately wanted to explain something. He began to tremble, dropped his eyes away and took his hands back. Is could see what he was doing, drawing into himself, building walls, regaining control. She had seen this enough to know he had to do it. Otherwise, he would break into his high hysterical laughter. She never wanted to hear that again. But illogically she couldn't let him go either. She reached out and touched his arm.

"I love you." She was surprised at her own words, but John was even more so. His eyes sprang to hers. The emotions of joy, hope, fear, and doubt that ran through them left Is whirling. Then he put his arms around her and drew her against him.

His trembling subsided. She held him for a long gentle time.

She wasn't hungry but she ate because John ate, and because it postponed whatever they had to do next. She felt light and joyful in a way she had only had small glimpses of before. Saying three simple words had released her in some way. How much more would being able to talk release John?

Is could have stayed at that fire with him forever - even with the bizarre company of a dead man and a dead horse – but by late morning John was ready to go. He helped her retrieve her saddle and bedroll from under the berserker. A few late flies had found him. They buzzed out of his mouth as John rolled him on his side to allow Is to get her things. More flies droned up from the dead horse as they rode by. There was nothing worth doing for either of them. Carrion eaters were the next step in the chain.

They rode along in silence, Is letting John lead wherever they were going, until he brought Celeste to a halt in an open meadow. He sat staring intently at something Is couldn't see, and neither horse was responding to it.

"I can't see it," she told John.

He turned and gave her a wan smile. If it was meant to reassure her it didn't work. He dismounted and signaled her to stay where she was as he walked forward.

He stopped and bowed the way his people bowed to one another before they practiced their martial arts together, the way he had bowed to Amil. Is waited for something to happen. She was afraid that John saw some sort of adversary. She was terrified that he would fight and die the way the berserker had. Instead John knelt down on the ground. Then he just sat for a long time as though in meditation.

Is got off Lark and let him graze with the mare. She sat down nearby, keeping her eyes on John in case he needed her help.

She woke, not quite sure where she was or why. Then she remembered and sat up quickly. She couldn't believe she had fallen asleep. She wondered if some trick had been played on her mind. There was no sign of John or the horses, or the meadow. In front of her stood a large reflective building. In all other directions all she could see was thick fog.

Is scrambled to her feet and started to walk toward the building. Almost immediately she was inside it. She didn't think she had taken enough steps to get there and she hadn't opened any doors.

There didn't seem to be anything in the building, yet it wasn't an empty shell. The space was filled with a glistening, foggy stuff, maybe the way the fog outside would look if it were somehow compacted and backlit. Whatever it was felt denser than fog. It wasn't so much like walking through a substance, like water, as it was like moving through an electrical current. But it wasn't that either.

Is gave up trying to figure it out when she saw John. He didn't see her. It was as though he was in another room. Only there were no walls to section this thing off into rooms.

He was kneeling the way he had been when she last saw him, and he was talking. Is couldn't quite make out what he was saying. She could hear his pitch get higher, then lower, and his volume get louder, then softer. She had the eerie feeling that someone was tuning him as they might tune a musical instrument.

Even though she seriously doubted she could do it, she began to walk toward him. He was only a few steps away. He remained at that distance as she walked.

A berserker and his horse appeared in front of her rearing. She flinched back, but they were not attacking her. They were fighting something invisible. She had never seen a video image or a hologram so she recognized what she was seeing as a memory. It was not her memory, so she concluded it was the building's memory. That changed her thinking about the building. It had seemed to be a structure. Now she wondered if it were a living thing, this Mirror-non-mirror. A mirror reflects things, she thought, perhaps it held the reflection of everything it had ever seen.

She continued to walk, passing more berserkers and more horses. They were all fighting something. They were as three-dimensional as life. She could hear their heavy breathing and smell their sweat. They were more than reflections. How could there be that much room in here? Then she thought, *how much room is in a memory anyway?*

Some of the berserkers were from the distant past. She recognized their costumes and tack from pictures that had hung on the walls of the indoor arena. The weapons they carried had always been the same. But the berserkers and their horses had gotten bigger, more powerful and better trained as time progressed.

This made Is realize how much research and development had gone into improving the berserkers and their horses. She wondered why nothing had been done to improve their weapons and answered herself, *because they were never fighting against anything.*

Distracted by her thoughts, she blundered into one of the images. The same tingling sensation she had felt before shot through her. All the hair on her body stood on end, but the slashing sword did not cut her. In fact berserker and horse dissolved into a much more complex and confusing image. Part of it was similar to the words and letters and numbers that had been so off-limits to her, part of it was intense feeling. A strange curiosity swept over her. As though from someone else's perspective she experienced the desire to learn what made humans and horses work. At her command were ways to experience these animals most thoroughly.

So Is brought the Mirror's abilities to bear on exploring the thing that interested her most: The augmented psychic connection between horse and rider. If she could understand how that connection was forged perhaps she could break Lark free from it. Momentarily she was engulfed in a white flash of loud light. The sound rattled inside her skull. It didn't occur to her to question how a light could be loud. It didn't hurt, exactly, and she wasn't afraid until later because at that moment there wasn't room to be afraid.

For a long while - or perhaps nanoseconds - her mind worked completely differently from any way she'd ever used it before. Thinking seemed a totally alien process.

Then the light/noise became too much for her small brain to hold. She felt it go crashing down her spinal cord and out into every nerve in her body. That did hurt as each nerve lit up with the screaming light.

If her skull had been a cage, her skin was absolutely no barrier to the light/noise. It flowed out every nerve ending, right through the pores of her skin and was gone. She was left behind, physically and mentally shaken, gasping from relieved pain, and clutching frantically at the fading wisps of white-hot understanding.

The best her ordinary mind could grasp as that there was something like a "fast" station which had been shrunk down to fit inside the berserker's head, and was somehow powered by the death process itself. The horse's energy, and its death agony, added to the strength of the transmission. But it was the rider's mind that went back and was received by someone the Mirror thought of as the Watcher.

There was more, much more, but Is couldn't take any more. If she didn't stop and organize what she already had something would surely snap and she'd forget everything.

She tried to walk away. Her body reeled drunkenly as though under the physical impact of the blows her mind had taken. She staggered and fell to her knees . . . and somehow right through the floor of what had appeared to be a solid building set solidly on the solid ground. When she looked around, the "building" was sitting on the meadow apparently the same distance from her as it had been when she had started to walk toward it before.

A moan drew her attention in the opposite direction.

John!

He was lying only feet away from her, huddled into himself, moaning as though he was experiencing deep pain.

She scuttled to him on all fours.

"John! John!" He didn't seem to be aware of her. He looked right through her and began to talk as he had been talking in the "building." Only now it was a quick dull monotone, all in one pitch, all at one volume. Is grabbed him by the shoulders and shook him, trying to stop him, trying to make him see her.

His eyes seemed to look a little more at her instead of beyond her. She couldn't be sure. He kept talking. He might as well be speaking a foreign language. She could understand the words but not their meanings. She had wanted so badly to hear him talk, and now all she wanted was for him to stop.

She began screaming at him, shaking him by the shoulders . . . and caught herself. The monologue had stopped. He looked *at* her.

Her nerves had had all they could take. Now she was the one going to pieces. He pulled her against him and held her, hard.

When she had herself under control she sat back from him. He looked at her with sane gentle eyes. She would have preferred to just leave it like that. She didn't need to hear him speak ever again if it was going to be that awful monotone but she felt compelled to know.

"Can you talk? Normally?

"I ... think." His voice was hoarse. He had to clear his throat. But the grin that spread across his face was gorgeous. Is was ready to celebrate with him.

"Is," he said and caught her hands. "I've got so much to tell you. You must understand. You have to make Ondre understand." His eyes bored into hers, pleading, demanding.

But all Is understood was that if she was the one who had to make Ondre understand, then John wasn't going back to his people. He was going to go inside the Mirror again.

Her fear was as hot as the light that had crashed through her nerves, as sharp as a knife ripping her open, bowels to heart. The Mirror would kill him. She was certain of it, and she knew with the certainty of her pain that she could not stop him.

He began talking rapidly, urgently.

"I'm so sorry to have to put you through this, but you're the only person I can do it with. We have to go back into the Mirror. You and I can connect the way a berserker and his horse are connected. It has to be you because we've already done it partly, that's how you took me to Amil's cabin, you and Lark." He got the rush of his words stopped. Gently he touched her face.

"Isadora," he said each syllable of her name slowly, delighting in saying them as she was delighting in hearing them.

"I better start at the beginning," he said. Then he smiled. "Thank you for helping me when it must have seemed like the worst thing to do, and thank you so much for hanging in there when I must have seemed totally insane. I'm sorry for all the times I frightened you."

Is had already forgiven anything that needed forgiving. She had nothing to say.

"I want to tell you what I've learned about the Mirror. It's an experiment the Alliance set up. It's a computer ... a thinking machine.

"But it's more than just a com...a machine. It doesn't just do, or think, the things it has been programmed, trained, to think; it can teach itself new things, and new ways to think." He watched to see if she would understand. The government school would never have taught her about computers.

"I felt how it thinks," she said, and she told him about her experience inside the Mirror. He watched her, deep excitement in his eyes, energy like electricity springing from him.

"If the Alliance made it, then why do they keep sending the berserkers against it?" she asked.

"Because they created it especially to kill berserkers, and they created the berserkers especially to be killed by it. That is the berserker's whole purpose, to be killed by the Mirror. But it doesn't just kill them, Is. It downloads ... it keeps them . . . in holo images. . . you saw, complete images. Sound, sight, smell, everything. And it can project them.

"Interactive holo images of complete downloaded personalities," he said to himself.

The words could have been a language Is had never heard before, but her experiences had given her their meaning.

"It keeps them alive after it's killed them."

"Yes! Exactly! What else could command so much of the Alliance's attention, so many resources, such secrecy for so long? They are trying to create life after death. They want to live forever."

Is felt the truth of it. The highest of the high government officials wanted to live after death, and of course they would keep that for only a select few. They would rule forever. No good would come of it.

"I have to go back in there," John said. "We have to know how far they've succeeded."

Is rebelled. "It will kill you," she practically screamed at him. "What good will it do you to know? You'll be dead."

He met her eyes. He didn't refute what she'd said. He believed it might kill him.

"It will not matter," he said about his own death. "You can tell Ondre what I've learned."

Fear came up from places Is hadn't known were inside her.

"I don't understand half of what you're saying," she protested. "I won't be able to explain it right."

"There is a way," John said, and then he changed it to, "I think there is a way. If you come into the Mirror with me, I think I can forge a link between us . . ." Is didn't let him finish.

"I was in there with you," she cried. "You were totally unaware of me and I couldn't reach you."

"I was fixing the linkages in my mind. I was busy. And I was not totally unaware of you."

"You were fixing yourself? The Mirror wasn't doing that to you?"

"No. I don't think it realized we were there. It is sort of 'blind' to . . . to physical manifestations - us, you and me and our horses - unless we respond to its probes, its holo manifestations. It couldn't 'see' either of us because we responded in ways outside its experience, its programming. It's sort of like the way you can't see the pictures in written words because you have not been trained, programmed, to read."

"But you said it trains itself."

"Yes," John answered slowly. "It may train itself to see me. Or it may not. But meanwhile it is also a machine. I used some of the machine-like aspects of it to repair what had been done to my mind, and it ignored me like a building ignores a rat wandering around in the basement."

Is had had the same impression. She was ignored as she walked through the Mirror's memory/thoughts.

"Could you make it 'fix' Lark?" She saw John's eyes change.

"I don't know. That's really a different sort of fixing. Lark has a chip, a physical thing, in his brain. I can't remove it. I might be able to tell it never to turn on . . ." His voice faded into nothing. His eyes came back from staring at something Is couldn't see.

"Is, I think it's more likely I'd kill Lark than help him." He met her eyes until she lowered hers. He began to talk again, believing that he owed her more explanation.

"In my mind, they used a ... light, to damage very select areas. I couldn't repair that physical damage, but I could bypass it. It was a matter of reestablishing pathways that used to be there, only putting them in different places. Like making new roads around obstructions." His eyes questioned if she understood. "I was fairly confident because it is my own mind. But the horse's mind is so different. I'd be lost in there. And what if he panicked inside the Mirror? The Mirror would notice that. It would do to him what it's done to the other horses." John shook his head. "Is, I'm sorry. I don't think I can do it. I'm afraid to try. I'm afraid of ruining the chance we do have. A chance to explain to my people what's going on, a chance to, maybe, stop it."

Is understood, one horse's life stacked against something enormously important to the Hluit people, something so enormous that John was ready to die to see it through.

"I know how much he means to you. I'm sorry."

"I understand," Is said but there was deadness in her voice that hid her emotions. One horse, who had been bred and trained and destined to die from the beginning, weighed against the need to find out what the Alliance was really up to and warn Ondre, Ellie, Petre, and all the Hluit.

"When your people know what is happening, what good will it do them? Can they stop it?" They were a few hundred nomads against the Alliance and all its troops and technology.

John looked away. "I don't know that yet, Is. I do know that sometime, in some way we are going to have to get leverage over the Alliance. They will not let us live in peace forever. There could be something in all this stuff with the Mirror that will give us that advantage."

But you'll be dead, she thought, her eyes clouding with tears.

"Will you help me?" he pressed her. "It has to be me, Is. I know enough of the language they programmed this computer with that I can probe it. I need to know, Is. My people need to know."

She could understand the need for knowledge. She had always wanted to learn more than was allowed her. But she was afraid; and she did not want to lose John.

"I don't know how to help you."

"If you come inside the Mirror with me, I think I can forge a link between us. That's another 'tool' function the Mirror has. That's how it makes the holo images interactive. If I open that link from my side, I think you will be able to respond. I think you'll be able to hear my thoughts, then you'll come back outside the Mirror and you'll 'hear' the things I learn. As I go deeper into its programming, it will become more dangerous. Sooner or later I think it will notice me. At that point I may be able to have a dialogue with it, or I may not. But you'll be outside. You'll be safe, and you can take everything I've learned back to Ondre."

"Will it ... download . . . you, like the berserkers?"

"Possibly."

"Then you won't really be dead?"

"I don't know. Those images are not really 'alive' either."

"You could be trapped like that. You want that?"

John shook his head. "I don't know enough. I would say if I'm trapped like that, I am dead."

Is could tell he hadn't said everything. She waited for him to continue, and finally he said, "Remember the dark bodies?"

"Yes?" Something flipped over inside Is. "What are they?"

"I think they are what's left of the berserkers after the Mirror disassembles them. The Mirror doesn't download everything into the holo images. There's something leftover, the spiritual part of the man, I guess."

"Are the dark bodies alive then?"

"Sort of, at least more so than the holo images."

"So has the Mirror succeeded? Has it created life after death for the Alliance."

John hesitated before he replied. "I would say it has not completely succeeded. Yet. I need to know more, Is. How do the dark bodies get created? They're like ghosts. Real ghosts. All people who die don't have ghosts. At least not ones we can see and hear. What's really going on here? How much is the Mirror's doing? And how much does the Alliance know? They didn't seem to know anything about the dark bodies. In all the time I was a spy I never heard, read or saw anything about them. Could the Mirror be hiding the dark bodies from the Alliance? If so, why?"

Is remembered the night the dark bodies had come and surrounded John, caressing him. "They communicated with you?"

"Yes. Not well. And there was danger. They have little of what you might call life energy. They exist in sort of a dream state, physically as well as mentally. To get enough energy together to communicate they must draw on the life forces of a living person."

"They could kill that way?"

"Possibly."

"Like the dog?" Is wanted to know. "He looked dead the whole time you were with the dark bodies. But he wasn't really . . ." She trailed off in confusion.

John gave a little laugh. "That dog is very interesting. You know, I never did see him."

That shocked Is. She had never questioned the dog's reality. He had seemed just like any other dog to her. She remembered trying to chase him back to Amil's cabin. He had dodged around Lark until Lark had under-stood the game and pinned his ears and gone after the dog as a horse will go after a cow.

"Lark saw it," she said to defend herself.

"I don't doubt you," John said. Then he was quiet for a long time until Is asked him what he was thinking.

"Crazy stuff," he said and wanted to stop. But when he saw that Is real-ly wanted to know, he continued. "Ondre told you that Amil and his cabin don't exist in our lifetimes. But when you and I went there, we could both see them, but when the dog followed us only you could see it. And Lark," he added, shaking his head.

"What does that mean?"

"I don't know. But maybe since you and Lark are the ones who can cross time boundaries, and you were able to bring me and Celeste to Amil's, maybe you somehow brought the dog across time when we left Amil's and returned to our own time."

Is shook her head. "I didn't do anything, just sat on Lark. Maybe it was something Amil did. We should go back and try to find answers there, not go inside the Mirror again," Is suggested.

"Maybe," John said pensively, "and maybe I'm totally wrong."

Is jumped on his hesitation. "You should wait. We should go back to see Amil before you go into the Mirror."

John was silent a long time thinking it over while Is held her mental breath. Then he shook his head.

"Amil might have some answers. We might even be able to find him again. But I can't take the time now. I have to do this now. I have the right knowledge. I understand this computer better than anyone. I suffered to get here and now is the right time. I can't explain why, but I know it. Do you understand?"

Reluctantly Is nodded. This was too important for lies. "Yes." Her voice was thick. She understood about right timing. It was part of the chain, like death, it came when it would.

"Isadora," he said soft-voiced, "I never wanted to get you involved in this. I wish I could do this alone. But I can't. I would have chosen someone else, even Ondre over you. He would do it in a heartbeat, but as much as I love him I don't have the same connection with him. You and I have something special, some entwinement that seems to be partly of the horses and even the land. Do you feel it?"

She nodded slowly. She had never been in love before. She didn't know if this was different from what other people felt. She thought of Petre who offered her love and made her feel good. But there had never been any contest in her mind between him and John. She was attached to John, connected, entwined. Nothing else drew her.

"You don't know how much I wish I didn't have to ask this of you," he said gently. "You've been hurt enough. But," he hesitated wanting desperately to explain so she would understand, "it might be precisely because of that pain that you have to be the one. I've seen you do things no one else can do. The ruin was a cabin when you were there, the Blueskins have a legend about you, you heard the dark bodies, you withstood the Mirror's attacks, and escaped its herd fogs." He spread his hands wide to show the enormity of the things she had done. "You've been inside the Mirror. I know of exactly one other person who ever got that close to the Mirror and lived to tell about it." He gave her a crooked little smile. "Me." Then serious, he said, "And we're connected, aren't we, you and I, somehow? This link might work between us when it might not work with someone else."

Is could only nod. The lump in her throat was too big.

"I love you," he said simply. "I wish this could have been different." Then he drew her against him and held her a very long while.

Is understood that more than life itself John wanted to know about the Mirror. Is could understand not caring about living. Many times in her life she had wished to be dead. If the Mirror killed her - she was willing to risk that. But she didn't have much to lose. John did. He had his people and their love, and Ondre's love. If she had had such things she was not sure she would be able to give them up. She did not even want to give John up, and they had not had anything but a very strange and mixed-up friendship. It was one thing to desire knowledge. It was another for John to be willing to lose everything he had in the pursuit of that knowledge. Is did not think she had that kind of courage, but she would help John because he did have it.

There was no need for more talk. John stood up and took her hand and they walked into the Mirror.

It looked the same. There was the same silvery-gray fog that wasn't fog that tingled her skin. But Is thought they had entered a different "room" this time. There were no berserker memories to see here, and it felt different. The tingling wasn't just on her skin, it was somehow inside her mind. She felt as if she wanted to scratch but didn't know where she itched. It was intensely unpleasant. She began to feel very irritated. She wanted to pull away from John. She wanted to leave this stupid place. It was hard to remember why she was supposed to stay. She tried to focus her attention on John. It was important that she help John, but she was in a strange mindset where emotions were just an irritation.

In an instant all that changed. She was swept by one emotion after another - rage, terror, love, sorrow - complete with their physical manifestations in her body. Fortunately each one only lasted a moment. She did not have time to act on any of them.

Then she became calm, suspended somehow with no emotion and no thought. Radiant. Silent. Cessation of all.

That lasted an amount of time that was neither long nor short.

Suddenly an "other" presence swept her with an embrace so loving, so radiant, so filled with joy it was indescribable. Is lost herself in that union.

. . . This is of me, he tried to instruct her, and she could hear/feel how there was something other-than-self. That is of the Mirror, and she could see/taste how that was so. This is how to access memory, he told her, and she was flooded with sight, sound, smell, sensation in a confusing blur. This is how to sort your memories from mine, he instructed her, but she didn't try. She was inside his mind and his heart not just his memories. She could find out how he really felt about her. Was he, deep down, just like the men in the Alliance? Was Ondre? Was Petre?

She felt how he only meant to let her in so far but she plunged ahead. He resisted her until he understood that this was about trust. Could she trust him the way she had not trusted anyone since she was a small child? He did something in his mind and the shield went down, she was engulfed in love – his love for her, for Ondre, Petre and all of his people, but it was not just his love for them it was also their love for him. She was awed into silence, embraced in a place of reverence she had not imagined could exist. She rested there in a total and complete rest where no fear or worry could reach her.

In time, she felt healed and a high-spirited reckless joy swept her. She was having fun being John. This was how it felt to be a boy having boy problems. This was how it felt to be loved by a family, to have real friends, teachers who loved you, to have love and support everywhere.

Is knew how it was to be a boy becoming a man, a man with a woman, and a man without one. She knew his worst disasters, his secret fears, his hopes, and the things that shamed him.

A long time passed before she reined herself in. By then she'd run through all of John's most intimate, most tender and most embarrassing moments. Through it all he hadn't made a move to stop her.

Now she was ashamed of herself. She had had no right to take all that. She wouldn't want him running through her memories that way. She wanted to withdraw.

He showed her how to do that too.

From the distance of the encapsulated other-excluding self Is formed around herself, she extended a tentative touch. Yes, he was still there. She formed an apology. He accepted it, she thought. It was hard to tell. Everything was getting very distant. It was beginning to be a little frightening. She had started the process of building a wall around herself but it kept on building.

Then she felt him push against her wall. He was seeking a way into her sanctuary. He would break in and take from her what she didn't want him to know. Abruptly she was no longer afraid of the walls building around her, she wanted them to increase. She felt him try again to reach her but she would not let him. Sudden sharp pain shot through her. Blinding light. Searing heat. No oxygen. *This is how to let me reach you,* he said in her mind and was gone.

She clung to her shattered walls, shaken, frightened, violated. Nothing else happened, but she was afraid of the power John had shown he had over her. She had always hated the power men had over women. Because he was stronger, because he could rape, she had to fear him. After an immeasurable period of time, after she was done being angry with him - with all men - she got angry with herself. It was her fear that gave men power over her. If she took away that fear, she took away that power.

How could she not fear the kind of violation she had just been through?

How could she not fear rape?

She worked on these things a long time. Mental understanding was a start, but only a start. She could not erase the fear with it. Action was needed.

She used the information John had thrust into her to open her shield. Yes, he was still there. She could bridge across to him.

He was full of apology. *I was going to lose you. You wouldn't have known how to get back out of there. I'm sorry. I should have taught you the bridge before the wall. I really didn't know how much I'd hurt you. I felt I had to do it. I'm sorry . . . sorry . . . sorry . . .*

She withdrew and he didn't try to follow. Okay, that had been very brave of her, she thought, cynical of herself. She could reach out and withdraw. Very brave. So why was she still afraid? Because that wasn't good enough. Is knew what she had to do.

She reached out tentatively and touched him. His quick joy and profuse apology reached her. She gave him a bit of a mental push, akin to saying, "Shut up," startling him into silence.

When she had his attention she began disassembling the wall until she had the link opened wide.

You don't have to do this, he pleaded, *the link is good enough.* She could feel him trying to hold back. He wasn't able to. He came flowing into her, into all her most intimate moments, her fears, her embarrassments, her hopes, her woman-ness.

The memories washed through them - sight, sound, smell, and pain. Her mother's blood was as vivid as Riding Master Masley's touch. She laid it all bare and she was defenseless and very, very sorry. John would see how twisted and frightened and truly ugly she was. She could never be someone as beautiful, confident, loving, or loved as any one of his people. He would abhor her.

He was saying something over and over again. There were no words, yet his message was clear. He cared for her. He forgave her the things she hadn't forgiven herself. He deeply appreciated her allowing him to do this. He understood her fear, and the courage it had taken to let him see her this way. He cherished her beauty.

Beauty? she asked.

Yes, her uniqueness. Her intricateness. Her difference. She accepted that because that was the way she welcomed and loved him.

His joy sparked hers. They were together in their intimacy a long time.

We must go on now, he finally said.

Yes. It wasn't possible for either one of them to be sad. They rearranged the linkage until it was more distant and more formal, more like speech. But what they had shared was inside both of them.

How do I go? she asked him, and suddenly she was falling. She landed on the meadow. There was no fog, no Mirror. Both horses grazed nearby.

John!

Wait. Please. Though she couldn't see him, he was inside her mind.

Chapter 19

Is rode Lark. The mare followed behind. She'd put John's saddle and all of his equipment on the mare. His people never wasted anything.

The meadow where she had last seen Ondre's group was empty, hay stacked neatly. The horse droppings were old and cold.

The wagon tracks were easy to follow. At the edge of a bowl overlooking a meadow Is spotted three scouts. They stood with their horses silhouetted against the skyline so she would see them. She let Lark move toward them at his own pace. Only two scouts came down to ride with her. The other had disappeared over the ridge. They could see John's empty saddle. They didn't say anything. Is left it like that.

The next day Ondre met her. His mare looked as if he had ridden all night. He didn't question her, just rode up and dismounted. After a moment Is dismounted too and he took her in his arms and held her. He didn't say a word. When he let her go he stroked Celeste's face. Is saw the tears in his eyes as he remounted his own horse.

She remembered the first time she had seen Ondre, galloping to meet his brother, and how they had hugged and laughed, and the spontaneous, playful teasing. For the first time in what seemed a very long time she thought of Petre.

The people came out of the camp to watch them approach. This time no one ran from the crowd to welcome John. No children cantered out on reluctant brood mares. Is watched as if this were happening to someone else, cataloging the similarities and differences. Even Lark seemed to feel the difference. Although he arched his neck and whinnied a few times, he did not prance and rear. He was tired and underfed. Is stroked his neck, promising him better care now.

Ellie appeared at her side when she dismounted. "I'm so sorry," she said, with her usual warmth and compassion. Is let Ellie hug her. Other people touched her, saying gentle things to her.

"Can we talk now?" she asked Ellie.

"Wouldn't you rather rest first?"

Is shook her head. *Rest?* Rest was not something that applied to her anymore. There was sleep with its dreams of horror, and painful awakenings. There had been hours of sitting, doing nothing, staring at nothing, and not caring, but not rest. There had been hours of sitting in the saddle, hypnotized by the horse's steady rhythm, thinking nothing, but not rest.

She heard Ellie speak to other people around them. She watched Ondre give the horses to a young man, who led them away to care for them. John's mare would be Ondre's now. Is felt an unexpected tug of pain, but it was gone in an instant. She would never feel anything again. She slipped Lark's saddle off and let him follow the mares. She let Ellie lead her. She drank the water Ellie gave her. She looked at the people who spoke to her. She tried to see them. She tried to respond. She couldn't remember their names. They didn't seem real. She did not seem real.

She realized people were seated, waiting for her to speak.

Is began to talk. She heard her voice as though it were someone else speaking. She listened to herself telling them about finding the Mirror. She told them how she and John had gone inside it and John had used it to fix his speech. She told them what he had wanted to tell them: The Mirror was made by the Alliance for the express purpose of killing the berserkers.

"He had found that out as a spy, what he didn't know was why. What purpose the whole thing had. The knowledge was off-limits to him as a research scholar. He was just supposed to do what he was told. There were people, higher up, who knew what it was all for.

"John got caught trying to find out more. The Alliance probably didn't realize he was a spy from the Hluit. They did what they usually do to people who want to know too much. They made it so he couldn't tell anyone anything he learned. He said it was a refined version of cutting out a person's tongue. They can do it without ruining the person's mind. In some cases the person can keep right on working for them; they haven't ruined their 'tool.'" Is listened to her own expressionless voice and felt none of the anger and horror she knew other people were feeling.

"They didn't try to kill John until he tried to escape. He would never have eaten the poisoned trail rations if he had stayed there and continued to do his job. It was sort of a trial and execution all wrapped up in one."

She found Ondre's face in the group. What his brother had been through should have been enough. John had shown enough courage by getting into the Alliance and spying on them. He had suffered enough. He did not have to go to the Mirror. No one would have blamed him. No one would even have known. But that had not been enough for John. Even after he had repaired the linkage in his brain and could have returned to his people and told them what he knew, he had needed to do more.

"John wanted to learn more," she told Ondre. "He was in the position to learn the most, the fastest. He thought it was very important for all of you. He knew there was a good chance the Mirror would kill him. But he knew I would report everything to you." She could have refused. She could have run away from him. She could have saved his life. Ondre must know that.

But there had been the other thing, the way John had made her feel. What he had done stemmed from a feeling of incredible love for his people and gratitude for all he had been given. It was right. It was more important than his life. In the end he was not afraid. His life was joyously given because of his devotion to his people, his appreciation for what the Hluit had made of their society, and his need to protect that.

While Is had been with him she had been caught up in his feeling of optimism and gratitude. She had experienced love and joy and generosity the way John did. She had understood the rightness of his actions.

Now it was all gone, changed to pain and then to deadness inside her. Even her memory of that feeling no longer made sense.

She had stopped talking. People were waiting.

"I'm sorry." Her lips moved. There was no sound in the words.

Ondre came across the circle to her. He took her hands. She could not bring herself to look away from his eyes.

"You did the right thing for John. I know him. He needed to do what he did. You gave him a great gift by understanding and helping him."

That was how it had seemed.

"You did a great thing for all of us, Is. Forgive yourself." That was Ellie. Is had seen how much Ellie loved John, and she loved John's brother even more. Ondre's pain was her pain.

"Aren't you . . . doesn't it ... ?" Is asked.

"Hurt? Yes," Ondre said. "Many things in life hurt. But you can stand them. You can always stand them, if you stay true in your heart."

Is looked away from them then. She could not let them see that there was nothing left in her heart except pain. Pain and confusion. She didn't have their confidence. She didn't have their broad base of love, or their belief system. They had given her a glimpse of all those things, but they were not "hers." She had seen something bigger and more wonderful than she had ever understood love to be, and now it was gone. Gone with John. Gone from her heart, taken from her forever. She would deliver the rest of John's message, then she would go. She could not stay among the Hluit with her false heart. And she could not stay because the Alliance knew she and Lark were alive. The berserker she had helped had seen her and Lark. He would have "fasted" that back to the Alliance at his death. She listened to her voice resume its story.

She told how she and John had gone into the Mirror a second time and John had forged the link with her. All she said of that unbelievable link was that it worked. She could see and feel what John did while he was inside the Mirror and she was outside.

He'd gotten really clever at accessing its memories, and Is tried to explain about walking through those memories. You could see them, and then you could get inside them as well.

John had done that for five or six days. Is didn't tell them about the nights when he would come back out of the Mirror and they lay together in that link making love. She didn't try to explain how there had been no room for anything but joy in that link even though the end was so near.

She told the people about downloaded berserkers, about interactive holograms, about death agonies powering "fast" transmissions to the Alliance. She was vaguely amazed that she understood the language she was using.

She explained how the Mirror disassembled the berserkers and reassembled them, and how the Alliance sent continually more complex berserkers.

"The Mirror does not think of itself as killing the berserkers, it thinks of preserving them. That is what the Alliance wants it to do, but not just preserve someone after they're dead; they want it to actually keep them in some living, changing form." She let them think a moment about that. "A few of the very highest people in the Alliance are trying to create eternal life for themselves.

"The Alliance keeps track of the Mirror's progress by what the berserkers "fast" back to them. The Mirror thinks of the Alliance as the Watcher. It wasn't troubled by being watched. It was not programmed to fear, or distrust, or really to question anything about itself or its program.

"But it's a special kind of computer. It can learn, and it can teach itself to learn. It was set up that way because it must be able to learn to do something its makers don't know how to do. They can't teach it. It has to teach itself. They could only give it the program, the desire, to learn this thing.

"That was all fine until the Mirror happened to kill a Hluit. It 'preserved' that man too. In his mind it found more complex things than in any berserker's mind. It found things it wasn't ready to understand. From the Hluit's distrust of the Alliance, it learned distrust. From that man's fear of death - which none of the berserkers had - it learned something about death. Before that it had killed without malice, or anger, or any understanding of what it was doing. It was obeying its program without questions.

"But the Hluit had many questions in his mind. From his questions the Mirror learned to question the motivation of the Watcher.

"It also downloaded outlaws it caught. Because the Mirror is capable of teaching itself to learn, and it is not under anyone's guidance when it learns, it draws its own conclusions. With astonishing speed, it put together the concepts of placing one's self above another, of winning and losing, of lying, of hiding, of war. And of what death means to people.

"John wasn't able to determine what it really 'thinks' about the Alliance, but we know that it is now hiding its best work from them. It has completed what the Alliance programmed it to do, but the Alliance doesn't know. We think the Mirror understands that the Alliance can 'kill' it, turn it off. We think it's trying to preserve itself by pretending it hasn't completed its program.

"The Alliance believes all the Mirror can do is download berserkers and store them as interactive holos. That isn't good enough. That isn't really life after death. They want the Mirror to take the next step and learn how to capture the living/changing personality. So the Alliance keeps feeding it more complex berserkers in hopes it will create something more suitable for their ambitions of life after death.

"Meanwhile the Mirror has created what the Alliance wanted."

"The Dark Bodies." Ondre said.

"Yes."

Ellie breathed a curse.

"They're alive. They are the real persons, not just up to the moment they died, but after too. But the Mirror cannot bring them inside itself because it fears the Alliance will be able to find out about them. So it leaves them outside and un-powered. They have no energy except other people's life force. The easiest life force for them to 'feed' on is pain or fear.

"The Mirror created the herd fogs, in part, to feed the Dark Bodies with people's fear. But sometimes some of the Dark Bodies do unexpected things, like rescuing the people the herd fogs have captured. They are alive, after all, and the Mirror either doesn't care to control them, or it can't."

"The Dark Bodies could speak to John, because of the pain he was in, not being able to tell us what he had learned," Ondre concluded. "And you could hear them, because of what the Alliance has put you through."

"Yes."

Ondre held her gaze for a long moment. "Did it make John into a Dark Body?"

"Not that I . . . could find. He was trying to find out more about the Dark Bodies, then there was a flash. Like . . . I'm not sure if it was bright or loud. I could feel . . . I could feel John's mind unraveling. I felt his body stop breathing, his heart stop pumping. I don't think he felt pain, just everything going away, disappearing." She had lived with the feeling so long it was almost a relief to say the words. "I stayed with that link as long as I could." She had not cared if the Mirror traced the link to her and killed her too. "I would have felt something if he had become a Dark Body. I know I would have.

"I was with that berserker when he died and became a Dark Body. I know how that felt. I know I would have felt it if John had become a Dark Body."

No one refuted her.

"After I could no longer hold the link open," she began, not knowing if that had been minutes, hours, or days, "there was…my brain…was different. I can remember these things, to tell them to you, because I was told, programmed, to do it, by John. But before that, I remember that I could taste memory, and smell sight, and touch..." She stopped because she couldn't tell them how she had touched John.

At last her voice broke. "I couldn't find his body."

She should have been able to bury him, she should have at least had that! "When I came out of the link I was in such a dense fog. I could barely see anything. I searched and searched . . ." She had walked slowly, dragging her feet, trying to feel for him with her feet. When that hadn't worked she had crawled on hands and knees all over that meadow.

"We'll find him," Ondre said to soothe her, though he couldn't know if they would. Some people who had disappeared in herd fogs had never been found.

Ellie was touching her. Outside, distant, incompletely.

"That's enough for now. You need food and sleep." Ellie lifted Is by the shoulders, telling her body to stand up, telling her body to walk. Is watched the interaction, incurious and distant.

Only a few mouthfuls of food would go down. The rest was impossible beyond even Ellie's control of her body. The tea was bitter and it made Is sleep. Her voice told one last thing.

"The Alliance knows I'm here. The berserker saw me before he died. He spoke to me. I touched him. He saw Lark. Troopers must be on their way here."

Chapter 20

Is woke to heavy pain, like a thick blanket pressing her down. There was no place in her it didn't reach. She opened her eyes. She was inside her tent. She should get up . . . but she was unable to find the energy. She didn't notice Petre until he spoke.

"Hello."

She didn't even try to use her voice. She couldn't respond to him. He had not been here when she arrived yesterday. Word must have reached him that she was back so he had come in from scout duty. He looked dirty and tired like he had come straight to her tent.

He began to talk. He told her things she should have wanted to know. A special regrouping had been called. A full council would meet. All the people would hear John's story.

When she turned her head away, he fell silent. After a while he said, "I just want you to know I'm so sorry. Ellie told me what you've been through. I . . .I'm so sorry." She could hear the sincerity in his voice. John had been his best friend.

"Thank you." She had to try twice to get sound into the words. Because it was polite. Because it wasn't Petre's fault. He'd always been good to her. He just didn't know, didn't understand anything of what she'd been through.

She heard him get up. "I'll go now."

She heard the tent flap lifting and she wanted to just let him go but she owed him better than that.

"Petre." He paused and Is brought up the words John would want her to say. "He loved you."

He didn't answer. After a moment he went out.

Is lay awhile relieved of his presence, left with the aloneness that had become the only presence she could tolerate. Yet she knew she was not done. People would have questions. She would answer everything she could. Then she would leave. She would go back to the Mirror. She had no doubt she would find it. She wouldn't take Lark. It didn't matter how she got herself killed. The people could have Lark, maybe they'd give him back to the Alliance. That might save a lot of lives. She'd take one of Ondre's horses to get to the Mirror. He'd understand, and a canny old brood mare would be able to find her way back to the people once Is was dead.

She got up and went out. It was a bright sunny day. People were stacking hay. For a moment it was as though nothing had changed for them. They had not understood the enormity of what John had given them. Their lives were no different. For a moment Is was furious with all of them. Then as suddenly as it had come, the emotion was gone, swallowed by the colorless void in which she now lived.

Ellie came over and tried to get her to eat some breakfast, but Is could not swallow anything, so Ellie began to talk.

"I know you are devastated. You had a very special relationship with John even before you experienced the link with him in the Mirror. I suspect there's no way any of us can fully understand how that felt. I just want you to know we are all with you, Is. As incomplete as that must feel to you now we love you and want to help you."

Is tried to nod. She knew she would not be able to force her voice past the constriction in her throat. There were no words anyway.

"Many of us loved John too." Ellie's hand rested on Is's arm trying to impart comfort, but Is could feel nothing.

"When everyone can be recalled we are going to have a ceremony for him even if we don't have his body. We'll do it in the Hluit fashion which means that any person who wants to participate can speak or sing or play music. Some people will write their own poetry or music. Some will fast. Some will dance. Many will cry, but also laugh. There may be chanting. If you want anything we will include it."

Ellie deserved a response so Is nodded. She would not be here when they had their ceremony.

"But in the meantime each person will mourn in their own private way," Ellie continued. "I just want you to know that if there is anything any of us can do, we are here with you."

Is could not even look at Ellie. This was what people did, then, when they were faced with so much pain. They made words. They came together in a group. They found comfort that Is knew she would not find.

Other people were gathering around. Is could not stand their sympathy. They could not understand her aloneness or her need to be alone. She felt almost panicked by their presence. She had to finish what she had come here to do and she had to leave.

"You can't stay here," she said rather abruptly. "The Alliance will find you." She told them about the dying berserker. "Troopers are probably already on their way."

She could feel people recoil a bit at her tone of voice. They had expected to offer sympathy and give her time to mourn before they talked about what faced them all. They were not prepared for this. Petre came to her rescue.

"Yes, troopers are on the way," he said in a matter of fact way. "I ran into them on my way back here. They want Lark and they want you."

Someone drew in her breath audibly and someone else reprimanded Petre softly for being so direct.

"No," Petre said to them. "She is ready to know."

People murmured in what sounded like disagreement, so Is spoke.

"I want to know. What has happened while I was gone?"

"Troopers picked up Petre when he was on scout," Ondre said, saving Petre from having to hide how bad that had been. "They made it plain that they want you and the stallion back. That's not new. But they've stepped up their threats against us. We're supposed to turn you over to them and they're going to bring Lark's berserker to find him."

"Then I'd better take him to them." Is heard the emotionless quality of her voice. It made her wonder if she could really do that - turn herself and Lark over to the Alliance. Could there be such a void of all emotion in her that even going back to the Alliance would not matter? Or could she pretend to be going back, but go to the Mirror instead? Once she was dead, Lark's berserker would find him easily enough. Would the Alliance accept that? Or would they kill Ondre's people anyway?

"It's hard to believe the Alliance would go to this much trouble over one war horse." someone said.

"He's not just a war horse," Is said. "He took me to Amil's cabin."

Ondre spoke to her gently, "If the Alliance created Lark, surely they made more like him, or they can. You've handled war horses most of your life, is Lark really different from the others?"

Is tried to focus and think. The bond she had with Lark was deeper than with any horse before but it wasn't, in essence, different. Lark had been easier to train than most, but again, not essentially different. He was smart, willing and cooperative, but she could say that about a lot of horses. He was certainly the gentlest stallion she'd ever handled.

"It just seems strange that they have to have him back if they can make more like him," Ondre said.

"Maybe they can't," Petre hazarded. "Maybe it's not just the chip in his brain. Maybe there are so many variables and Lark's the only one where all of them worked."

"Or maybe they just don't want *us* to have him," someone else guessed.

"But John and his mare went to Amil's too," a woman objected. "Maybe they're the ones who took Is and Lark there."

"But that wasn't the only time something of that nature happened to Is," Petre reminded them. "Remember, she told us of a time before she met John, when she saw the Blueskins and started a landslide running away, but they never heard her. They never came to investigate. And the time she saw the government riders talking to Blueskins, and rode by them right out in the open because they couldn't see her."

There had been another time too. Although Is had not realized it then. The time she had run away from John. Lark had stumbled, but instead of falling they were suddenly standing in a meadow. She remembered how she had noticed that the grass was spring green. No one had found her there all day. But when she slept, the Blueskins had come, and she remembered how she had noticed as they walked out of the valley that the grass swished with the dry sound of late summer. She had not thought much about it then, but she had noticed. She came out of her own thoughts in time to hear Ondre speak.

"I'm afraid the Alliance may know a good deal more than John supposed. How else could they have created a horse like Lark? His ability to move through time is similar to the Mirror's ability to throw images back in time, and perhaps forward, for all we know."

"Yes," a woman whose name Is had forgotten, said. "The disorienting effects of the herd fogs also seem related. And whether the Alliance has learned from the Mirror how to manipulate these things, or whether the Alliance taught that to the Mirror, it doesn't matter. They both know now."

"So it might not be enough to just shut the Mirror off," Petre said, and Is was left whirling. She had not even tried to put any of this together. But the other people seemed unsurprised. They must have talked all night. They were way ahead of her.

"No, even if we knew how to do that," Ondre confirmed, "it would not stop the Alliance. They can build another Mirror and they can probably create another horse like Lark."

"So even if the Alliance doesn't know that the Mirror has succeeded in creating life after death with the Dark Bodies, they have still learned a lot about manipulating time."

"But is that going to be a threat to us?" someone asked hypothetically. "A horse that can travel through time, a computer that can make dead people into ghosts, what has that to do with whether the Alliance will let us continue to exist or not?"

"It may not be directly related," Ellie said, "but we know they have no regard for our rights, or even our lives. They consider us to be one of their experiments and whenever they decide to terminate our experiment they will do so even if that means killing all of us."

"We have always known that." "That has not changed," people murmured.

"So we're pretty much where we've always been – at their mercy."

"But there could be something in all of this that would give us an edge, some significant leverage we could use to ensure our future freedom."

"What if we could make ourselves an integral part of whether their experiment succeeds or fails. Or what if we could gain the control of the Mirror they have lost? We could bargain with that."

"Or they might just wipe us out that much faster."

"We have to make them need us."

"But how?"

"If Lark truly is the only horse they have who can travel through time, we have to make sure they don't get him back?"

"But they will come for him with his berserker and we can't control him then, even Is can't."

"But what if Lark wasn't here? What if he was somewhere where the Alliance couldn't get at him?"

"You mean Amil's cabin?"

"Yes. Maybe Is could try to take him back there. They could both be safe from the Alliance. And there might be other things to be learned from the research Amil stole. Even possibly some way to get the leverage we need to ensure our own survival."

Is sensed how much they wanted her help, but not one person would ask her outright. She was free to do, or not do, what she chose. She did not want choices. She did not want life.

"Even if Lark's gone, the Alliance may take it out on you anyway," Is said.

"We are not completely defenseless against the Alliance," Ondre said. "We have always known the day could arrive that they would come for us either to destroy us or take us back. We have contingency plans in place, which is part of the reason we all train in martial art and survival on the land. We know guerilla warfare, we have places to hide."

"But people will die and your whole way of life will be ruined," Is objected. "You can't seriously want to risk that?"

"Our way of life has always been at risk. Unless we can find a way to force the Alliance to recognize us as a sovereign people and make them negotiate a treaty with us - and find some way in which they can be forced to keep that treaty – our way of life will always be at risk."

Is had never thought about the Hluit having a chance against the Alliance. Her own problems had centered around Lark. But now turning him over to the Alliance seemed like a bad idea. Whatever use they intended for Lark, Is doubted it would be good for anyone except a few high officials. If she left him with the Hluit it sounded as though they would not turn him over to the Alliance either, but his berserker would come for him and the people would either have to kill him or let him go. Is didn't doubt that the Alliance wanted him back badly enough to kill all the Hluit if they had to.

Questions crowded her mind. If she took Lark to Amil's would he still go berserk? Maybe that was not built into him. Maybe he had never been intended to face the Mirror. Could he be trained to get control of his time-traveling ability? What triggered it? Could she train him to use it on some signal she gave him? Could that somehow help the Hluit? Or was it something only his specially developed berserker could control? Could Lark's ability somehow help the Hluit? She came back to that.

She had no answers, but more and more Amil's cabin seemed like the place to find them. Is walked away from the others to think. She had not wanted options. She wanted to go back to the Mirror and get herself killed. She did not want to be a hologram, or a Dark Body. She wanted to be plain and simply dead.

Then she wouldn't have to worry about there being some remnant of John left somewhere. She wouldn't have to worry about what happened to Lark, or to John's people.

She knew that was a wrong and selfish way to think. It was the antithesis of what John had felt and done. She was letting him down, and letting her parents down again, even worse than she'd ever let them down in the government school. She was letting Ondre and Ellie down, along with all the Hluit, and Lark too. But going on with this pain, looking for answers, trying to help the Hluit when they seemed so doomed was too much to ask. She tried to make herself want to do the right thing. But all she wanted was death.

By the time Is faced that decision it was too late in the day to set out for the Mirror, besides she did not want anyone to try to talk her out of it so she decided she would pretend to go to her tent to rest and then slip away when the moon was high. Then the people would have to decide what to do with Lark and the Alliance. Maybe someone else could get him to go to Amil's. But she knew in her heart that that was not so. There was a connection between her and Lark that was a necessary part of the mix.

Walking among John's family was like treason. Accepting more hospitality from them was impossible.

She went inside her tent, but she did not sleep. After dark she came back out to sit under the sky. She couldn't see much but she could feel the land all around her. She was not afraid of her decision to die, and yet she could not stay inside the tent alone with herself, cut off from the land this night. Her thoughts drifted idly – the bad times she had endured, the good times that had been snatched away from her – but she did not feel sorry for herself. At least she had had those good times. She had met the Hluit. She had had that fantastic link with John. She had had wonderful horses. But now there was too much pain and she was too small to hold it all.

The moon rose over the mountains, almost full. It was light enough to go now. It would get dark again before dawn, she'd have to stop then for a while, but by then she'd be miles away. No one would go after her, except maybe Petre. But by his people's moral code he could not stop her, he could only argue with her and make her feel worse, but she would not change her mind. If she went now he might never catch up to her.

It was as though thinking of him caused him to materialize at her side. She had not heard him come up before he was already sitting beside her.

Now she had to think of what to say to get rid of him without arousing suspicion. He spoke first.

"Is, don't let yourself down."

She didn't allow herself to know what he meant. "Oh, I'm not going to let anyone down," she lied to him.

"Oh," he said. "You are not about to ride out of here. You are not going to go get yourself killed."

They weren't even questions. He had stated her plans exactly and he had no right to know them.

"It's none of your business."

"No, of course not. A person I care more about than anyone in the world is about to make a huge mistake. Of course it's none of my business."

All the lies Is had been planning disappeared. "Petre, don't. I'm not John. I can't do this. I'm not like your people. I'm an Alliance thing. I'm broken. I'm dirty. I just want out."

"Then why does it bother you?"

"It doesn't."

"Don't lie, Is. This might be the last conversation we ever have."

"Okay," she agreed to the rule. "I can't do what your people want. I can't go back to Amil's. I don't have the strength. I don't love enough to do it for love. It was all John's love before. All of it. Now that he's gone, it's gone. I don't have any of my own. No love. No strength. No courage."

He'd asked for honesty, and damn him, she'd give it to him.

"So, I ask again, why does it bother you so much?"

"Because I know I should feel these things, and I don't."

"But you will again. You need to give yourself time."

"Sure, and watch your people get slaughtered."

"They won't get slaughtered."

"Good, then I don't have to worry about it."

"No, you don't have to worry about it when you're dead. You don't have to give us anything, Is. You're probably the only one who can ride Lark back to Amil's place. But you have chosen not to owe us anything."

"That's right," she said. "I am choosing my own freedom. I am being responsible only for myself. I do not choose to be responsible for your people." She spouted Hluit philosophy back at him. Let him answer that one.

But Petre didn't argue with her. He said, "It is not for our people that you have to do this. You have to do it for yourself. You owe yourself, not us."

That made no sense. "I owe myself what?" she asked angrily, and heard how her voice sounded like a petulant child's.

"You owe yourself the chance to prove to yourself that you are a good person. You can give from love. You are not 'an Alliance thing.' You're tougher than that, Is. You aren't going to let those Alliance bastards beat you in the end, are you?"

"They are going to kill your people, Petre. Slaughter them!" she nearly shouted. "They can't really want me to go to Amil's. It would be better for them if I were dead and the Alliance got Lark back.

"They do want it, Is. They want you to be safe. They want to do whatever it takes to break free of the Alliance. You should understand that."

"The Alliance will *kill* them, Petre," she said savagely. "You know it will.

"One day the Alliance will kill or enslave us anyway, Is."

"But I can't stand for that to be because of me."

"But because of you there is also a chance to change that."

"I don't believe that Petre. All I can see is people dying.

"You know every last one of us is a martial artist. We know this land. You heard Ondre."

"But there are old people and little children . . ."

"Who won't grow up as you did, Is, in Alliance schools where they tried to control you completely, withholding education, using bribes and brainwashing and sexual harassment. Is, when you had the chance, you risked death to get out of their enslavement. You should understand how my people feel. Because of you John didn't die from the poison. Because of you he got to deliver his message."

"What good is that!" she practically screamed at him. "He's dead now. And what possible good can what he learned be to your people now?"

"I don't know that yet, Is. But we know something the Alliance didn't want us to know. We know something the Alliance doesn't even know about its own experiment."

"They'll still kill you, maybe even quicker because of what they don't want you to know," she snapped.

"Not if we play our hand right. Knowledge is power. We have some, but we need more. We need to know more about Lark and we need to keep him out of Alliance hands. Whether you're here or not, we're not going to give him back to the Alliance."

"They'll bring his berserker. You won't be able to control him."

"That's why you should take him to Amil's."

"You think I know how to take him there, but I don't."

"But you could try."

"Even if I got him to Amil's, we don't know if that will work."

"That's true, we don't," he said honestly, "but it's our best chance." He could see how much she didn't want to try, she didn't believe it would work. She was broken and defeated – her heart torn out of her – all her toughness and courage and the healing she had begun to feel, crushed.

It broke his heart to see her this way. He sought for some way to put that toughness back in her, and he knew she would hate him for it. Her strong ethics and her unshakable sense of fair play had gotten her into trouble in the Alliance, but it had also seen her through many tough times. He had to reawaken that in her. He struck at the one thing she still cared about.

"You go ahead and quit." He made his voice angry. "If the Alliance gets Lark back you won't have to know how they use him, whether they let the Mirror kill him, or have some worse plan for him. I'll take Lark, I'll try to get to Amil's. "

"Lark won't do it for you."

"Probably not."

"They'll catch you and kill you, or Lark will."

He met her angry eyes with his own determination. Let her see he would do it anyway. She turned away first.

"That's not fair."

"Many things in your life have not been fair, but they were always things that were being done to you. They were not your fault. This time it's you who is not being fair. You might be able to do something that may save us, but you won't try."

"I can't, Petre. *I can't!*"

"John wouldn't want you to kill yourself."

"I've done what John wanted."

"But he wouldn't want you to die."

"Then he should have stayed alive," she returned angrily.

Petre understood the betrayal she felt. John had given himself to his people above her. Petre remembered the loneliness, and yes betrayal, he had felt when John had left him and Ondre to live in the Alliance for so many years. He understood, of course, how important it was for John to do that, but there was no reasoning with his heart. It hurt. This must be many times worse for Is, and she did not feel the support of friends and community that Petre had had. He wanted to tell her, *I love you. I'll support you.* But with all the pain in her heart he knew that wouldn't be enough for her.

He heard her ragged breath, caught the sob, quickly choked off at the end of it.

His heart melted. All the toughness went out of him. He could not cause her pain this way.

"Is . . ." his own voice caught.

"Petre, don't . . ." her voice faltered, high and thin at the breaking point.

He didn't know what she meant that he should not do. Not hurt her? Not force her to do this?

"I'm sorry," he whispered, apologizing to her, apologizing to his people for failing to convince her. "I can't hurt you like this." He stood to leave

185

and the pain in his heart caused him to stagger. He had failed her. He had lost her. He had failed John who would not want her to die like this. He turned blindly into the night.

"Petre?" His name from her lips froze him to the spot. He was afraid to turn, afraid to hope.

"I can't . . . alone. Will you go with me?"

"Yes," he managed instead of the wild exclamation of hope in his heart. "I will go with you, always." Too much had shown in his voice, he knew it the moment he'd said it.

"No, Petre don't misunderstand. I gave something to John - maybe more than one person should give to another - now it's gone. There's nothing left inside me without John. I can't love you. I can't give you anything. There is nothing left inside me to give.

"I know," He swallowed hard. "I have something to give you."

"No. I can't accept it."

"You can't accept it because you don't understand what it is. You can't accept it because you don't understand that you can't reject it. It is already given. You have no control of that. You never did."

His words brought her up short. *You don't understand what it is.* She closed her eyes against the sudden reawakening of emotions she didn't want to feel. He was right, she did not understand how his people could care anything about her except how she affected their own survival. She did not understand how he could love her when she did not love him and never would. She did not understand what he was offering her.

"I can't . . . ." The other decision was so much easier. So much safer. *You're tougher than that, Is.* "I can't promise anything."

"I know. Just try to get us to Amil's."

The other option, death, would always be there. If this didn't work, if she tried, and couldn't ... it was a coward's way to think, but she needed to know there was a way to get out of this pain. To continue in this suffering for the sake of other people, to allow herself to be loved, to risk caring - all were terrifying to her. She couldn't take more pain. She couldn't love again. She didn't owe anyone anything. But there was a place in her heart that knew none of that was the issue. The issue was what was right. Running away, when she was in the best position to help was wrong.

"It can't be worth it to you," *to keep loving me,* she added in her mind.

"Let me decide what's of what worth to me."

It was his decision. *If people would be responsible for their selves and let others be responsible for their selves . . .* He was in charge of himself. She had no more right to forbid than to allow.

"Thank you." His voice was almost a whisper, inappropriate words because there were none appropriate.

She heard him walk away.

He was waiting for her when she came out of her tent in the morning. He came up out of the mist leading John's mare, saddled and packed, ready to go. Is's heart wanted to stop. No, this would cause too much pain. She should never have agreed to this.

Celeste came forward and sniffed her hand. The mare's delicate ears pricked, her deep intelligent eyes looked into Is's. She brought her head forward and touched Is's check daintily with her soft nose.

Is let go of the breath she had been holding.

The moment passed and Is began to pack up her things into Lark's saddlebags. People came in one's and two's drifting out of the mist. Some of them carried small packages they handed to Petre or put in the saddlebags.

They spoke to Is saying simply, "Good luck," or "Thank you." They acknowledged Petre with a touch or a hug that said the same thing. And then they drifted on. There were no clinging goodbyes, no fanfare, just simple honesty.

Is met Petre's eyes. This was the right choice.

Lisa Maxwell lives on a farm in Weaverville, North Carolina, where she teaches riding and trains horses when she isn't traveling to teach horsemanship clinics. She also holds a second degree black belt in aikido.

The Horse Who Walked Through Time

The exciting conclusion of the saga of Isadora and her horse, Lark.

The Alliance has lost control of the Mirror and Lark is the key to re-gaining that control. The Alliance is poised to annihilate all the Hluit if they don't return Isadora and Lark. The Hluit realize their survival depends on who controls Lark. But how can they stand against the superior force of the Alliance?